ONCE
UPON
A
KISS

Books by Robin Palmer:

Cindy Ella

Geek Charming

Little Miss Red

Once Upon a Kiss

Wicked Jealous

ONCE UPON A KISS

ROBIN PALMER

speak

SPEAK

An imprint of Penguin Random House LLC

375 Hudson Street

New York, New York 10014

First published in the United States of America by Speak,

an imprint of Penguin Random House LLC, 2016

Library of Congress Cataloging-in-Publication data is available.

ISBN 978-0-14-750988-8

Printed in USA

Design by Danielle Calotta

1 3 5 7 9 10 8 6 4 2

For Eileen Kreit,
who not only came up with the title,
but gave me the chance of a lifetime

ONCE
UPON
A
KISS

CHAPTER One

1986

YOU KNOW THAT *SESAME STREET* SONG "One of These Things," where they show a bunch of stuff that's alike and then one thing that's "not like the others"?

Well, when it came to the Brenner household of Beverly Hills, California, I—Zoe Michelle Brenner—was not like the others. Not like my parents, Judy and Stan, founders of Discocize, which, according to the past week's *People* magazine, was the "hottest fitness fad not just of 1986 but the entire decade." And certainly not like my fourteen-year-old brother, Ethan, whose three goals in life were to be popular, be rich, and get into *The Guinness Book of Records* for the highest score on Super Mario Bros. He played it so often that in my dream the night before (the recurring one, where I'm just about to kiss Judd

Nelson, who ever since I saw *The Breakfast Club* had replaced Jake from *Sixteen Candles* as my ideal boyfriend), the Super Mario Bros. music started up and totally killed the moment. According to Judd, at least the dream version of him, he was very sensitive, which meant the soundtrack when kissing had to be just right.

"Judd Nelson told you that the make-out soundtrack has to be just right," my best friend, Jonah, said doubtfully as we sat at lunch in the Castle Heights High cafeteria that April afternoon.

"Uh-huh," I said as I tore off a piece of his Twinkie and popped it in my mouth. I wasn't a huge Twinkie fan—the after-taste reminded me of dishwashing liquid—but when you lived in a house like I did, where the snack choices were sunflower seeds or Wasa bread (think sand mixed with pebbles), you didn't miss a chance to eat sugar.

His right eyebrow shot up as he tore off a piece of Twinkie as well. As always, our snacking rhythms were synchronized. Which was a good thing, especially when we were eating popcorn or Cheez-Its. Otherwise, things would've gotten pretty messy.

"What?" I said.

"You really think that Judd Nelson would care what kind of music was playing as he kissed a girl."

I cocked my head as I thought about it. "Yeah, you're probably right." I sighed. I, on the other hand, definitely cared about what kind of music was playing when I made out with a guy. Not like that happened on a regular basis. "He's not going to work as my crush anymore," I announced. "Good music is imperative for the whole make-out experience."

"I agree," Jonah said, even though he had about as much experience with girls as I had with guys. In my sixteen years on the planet I had kissed only three guys: Stephen Roskoff, who I got stuck in the closet with at Heather Greene's house during Seven Minutes in Heaven, when I was thirteen. Ross Sherman, who gnawed at my botton lip so hard that he drew blood, at camp when I was fourteen. And my coworker Matt McDonald, during the Hot Dog on a Stick holiday party, who drooled so much, it looked like I had made out with a Great Dane. (I blamed my poor judgment on all the frozen blue raspberry lemonade I had consumed.)

"I'm thinking next time I make out with someone there's going to be some Psychedelic Furs playing."

His eyebrow went up again.

"What?" I asked, reaching for more Twinkie. Realizing it was the last bite, I drew my hand back.

Jonah pushed the cake toward me. "No one likes New Wave as much as me," he said. That was true. A total music freak, Jonah had a show on the school-run radio station called *New Wave for Numbskulls*. "But when it comes to swapping spit, it doesn't work. That's what Marvin Gaye is for."

"I bet Molly Ringwald listens to New Wave when she makes out," I said. Molly Ringwald was one of my idols. I kind of looked like her. Well, if Molly Ringwald had dirty blonde hair and blue eyes and a semi-big nose that her mother had offered to get made smaller as her sweet sixteen gift a few months earlier. (I turned it down.) Jonah, on the other hand, resembled Matthew Broderick: dark hair, blue eyes that looked a little buggy if he wasn't wearing his glasses (because he thought they made him look like a nerd, even though he really needed them to see).

"Okay, enough about make-out music. We need to get back to work," Jonah said as he picked up a notebook titled "Campaign Stuff."

"Right. Who do we have today?"

He flipped through the pages until he got to a very crooked homemade calendar that I had made. "Today is . . . the Dirtbags."

"Oh good. I've been looking forward to this one." I reached up and ran my hand through the long side of my asymmetrical haircut before looking down at my shirt to make sure none of my taco had ended up there.

"Food check," Jonah said before I stood up.

I leaned toward him and opened my mouth in a wide smile. "Anything?" I asked between gritted teeth.

He waved his hand in front of his nose. "No. But . . ." He reached into his pocket and pulled out a pack of breath mints. "You might want to try one of these."

I took one and popped it in my mouth. Only a best friend could tell you you had bad breath and not hurt your feelings. "Okay, food check on you now," I said.

"Why? I'm not the one running for class president. I'm just the campaign manager."

"But we're a *team*."

He opened his mouth to reveal braces flecked with all sorts of I didn't even want to know what. I cringed. "When was the last time you actually *brushed*?" I demanded.

"This morning!" he cried. "Or maybe it was last night," he sheepishly said.

"As difficult as it is for you, just try to keep your mouth closed," I teased as we got up.

Me running for class president had actually been Jonah's idea. Not because I had a gift for making people feel safe, or was particularly good at public speaking, or could tell believable lies. It was because, he explained, he was sick and tired of hearing me complain about how Andrea Manson—the current president—did nothing to try to bring all the various cliques in Castle Heights together, and everything to keep them apart. Or, more specifically, everything to keep them away from her so that the rarified air she breathed as the most popular and feared person in school would not be contaminated. And from her perch on the Ramp—the raised partition at the head of the cafeteria, where all the popular people sat—she was pretty successful at it.

"But class presidents are always popular kids," I had replied when he first brought it up.

"So you'll do it the other way around." He shrugged. "You'll become class president first, and then you'll become popular."

I wrinkled my nose. "Why would I want that? We hate people who are popular. They totally put people in boxes and judge them without knowing them."

"Kind of like you just did right there with that statement?" he retorted.

"That's not true. Because we're on the outside, I get a better view than they do, so I know that's what they're doing. They can't see it because they're so high up."

"So change it."

"What do you mean?"

"You're always going on about all these ideas you have to bring the school together," he said. "You know . . . getting rid of the Ramp; Cultural Kidnapping—"

"Not to sound full of myself, but I do think that Cultural Kidnapping one is a good one," I said. The idea had been that everyone would draw a name from a hat and would have to spend the day with that person, doing whatever it was they did as part of a normal day. "Who *wouldn't* want to spend the day with someone from a completely different social group?" I asked. "It would be like being an exchange student but without having to look in a pocket dictionary to figure out how to say 'Where's the bathroom?' in their language."

"So instead of talking my ear off about them, why don't you actually try to *do* something about it?"

He may as well have suggested I get into a time machine and fast-forward to the year 2000. "I don't know. I mean . . . it's just . . . I don't have time to be class president. I'm a very busy person," I said defensively.

"And by 'busy' do you mean calling the radio station and bothering me with song requests every five minutes?"

Okay, so maybe my social life hadn't been exactly heavy on the "social" part. Jonah was pretty much my only friend. We had met in eighth grade in a ballroom dancing class, which, it turned out, both of us had been bribed by our parents to take. Because my name followed his alphabetically (Brennan and Brenner), we were assigned each other as partners. We spent the next eight Friday evenings stepping on each other's feet and discovered we had a ton of stuff in common, such as a shared love of *Brady Bunch* reruns and apple slices smeared with peanut butter and honey. We were at different junior high schools then, but that didn't stop us from tying up the phone line almost every night. My dad was always complaining that every time he called from the health club to see if my mom wanted him to pick up dinner from Inaka, a macrobiotic restaurant that only served vegetarian food, there was a busy signal.

The fact that we both ended up at Castle Heights was a total score for me. Especially since the brains of all the girls I used to hang out with had gotten sun damaged over the summer. The minute high school started, all they wanted to talk about was how to get popular enough so we could sit up on the Ramp and which tanning salon in town was the least likely to give you any sort of gross disease. Soon enough I was spending not just every lunch period with Jonah, but my weekends as well. You'd think you'd get sick of spending all your time with one person, but Jonah and I never ran out of things to talk about.

But the truth was even though I may have had a weird haircut, and favored neon-colored Lycra miniskirts and gold sunglasses, I wasn't all that comfortable being seen. I complained about being on the sidelines, but I kind of liked being invisible. When you were invisible, you weren't a target for people to talk about. And yet, over the past few months, I had to admit I'd been getting antsy for something to change. I just didn't (a) know what or (b) have the guts to do something about it.

"You're doing it. You're running," Jonah had announced before I could come up with another excuse. "Here—we'll vote on it. All in favor of Zoe running for president?" His arm flew up. "Aye!" he said, before reaching for my arm and hoisting it up. "Aye, too," he said in a high-pitched voice, imitating me, before he let it drop. He smiled. "That was easy enough."

That had been a month earlier. The most common reaction to my entrance into the race was "Zoe Brenner? Who's that?"— which meant that I had to work extra hard to get in touch with voters, which is why every lunch period for the past week had been spent visiting with different cliques.

"Hey, guys," I said nervously as we stood in front of the Dirtbags' table. Finally being up close to them (they usually hung out outside, smoking), I saw that the name wasn't fair, as there was nothing dirty about them. Angela Brancusi, however, could have benefited from wiping a Stridex pad over her nose.

Barely a mumble in response. Maybe they were stoned.

I looked over at Jonah for help and mouthed, *Help!*

He sighed. "I'm Jonah Brennan, and this is my friend Zoe Brenner. You may have heard that she's running for class president?"

This didn't even get a response. Maybe because they were

too busy examining an onion ring in the shape of a pair of devil's horns and wondering whether it was a sign of something.

"And maybe you haven't. Well, she is, and she's awesome, and if you elect her, I can personally promise you that she will do her best to address whatever concerns you might have about how things are being run around here."

Still nothing.

"So . . . what might those concerns be?" Jonah asked.

Carl Nichols looked up. "How about better munchies in the vending machines?" His eyes were so red, *he* looked like the devil.

"I can absolutely, positively look into that!" I exclaimed.

Jonah nudged me and shook his head.

"What? I shouldn't look into that?" I hissed.

"No, you should. But you should also bring it down a notch so you don't sound like a game show host," he hissed back.

"Okay, okay." I took a deep breath. "So, uh, anything else?"

"Yeah," said Laura Preston as she put Visine in her eyes. "Do you think you guys can leave? You're really squashing my mellow."

Jonah and I looked at each other. "Sure. We can do that," Jonah replied. "If we can be sure to get your vote next week."

The table looked at each other and shrugged. "Sure. Why not?" Andy Faxson said.

"Cool. Thanks," I said, trying to not jump up and down and growl a big "Yeeeeeaaaaaahhhh!" like I wanted to. Instead I grabbed Jonah's arm and spun him around and tried to walk away in the most presidential manner possible.

"We got some votes!" I cried when we were far enough away for me to act non-presidential and not be seen. "Who can we go to next?" I asked excitedly. Now that I had gotten a taste of real power, I wanted more.

We hit the French Clubbers. Because they were so big on seeming French, they all looked pained when I talked to them, like they had just sucked on a lemon. But I think they really liked the Cultural Kidnapping idea. And the Computer Club. Jonah's friend Nerdy Wayne, who was the sound engineer at the radio station, was the president, and he was more than happy to promise me his vote, as was Michael Reston, even without me letting him take me to the *Star Wars/The Empire Strikes Back* double feature that was playing at the movie theater on Beverly Boulevard.

"Hey, Zoe—I've been thinking more about Socialize," Nerdy Wayne said. "Want me to tell you about it?"

Oh no. I couldn't listen to more about Socialize, even if it meant I wouldn't get his vote. Basically the idea was that once you signed up for it on the computer ("I'm telling you—in ten years or so, everyone's going to have one," he liked to say, "and not only that, but they're going to be portable, so you can take them with you instead of having to sit at your desk"), it would be like this giant bulletin board where you'd be able to write messages to other people and post photographs for everyone to see. (The idea that you'd be able to see your own pictures on the computer sounded nuts, but Wayne swore it would happen.) "I would love to hear about it—" I began.

Wayne's face lit up.

"—but I have to finish campaigning. Can I take a rain check?"

He nodded, and we started moving away. I was just about to tell the Recyclers about my promise to make sure not a single soda can was left behind—a promise that Andrea Manson had made but totally reneged on—when my nostrils were invaded by the powdery smell of Love's Baby Soft perfume.

"Poor Zoe," a high-pitched nasal voice sighed. "I see you still haven't been able to afford to get a whole haircut."

I turned. Standing there in a purple miniskirt, white puffy shirt with a big bow, and black patent leather pumps was Andrea herself. As usual, she had one of her favorite accessories with her: Cheryl Mancini, her best friend, who served as a combination lady-in-waiting and pet parrot.

"Omigod, that is *so* funny, Andrea!" Cheryl said. She was wearing the discount version of Andrea's outfit.

Andrea glanced at her. "I know. That's why I said it."

"That *is* pretty funny, Andrea," offered Lindsy Rauch, one of the Recyclers.

My mouth did the O thing it did when I was too stunned to talk. Lindsy had told me just the day before in the locker room as we got changed after gym that she liked my haircut. As we locked eyes, she sheepishly shrugged. Nothing drove me nuts more than people who talked out of both sides of their mouth. But I shouldn't have been surprised. Not only did no one want to risk pissing Andrea off, they all secretly wanted to be her friend.

"Actually, my hair's supposed to be like this, Andrea. It's called an asymmetrical cut," I replied.

Andrea had hated me since sixth grade, when I had beat her in the finals of the spelling bee (how she even got that far when she then went on to spell *Pac-Man* wrong was beyond me). But it felt like her disdain for me was about more than that. Maybe because with my neon-pink Lycra miniskirt, robin's-egg-blue T-shirt, and fingerless lace gloves, I was anything but cookie-cutter. If anything, I would be the poster child for what *not* to wear in a *Seventeen* magazine article.

"So what's going on here?" Andrea asked.

"Not that it's any of your business, but I was just telling the Recyclers about what I'd do if I were elected president," I replied icily.

"You mean, what you *will* do when you *are* president," Jonah corrected. "My mom says the whole positive-thinking thing really works," he whispered.

I smiled gratefully. I didn't know what I would have done without Jonah. I mean, I would have been friendless, but besides that. We were the perfect balance to each other.

Andrea snorted. "As if."

"Yeah. As if," Cheryl repeated before trying to copy her snort, but missing the mark so that it sounded like a snore.

Andrea's equally popular boyfriend (but with fewer IQ points), Brad Bundy, walked up. Maybe if I had been a Barbie fan, I would have found him cute, seeing that he was a carbon copy of Ken, but the trauma of discovering my entire Barbie family had suffered third-degree burns after I left them next to the stove top when I was nine turned me off from Barbies. That, and the fact that even at that age I was well aware that being tall and good-looking with no zits and 0 percent body fat was not representative of the real world.

"Oh. Hey, Brad," Cheryl said hopefully. You'd have to be blind to not see the enormity of Cheryl's crush on Brad. But even Tammy Morales—who *was* blind—knew about it, because I had overheard her in the bathroom talking about it the week before.

Brad didn't even acknowledge her. "Hey, babe," he said as he snaked his arm around Andrea's waist. "Wanna go get in some studying before our biology quiz?"

"What are you talking about?" Andrea asked. "We took biology last year."

"I know," he replied. "I was trying to be, you know . . . *sexy.* See, biology is the basis for—"

"I get the connection, Brad," Andrea interrupted.

"I get it, too," Cheryl said. "Omigod, that is *so* clever!"

Andrea patted him on the cheek. "Babe, instead of making jokes, maybe think about sticking to things you're good at." She smiled. "Like wearing the clothes I pick out for you."

Jonah and I exchanged a look. As usual, Brad was wearing one of his many pastel Izods with an upturned collar—this one was lavender—making him look like a preppy Easter egg.

"Excuse me, what was that?" Andrea asked.

"Yeah. What was that?" said Cheryl. While she tried to sound as threatening as Andrea, she couldn't quite match it.

"Um, I didn't say anything," I replied.

"Oh, I thought the look that you just gave your boyfriend meant you don't approve of Brad's fashion choices. Or rather, *my* choices for him."

"He's not my boyfriend."

"I'm not," Jonah agreed. "And she's not my girlfriend."

People were always mistaking us for boyfriend and girlfriend, a fact which we thought was a riot. I loved Jonah to death, and I knew he'd do anything for me, but the idea of kissing him was like the thought of kissing my cousin Aaron.

Andrea glared at him. "Was I talking to you?"

"Yeah," Cheryl said. "Was she talking—"

Andrea shot her a look.

"Sorry," Cheryl replied, chastised.

Brad smiled at me. "Cool haircut, Zoe."

"Thanks, Brad."

Jonah nudged me with his arm and mouthed *I told you so* before I mouthed back *You're nuts*. Jonah swore that Brad had some sort of crush on me, which was crazy. The only reason he knew my name was because we had been lab partners in chemistry, and he copied off me while I did the work. That being said, it *was* a little weird that whenever I saw him he went out of his way to say hi and compliment me on something. (Although, "I like how the green of your army surplus bag matches your eyes" when my eyes were actually blue was sort of a half compliment.) But he couldn't actually like *me*—I mean, he was dating the most popular girl in school.

"Okay, this conversation is over," Andrea announced, clutching Brad's arm. "And I really hope you haven't spent a lot of money on campaign buttons, because there's no way you're winning," she added as she began to stomp off.

"See you around, Zoe!" Brad yelled over his shoulder as she dragged him along.

It was kind of ironic that one of the few people who was nice to me all the time was him.

CHAPTER
Two

"MAYBE WE SHOULD MAKE MIXTAPES and hand them out to voters," Jonah said as we raided my kitchen for snacks after school later. "I heard Montana Russo telling Nick Shaffer that they have these double recorders now, so you can tape a tape."

Montana was a girl in our class who I had been meaning to get to know better. She had moved to town in the middle of the year before and sat by herself at lunch, but didn't seem to mind it at all. I don't know why I thought we'd hit it off as friends, but I did. "Love that," I replied. I opened the pantry only to find it full of nothing but Tab soda and paint tarps. Yet again, my mother was remodeling the house. Instead of the Southwestern motif from the past few months, everything in our house was now white and Lucite. It made me feel like I was living in a spaceship.

Jonah took a sip of some green juice he found in the fridge before immediately spitting it out in the sink. "What *is* this?!"

I looked over from the Reese's peanut butter cups I had pulled down from the top, top cupboard. My junk food stash was for emergencies, and the anxiety of running for office pretty much fit that bill. "Wheatgrass juice."

"We're hanging out at my house from now on," he said as he scraped at his tongue.

"Okay with me."

He reached into his pocket and pulled out a crumpled-up piece of notebook paper. "I worked on your speech during study hall," he said as he handed it to me.

"What's all this brown stuff?"

He peered at it. "Probably Milk Duds."

Just then my fourteen-year-old brother, Ethan, skidded into the kitchen à la Tom Cruise in *Risky Business*. He was obsessed with the movie. I had gotten used to him wearing Ray-Ban sunglasses at night, but I drew the line when he tried to walk around in his Jockey shorts. With his curly brown hair that looked like a perm (lucky—or unlucky—for him it was natural . . . unlike my parents': my mom *and* my dad paid a lot of money for their perms) and a scrawny body, with what looked like pale white spaghetti for arms and legs, there was nothing Tom Cruise–ish about Ethan.

"What's that paper with doody flecks on it?" he demanded as he opened a cabinet.

"It's Milk Duds. And hello to you, too, dear brother," I said. Ethan wasn't big on hellos. He liked to get right to the point.

"Hello is for people who aren't on the move like I am," he replied.

Jonah and I looked at each other and rolled our eyes. My brother was so dorky that he was almost funny.

"And where are the dishes?" he asked.

I pointed to the pantry. "In there."

"They're redoing the kitchen *again*?"

I shrugged. "It's been three whole months."

"I only just got used to the family room being where the dining room used to be," he grumbled as he reached for some banana chips I had found in a cupboard. Unlike Jonah and me, Ethan and I were not synchronized. Which in this case meant a hailstorm of chips rained down on the linoleum as we stuck our hands into the bag at the same time. "So what's the paper?"

"It's my speech for the election."

Ethan rolled his eyes. "You're *still* thinking of running?"

"She's not thinking about it—she's doing it," Jonah corrected. "Oh, and she's going to win." He closed his eyes. "In fact, I can see her right now, on the stage, hands in the air in victory as the crowd goes wild—"

Ethan stared at him like he was nuts.

Finally Jonah opened his eyes. "It's positive visualization, which goes along with positive thinking. My mother swears by it."

"Yeah, well, if you ask me, I positively think that her running for office is not only a waste of time, but an embarrassment to me," Ethan said. "Not to mention, if this gets out to the middle-school crowd, I can kiss my chances of becoming popular good-bye."

The only thing Ethan wanted more than to be rich was to be popular. I kept telling him that if he focused on the first one, then he could just buy the popularity, but he felt strongly about doing them separately.

"Way to support your big sister," I said as I yanked the banana chips back from him. I had found that one of the best ways to punish Ethan was by taking away food.

"You don't get it—I *am* supporting you. By keeping you from embarrassing yourself!" he said as he wrestled the bag from me and took another huge handful before going toward the dining room. Or what had been the dining room up until it became the family room.

"She's not just going to win—she's going to win by a land-slide!" Jonah called after him.

"You know, denial is not just a river in Israel!" Ethan shot back.

"I keep telling you—the Nile is in *Egypt*!" I called after him. Geography was not my brother's strong suit. Neither was math, science, English, or history. Basically he excelled in lunch, and that was about it.

"Why does everyone in this house always have to yell?" my mother yelled as she bounded into the kitchen, wearing one of her many Day-Glo leotards, this one hot pink. On top of her white tights were purple acrylic leg warmers. If all of that wasn't bad enough (and it was), she wore a braided pastel headband around her brunette permed Afro.

"Oh, you're both here! Faaaaaantastic!" she exclaimed as she began to do some side bends, adding a disco-y clap and a shimmy in between each one for good measure. Ever since my parents had filmed their first Discocize video, they had taken to talking like they were on camera even when they weren't. "Those two students we found at UCLA for the new video just dropped out because they didn't realize the *disco* in *Discocize* meant *disco disco*." She began walking backward in a Hustle-like move ("Only the most dynamite dance to come out of the disco era," my father had explained to me when I once asked him what he was doing). "Apparently it goes against their core beliefs," she explained. "But we really need young people so the audience sees that Discocize appeals to all ages."

Which would be false advertising, seeing that the average age of the students who had been in their class at the Jewish Community Center before they gave it up to make videos (this was their third) was fifty.

My father came jogging in, wearing royal-blue satin biker shorts and a white tank top with a matching headband around his matching perm. Like Ethan, his arms and legs were on the scrawnier side, although thanks to the tanning bed they had recently installed in the guest room, he was orange rather than pale.

"Look, Stan!" my mom said. "The kids are here—which means they can be in the video!"

"Dyyyyynamite!" my dad said, reaching for a pick to fluff his

Afro. Back before the perm, he had looked a lot like this singer Neil Diamond, but now he just looked . . . *weird*.

My mother began doing squats. With a clap, of course. "It'll only take about a half hour." While they had shot their first one in our family room–slash–dining room, now they rented a studio whenever they filmed. It was actually a Sons of Italy banquet hall, but they always made sure to take down the Italian flags before the cameras started rolling. "Ooh, and I have the *cutest* leotard for you to wear—it's got pink and white stripes, which will look just faaaaaaabulous with lavender leg warmers—"

Jonah and I looked at each other. "I have to practice my speech for the election," I said quickly.

"And I have to watch her practice it and make sure she enunciates properly," he added.

My parents exchanged a look. "So you're really going to go forward with this thing, huh?" my mother asked gently.

"If, by *this thing*, you mean running for office and doing my part to try and effect change in the world, then yes. Yes, I am," I said firmly.

My father patted my hand. "Well, sweetie, then we think it's dynamite that you're tackling such a big challenge like that." My father was very big on the word *dynamite*. "Maybe you can work this into your college essays. Admission boards love stories about brushing yourself off when you fail and continuing on."

"Thanks for the support," I said.

"Anytime," my mother said as she Hustled backward out of the room. "You know we're always here for you."

"Absolutely," said my dad as he followed her. "That is, if we're not off shooting a video."

Jonah reached into his pocket and pulled out a Peppermint Pattie. "Here. I was saving this as my snack for the radio show, but I think you need it more right now."

I smiled. While Jonah was super generous, when it came to Peppermint Patties—his favorite candy of all time—he tended to not only hoard them, but downright lie if asked if he had one. "Thanks," I said as I took it. Granted it was mushy and melted after having been in his pocket for who knew how long, it was the thought that counted. "What would I do without you?"

"Lucky for you, you won't ever have to find out," he replied.

The days leading up to the election were a blur. Between campaigning and smiling and scouring the Galleria mall to find the perfect outfit that said "yes, I'm stylish, but I'm way more about substance over style" I was exhausted. Every time I thought I couldn't go on—that maybe everyone was right, that I was just fooling myself and wasting my time—Jonah would dedicate a song to me during his radio show. "And now, for the girl most likely to be president next week, we have the Talking Heads' 'Burning Down the House.'" "Here's another one to get you in the mood for the upcoming election: Devo's 'Whip It.'"

Finally the day arrived.

"You're going to be great. You already *are* great," Jonah said as he karate-chopped my shoulders while we stood backstage waiting for Mrs. Carlson, our principal, to introduce me.

"Why are you hitting my shoulders?"

"I'm massaging them. You know, like you see them do in movies about boxers."

"But I'm not a boxer."

"Zoe? As your campaign manager, I'm going to suggest that you loosen up in your thinking and not be so literal. Class presidents are supposed to be *visionaries*."

"Okay. Fine. Whatever," I said.

"It's time!" he said, pushing me toward the curtain.

"I can't do this," I said nervously.

"You can," he said, pushing me again. "And you will. Break a leg. But not literally. Only figuratively."

With one more push, I was out there, in front of what seemed like four high schools' worth of students. I cleared my throat, and after a slight feedback issue with the microphone because, in my nervousness, I had forgotten you didn't have to actually *yell* when you used a microphone, I was off and running. Well, off and walking (lots of *and . . . um*s in the beginning) but *soon* I was running, detailing the more brilliant of my campaign promises: Cultural Kidnapping; a promise to get better snacks in the vending machines; and—the shining jewel in my class president crown and the thing that I hoped my administration to be remembered for—my pledge to get rid of the Ramp.

"I know that some of you might consider the Ramp an institution, but think about what it really does," I preached. "It separates the school into Haves and Have-nots. It's like the caste system in India, but with air-conditioning."

I waited for the excited buzzing that Jonah and I had been sure this would prompt, but all I got was crickets.

"Hello? Is this thing on?" I said into the microphone.

Still nothing. Well, other than feedback.

Panicked, I looked over at Jonah for help.

"Don't scream into the mike!" was all he offered.

And then, one lone clap. I squinted to see who it was, surprised to see it was Brad.

"What are you *doing*?" Andrea barked. "*You* sit on the Ramp."

"Yeah, I know, but that was kind of a funny line. You know, the India thing," he said.

I cleared my throat and stepped back. "So, uh, from your lack of enthusiasm to my idea, am I supposed to take it that absolutely no one in this entire school thinks getting rid of the Ramp is a good idea?"

Alan Sharp's hand went up. I smiled. The first one in school to get a Mohawk, Alan was all for bucking the establishment.

"I knew I could count on you, Alan!" I said.

"For what? I was just wondering whether you could repeat what you just said. I've got a ton of earwax and have been having a lot of problems with my hearing."

I sighed. Even if Alan did back me, three votes was not going to win me the election.

Before I could even attempt to come up with some sort of save, Andrea Manson stood and *click-clack*ed over to the microphone. "Okay, well, thanks for giving this a try, Zoe," she said in the sickly sweet voice she used when teachers were around. "But

I'm assuming from the complete lack of interest from our class-mates in what you have to say that you've now realized that you're not going to win the election and you're now ready to hand the mike over to me?" she added as she pushed me out of the way.

"Hey, guys," she purred.

Everyone looked at each other, unsure about whether they should respond. That's how intimidated people were by her.

"I said—*hey, guys,*" she repeated more forcefully.

"Hey, Andrea!" everyone in the crowd except for me and Jonah yelled back. Including the Dirtbags.

"So I know you're all probably real sick of sitting here by now, so I'm just going to get right to the point. If you reelect me, I think I'm just going to keep doing what I was doing, because—and correct me if I'm wrong—that seemed to be working pretty well."

All the applause I thought I would be getting for my Ramp-demolition idea filled the room. My shoulders slumped as Andrea flashed a huge nothing-in-her-teeth smile. "That's what I thought. Okay. Well, bye!" she said as she flounced off the stage as Michael Jackson's "P.Y.T." played, leaving me standing alone on the stage like a total dork.

And just like that, my political career was over as quickly as it had started.

CHAPTER Three

IT WAS SO CLEAR WHO THE WINNER WAS that after Andrea's speech, Mrs. Carlson announced that instead of waiting until the following week to vote, we'd do it when we got back to homeroom and that the results would be announced before the last bell. It was pathetic enough to lose an election by 237 votes when your class had 239 students in it. But to then have to put on cherry-red polyester pants and a red, white, yellow, and blue top made me feel like I had a big *L* tattooed on my forehead.

Unlike having a cool after-school job, like Jonah (he worked at Vinnie's Vinyl), the only one I had been able to get was at Hot Dog on a Stick at the Galleria mall. Every time I itched at my skin under my uniform, I silently cursed myself for spilling an Orange Julius all over my Spencer Gifts application before I could hand it in, which meant that Toby McCall got the job instead. (Ethan was even more disappointed than I was, seeing that Spencer's, with its wide variety of fart machines and lava lamps, was the store of choice for fourteen-year-old boys all across America.)

"Is it straight?" I asked Jonah, balancing my hat on my head as we stood in front of the escalator. The striped hat that went along with my Hot Dog on a Stick uniform was big and bulky, like something you'd see on a drum majorette, which meant that if it wasn't perfectly balanced, it fell off.

He reached up and adjusted it. "Now it is. Okay, I've gotta get to work. I'll come by during my break." Lucky for us, Vinnie's was also in the mall, which meant that we got to spend our breaks together.

"Okay."

He started to turn to go, but stopped and looked at me. Like *really* looked at me in a way that made me feel both grateful and completely uncomfortable at the same time.

"You're still upset about today."

"No, I'm not," I said as I looked away and started to pick at my cuticles. "I told you before—I only decided to run because you wanted me to. It's not like I actually wanted to win," I scoffed. "I mean, me as the president of the junior class? As if!"

"You're lying."

"I am not."

"Yes, you are. You're picking at your cuticles. That's the number two telltale sign that you're lying."

"What's number one?"

"You twirl your hair," he replied. "But since your haircut you can't do that anymore, except for that one long piece in the front."

Okay, Jonah was my best friend, but at that moment I really couldn't stand him. How dare he know me so well without my permission?

"You're allowed to be upset," he said. "I mean, you wouldn't be human if you weren't. You'd be . . . I don't know . . . a sociopath or something." He thought about it. "Or is it a psychopath? I can never remember. At any rate, the ideas you had were awesome. Because *you're* awesome."

I shook my head.

"You are! You think I would be best friends with someone who wasn't totally awesome? I have a reputation to protect. Maybe that reputation is not yet world-known and still only within the walls of the radio station, but still."

I could feel a smile starting to creep across my face.

"I keep telling you—Andrea Manson and those guys? When we come back for our twentieth reunion from wherever we're living—New York, London, Berlin—"

"I thought we had nixed the Berlin thing. Because German food gives you gas," I said.

"Right. Forget I said that. Anyways, the point is, what's going to happen is that we're gonna see that they peaked here in high school. But us? We've barely even sprouted yet, let alone bloomed." He cocked his head. "That sounds like the inside of a greeting card, huh?"

My smile got bigger. "It does," I agreed. "But a good one. Not a cheesy one with sparkles on the front that you can never get off your hands."

"Zoe Brenner, you will always have my vote for the coolest, funniest, smartest person at Castle Heights."

I swiped at my face. "Okay, you're going to have to stop because you're totally making me cry right now, and I never ended up taking off that mascara my mom forced me to put on this morning because it was a special occasion."

"Fine. Pep talk aborted." He looked at his watch. "I gotta go."

"Okay. But one thing—anything cool about me I got from being friends with you," I said. "I know we hate when we get all mushy and stuff, but you are literally the best friend anyone could ever have."

"Yeah, I know," he said with a smile as he started to walk away. He was about as comfortable receiving compliments as I was. "It's tough, but someone's got to do it. Now go sell some dogs!"

"Welcome to Hot Dog on a Stick," I said pleasantly to a frazzled-looking mom and her three small children about an hour into my shift. Well, as pleasantly as possible for someone who had a neck ache from holding her head still for so long. The early-evening shift was bananas due to the fact that a lot of mothers in the area considered corn dogs to be a completely nutritious dinner for their kids, seeing that it was both a protein and a vegetable. If cornmeal was a vegetable, which I was pretty sure it was not. "What can I get you?"

"Three corn dogs," the woman snapped as one of her kids wiped his nose on her jeans while another kept trying to climb up on the glass wall that stopped small children like himself from falling down three levels to their deaths.

"Actually, ma'am, these are not corn dogs," I corrected in what I hoped was still my pleasant voice.

"Whatta you talking about, they're not corn dogs?" she barked. She pointed to one. "See? There's the corn right there."

I turned to see if Wally, my manager, was hanging around eavesdropping. He was. Wally took his job—and all the other employees' jobs—very seriously. In fact, on my first day, he had admitted to me that he had chosen not to go to college so that he could pursue a career with Hot Dog on a Stick, with the plan to move up through the ranks and one day join their corporate office, where he would get business cards and an engraved nameplate.

"Actually, corn dogs are frozen and reheated," I explained. "These Hot Dogs on a Stick, however, are made fresh to order, so you and your loved ones can be sure that not only are you enjoying something delicious but also nutritious." The whole thing sounded canned because it was. It was straight from the employee manual, verbatim. As I glanced over at Wally he gave what seemed to be an approving nod. Although the fact that he was three inches shorter than me with a very small head that got swallowed up by his hat made it difficult to tell for sure.

By this time, the third kid—who a moment earlier had been sleeping in her stroller—was now screaming at the top of her lungs, thanks to a few bops on the head courtesy of her brother's *Star Wars* lightsaber. "Listen, missy," the woman yelled over the noise, "I don't care what they're made of. Just give me three, okay?"

"Of course," I said politely as I reached for them.

"You didn't ask her if she wanted lemonade," Wally hissed.

"Right." I always forgot that part. As the woman went to grab for whatever everyone knew was a corn dog, I held them back. "Can I interest you in some fresh lemonade? We have four delicious flavors—original, cherry, lime, and blue raspberry—which you can have regular *or* frozen. Not only does it quench your thirst, but it's made every two hours right here on the premises."

"Just because you don't have a life doesn't mean you have to stop the rest of us from getting on with ours. Now just give me the corn dogs!" she ordered, reaching over the counter to grab them.

"I'd be happy to give you your *Hot Dogs on Sticks*, ma'am," I said, holding them away from her, "as soon as you pay me for them." Due to a recent string of dine-and-ditch incidents in the food court, Wally was very firm that we not hand anything over to the customer before getting the money.

"I'll *pay* you as soon as you *give* them to me!" she snapped as she lunged for them.

The next few moments were a blur. As we struggled, one of the corn dogs fell in the vat of blue raspberry lemonade; which splashed up into my eye and made me throw my head back, causing my hat to go flying off and into Wally's nose. This resulted in some screaming along the lines of "Oh, my nose!" à la Marcia Brady from the *Brady Bunch* episode where she gets hit with the football, tipping me off to the fact that I had probably just lost my job. After that, one of the corn dogs then flew out of my hand and soared through the air before landing in the back of some blonde girl's hair and remaining stuck there.

"Oh, my hair!" I heard the girl cry as she tried, unsuccessfully, to fish it out.

Even though I couldn't see because of the lemonade in my eyes, I knew that voice. I quickly put my hat back on in hopes of hiding under it.

"Hey, I think that's a corn dog," said the guy next to her.

"What?!" the girl cried. "Well, don't just stand there—*get it out!*"

"It's not a corn dog!" Wally yelled with his hands cupped around his nose. I cringed as a few drops of blood dripped through them. "It's a Hot Dog on a Stick—*there's a difference!*"

As the couple turned around, I saw that I was right. It was none other than Andrea Manson and Brad Bundy. I pulled my hat down even farther.

"You do realize you're fired, right?" I heard Wally say.

"Yeah, that's kind of the least of my problems at the moment," I said as I watched Andrea march toward me.

"It's you!" she cried. "I should have known. Do you know how long it took me to get my hair just right this morning?!" she shrieked when she got there.

I shrugged. "A half hour?"

"An *hour*!" she corrected. "And it was totally perfect. At least until you decided to throw a corn dog at me and ruin it because you totally humiliated yourself today thinking you had the slightest chance of getting anyone to vote for you other than your weird boyfriend—"

"He's not my boyfriend," I corrected her again. "He's my best friend."

"Of course he's not your boyfriend," she said. "What was I thinking? You don't have a boyfriend! All you have is a job at this *stupid* place with a *stupid* hat covering your *stupid* hair that looks like it was cut with a chain saw!"

"Okay, first of all," I said as I reached up and took off the hat and placed it on the counter, "I no longer have this job because I was just fired." As I reached up to touch my hair, I realized the ends were all sticky with blue raspberry lemonade.

"What's the second of all?" Brad asked.

"Huh?"

"You said *first of all*," he replied. "Usually when people say *first of all*, there's a *second of all* that comes after that." He turned to Andrea. "Isn't there? Or did I just dream that?"

It was amazing to me that Brad had been held back in school only once. It was a good thing he and Andrea spent so much time lip-locked, because conversation with him would have been impossible.

"What does it matter what the second of all is when I'm having a hair emergency?!" cried Andrea.

"Okay, okay." He leaned in toward me. "Hey, do you think I can have that corn dog for free?" he whispered, pointing to the blue one that Wally had fished out of the lemonade vat. "Seeing that it's got lemonade on it, no one's going to want it, right?"

"I can't believe you're talking about food right now!" Andrea yelled.

"You heard that? I thought I was using my inside whisper."

"You don't have an inside *voice*, let alone an inside *whisper*!" She turned to me, eyes narrowed. "I know what this is about," she said as a small crowd started to gather. "This is about you being so jealous of me you couldn't *stand* it anymore, which caused you to hurt the most important thing in the world to me."

"Whoa, babe, I'm fine," Brad said, squeezing her arm. "The corn dog didn't even come near me."

"Not *you*. I'm talking about my *hair*!" She turned back to me. "You're jealous of me because you're a total loser and you always have been and you always will be," she said as she turned on her heel and stomped off.

Andrea had a reputation for exaggerating. But at that moment, with a crowd of people staring at me and my blue-tinged hair, I sure felt like she was right.

Being considered "the girl with the weird haircut" at Castle Heights had been bad enough. But becoming known as "the girl who was dumb enough to run for office against Andrea Manson and throws corn dogs at people for no reason other than she's bitter" definitely didn't help my social life.

"Hey, Zoe," Tommy Melhado called out as he passed our lunch table the next day. "You wanna buy some ammo from me?" he said as he held up a hot dog before cracking himself up.

I put my head down on the table. Great. I had gotten to the point where the most unpopular of the unpopular kids was now teasing me.

"Watch out—your hair is going to get in your chili," Jonah said as he went to move the bowl away from my head.

"What does it matter? It's already blue," I replied. I had washed it twice and the color still hadn't come out.

"That's kind of an upside to all this, right?" Jonah said. "Now you don't have to try to convince your parents to let you dye your hair!"

I smiled at him. I was grateful that he was such a glass-half-full kind of person. Especially since my glass had about only two drops left in it.

"Hey, Zoe."

I turned around to see Matt Wychowski standing in back of me. Actually, Matt was the most unpopular of the unpopular kids. Which may have had something to do with the fact that he was a klepto- *and* pyromaniac and had spent some time in a special school where they confiscated your shoelaces.

"Yeah, Matt?" I said warily.

"So now that you're, like, a social pariah like me, you wanna hang out some time?"

Seriously? *This* was where it was at now? "Thanks, but I can't."

"'Cause you guys are together?"

"*No.* Just friends," Jonah and I said in stereo.

"Then how come?"

Not like I had ever been asked before, but it was hard to believe that guys actually asked why you were saying no. "Because . . . I'm one of those pariahs who likes to really embrace the whole pariah-ness of it all, if you get what I'm saying."

He cocked his head and thought about it. "Not really, but okay," he replied as he wandered off.

"Nice save," Jonah said.

"Thanks," I replied. I started to open my mouth to speak before closing it again.

"What?" Jonah asked.

"Nothing."

"Oh, it's definitely something. It's always something when you do that guppy thing."

I sighed. Would this being known really well stuff ever feel comfortable? "I don't know," I said as I reached for some fries. "I was just thinking about whether I'll ever be asked out by some-one who's not, you know, a criminal."

"Sure you will," he said, taking his own handful. "Why wouldn't you be? I told you the other day—you're awesome." He reached for more fries. "In fact, I think the problem is that, actu-ally, you're *too* awesome. You're intimidating."

At that I snorted. "Yeah right."

"You are. I mean, if we weren't best friends, I'd be intimi-dated by you."

I shook my head. "That's crazy."

"It's true. You're smart. Funny. You have excellent taste in music. Because of me, of course."

I rolled my eyes.

"And, you're, you know . . . *pretty*."

It was weird to hear him say something like that.

"I can say that because we're best friends," he quickly added. "Not because you're my type or anything."

"Well, right, of course." I cocked my head. "What *is* your type?"

He shrugged. "I don't know. Someone with good taste in music."

"Obviously."

"And funny."

"Of course."

"Smart."

"Sure."

"Can we talk about something else?" he asked.

"Yes," I said quickly.

Luckily we never ran out of things to say. Pretty much the only thing wrong with Jonah was that he didn't like shopping, which meant I was on my own that afternoon at Terri's Totally Bitchin' Treasures, my favorite clothing store in town. It was on Fairfax Avenue, a bit away from the shops on Melrose, but that was how Terri was—just a little bit off the beaten path with everything.

"What's the story, my favorite mini New Waver?" Terri asked, looking up from pressing on a purple Lee Press-On Nail.

Terri was my dream version of an older sister. With her long hair that changed styles and colors weekly, and a wardrobe that came exclusively from thrift stores, she was like a human paper doll.

"Where should I start?" I replied as I started going through the sale rack. "The part where I only got two votes for president? Or should I just skip to the part at the Galleria when I threw a Hot Dog on a Stick into Andrea Manson's hair?"

Terri's false-eyelashed eyes widened so much you could no longer see the cornflower-blue eye shadow that was her trademark. "You've turned into a total rebel—I love it!"

"The rebelling wasn't exactly planned." I looked up from a pair of fuchsia ribbed cotton leggings. "Hey, if I dropped out of school, could I get a job here?"

"I wish," she replied. "But not selling out does not make one rich. I can barely afford my rent on my apartment in Koreatown as it is." I loved Terri's apartment. It was a huge loft with high ceilings. She said that the smell of kimchi—Korean cabbage salad—wafting in her windows in the summer got annoying, but I loved kimchi and didn't think I'd ever get sick of it.

She walked out from behind the counter and over to the New Arrivals rack. "How do you walk in those without breaking your neck?" I asked, pointing to the five-inch black patent leather pumps on her feet.

"They're great, right? My friend who works in the Costume Department on *General Hospital* snagged them for me." As she reached into her pocket and started feeling around for something, I opened my purse and took out a pack of gum and handed it to her.

"What would I do without you?" she asked as she shoved two pieces of Trident cinnamon in her mouth. "You're, like, psychic." She flipped through the rack and pulled out a robin's-egg-blue Lycra minidress with black piping.

"It's gorgeous," I gasped.

"I knew you'd like it," she replied, handing it to me.

"But it's a size fourteen," I said, disappointed, as I looked at the tag.

"Yeah, unfortunately that was the only size they had left," she said, "which is why you can have it for the low, low price of twelve ninety-nine. That's half off. And because you've had such a sucky week, I'll throw in the tailoring for free."

I hugged her. If there was anything I loved more than Lycra in neon colors, it was a bargain. "You're the best," I said as I ran into the dressing room to put it on. Seeing that I was a size six, I was swimming in it, so I was glad I had stopped at the candy store and gotten some Fun Dip, because this was going to take a while.

I had made my way through the grape powder and was completely engrossed in Terri's story about her latest waiter-but-really-he's-a-musician-who's-*thisclose*-away-from-his-big-break boyfriend when the door to the shop opened.

"Hello?" a guy's voice called out. "I was wondering if you had the new Super Mario Bros. . . . Oh wait. This isn't the video store."

Uh-oh. I recognized that voice. It belonged to Brad Bundy. As I heard his footsteps coming toward us, I tried to slide my head down into my neck like a turtle so he wouldn't know it was me and took the Fun Dip stick out of my mouth. "Nope. It's next door," I mumbled.

"Zoe? Is that you?" Brad asked when he saw me. His Izod shirt was peach, one of the many colors in his Easter egg–like palette of polo shirts.

So much for that plan.

I unfolded myself. "Yup. Yeah, it is."

"Nice dress," he said. "The pins are a cool touch. Is that one of those New Wave things?"

"Uh, no. It's one of those tailoring things," I replied.

Brad looked at Terri and smiled. He really did look like a golden retriever when he did that. But a really dumb one. Like one that was inbred. "I'm Brad."

"Ohhh, so *you're* Brad."

He looked confused. "Didn't I just say that?"

Terri looked at me. "You weren't kidding about the dull tool in the shed thing," she whispered. As she went back to pinning the dress, she wobbled on her heels and pricked my arm with a pin. As I opened my mouth to say "Ow" I began to choke on the Fun Dip stick.

"Omigod, honey, I'm so sorry!" she cried.

"Zoe, are you okay?" Brad asked.

I tried to say "No, because I'm choking" but all I could get out was a *glug-glug-glug* as I choked some more.

"Do you need me to do some mouth-to-mouth resuscitation?" he asked. "I'm a lifeguard, so I know how to do that CPR stuff without killing people. Whoa—you're turning blue. Or is it the grape powder?"

My legs gave out as I fell to the floor. I may have been choking to death, but I was still with it enough to know that I did not want Brad Bundy's lips anywhere near mine.

Which turned out to be the last thing I saw before everything went black.

CHAPTER Four

I AM NOT A MORNING PERSON.

In fact, Jonah's always teasing me that I could have three alarm clocks, a ringing telephone, *and* a fire alarm go off, and I'd still sleep through it. But that morning, when the sound of thumping bass began to rattle my bed, and I reached up to wipe away the sweat on the side of my neck only to have my hand get caught in a bunch of hair, I shot up in bed so fast that I smacked the back of my head on my headboard.

"Owww!" I cried. I had told my mother the sharp edges on the newly installed Lucite headboard could take out someone's eye, but when I turned around to give it a dirty look, it wasn't Lucite. It was smooth blond wood. In fact, when I looked around the room, there wasn't an ounce of Lucite to be seen. Not the desk. Not the chair. Not the dresser. Not the shelf that held my TV and my boom box. In fact, my TV wasn't even there. Instead there was a flat screen attached to the wall. And instead of a boom box, there was a stand with what looked like speakers, with a little pink thing attached to the top of it.

I had to be seeing things. For the past few months, I had been getting headaches when I read for long periods of time (interestingly, they seemed to correspond with any books I had to read for English class, like *Great Expectations* or *Madame Bovary*). Apparently something had happened during the night where my eyes just went completely, like a battery going dead. "Ethan! Get in here! *Now!*" I bellowed. I wasn't sure how someone with his lack of coordination and inability to do anything quietly, including breathing, would have been able to come in while I was sleeping and switch out my furniture, but he had to be behind it. Third on his To Do list, behind becoming rich and popular, was annoying me whenever and however possible.

As I hauled myself to my feet and threw on a robe, I realized that it wasn't just my eyes that were weird—it was my entire body, especially my head. It felt like a combination of swimming through Jell-O and eating too much raw brownie mix. (Raw brownie mix equals one of Jonah's and my favorite snack foods.) Maybe I had food poisoning. I tried to remember what I had had for dinner the night before but couldn't, which was another clue that something weird was going on: when it came to food, I had this bizarre gift for being able to remember every meal I had eaten going all the way back to when I was six years old. (My sixth birthday party: Domino's pizza with extra cheese, pepperoni, and olives. Carvel birthday cake in the shape of Snoopy.) The last thing I remembered was standing in front of the mirror at Terri's with a Fun Dip stick in my mouth.

"Dude, *what* is your problem?" Ethan asked from my doorway. "I know you don't like Lil Wayne, but you need to *chill*."

Okay, at least he looked the same. Other than the fact that instead of that gross Pac-Man T-shirt that he wore almost every day, he was wearing one that had a picture of an apple with a little bite taken out of it. "Nerdy Wayne?" I asked, confused.

As the sound of a horn came from the pocket of his jeans, he reached in and took out a silver thing that was the size of a business card and started pushing buttons on it.

"What is that, and what are you doing?" I asked, even more confused.

"I'm texting Martin. Why are you acting so weird?"

"Text?" I jumped as a *ding* came from the silver thing. "Ahh!" What *was* that? A pager? I knew from a PSA I had seen on TV that drug dealers carried them, but I didn't know a real person who did.

"What is your deal?" Ethan demanded. "Have you already started in on the Red Bulls?"

"What's a Red Bull? And do you not notice anything different about this room?!" I demanded. "Or me?!"

"Other than the zit on your chin? Nope." He took the silver thing and aimed it at my face. A second later a clicking sound could be heard, like a camera.

"Instagram, here you come," he cackled as he ran out of the room.

If my head hadn't been hurting before, it definitely was now. Text, bells, whistles, silver things—what was going on?! I walked over to my phone to call Jonah to ask him if he knew what I had for dinner the night before, but it wasn't there. All I could find was a thing that looked like Ethan's silver thing, but this one was pink. As I pushed the button on the bottom, the screen filled with all these little pictures—a little bubble like the kind that was in comics that said *Messages*; the date that said *Calendar* underneath it; a picture of a sunflower that said *Photos*; a lens that said *Camera*. As I touched the screen and a bunch of different little pictures showed up, the sound of a chime could be heard.

"Ahh!" I yelped, dropping it. As I went to pick it up, it *ding*ed again. "*What* is that thing?" I said aloud. I picked it up and looked at the screen. **Stopping at Bucks. Will get u a mochaccino. B there in 15.** flashed across the screen. In the top left-hand corner, the word *Andrea* could be seen. Who was Andrea? And what the heck was a mochawhatever?

"Ethan!" I yelled.

"What?" he yelled back from his room.

"Can you come here, please!"

"I was just there!"

"I told you kids—I don't like all this yelling in the house!" my father yelled from the bedroom.

"Just come here!"

"Just because you're older doesn't mean you can order me around!"

"Yes, it does!"

"Your father isn't going to say it again!" my mother yelled from downstairs. "Enough with the yelling!" She sighed. "I can't deal with this. Rain, can you go deal with this?"

A moment later the sound of footsteps could be heard on the stairs, followed by a head of very long brown dreadlocks on a very short woman in my doorway.

"Hey, Zoe!" chirped the woman.

"Hey . . ." Since I didn't know her name—or who the heck she was and what she was doing in our house at 7:45 a.m.—I nodded a few times.

"May I enter your personal space?" she asked in a calm voice, like the one used by the woman who gave me a massage when we were on vacation in Hawaii over Christmas.

"Huh?"

"Can I come in your room?"

"Oh. Sure. I guess so."

She came over and took both my hands in hers and looked at me. "What's underneath the yelling?"

"What?" I tried not to stare at the silver ring on her right nostril, but it was next to impossible.

"Your mother sent me up here to ask you to stop yelling, but I'm wondering what's *underneath* it." She took her finger and gently poked me on my robe above my left boob. "What's *here*?"

"My tank top?" I said, baffled.

"No. What are you feeling in your *heart*?"

"Umm . . ."

"One of the greatest insights that Rhiannon shared with me—"

"Rhiannon."

"My psychic. I've told you about her before."

If she had, then it was psychically, because I had never seen this woman before in my life.

"Anyways, Rhiannon once told me that anger and its manifestations—in this case, that would include yelling—are depression turned inward." She looked at me, waiting for a response.

"Wow. That's, uh, deep," I finally said.

"Right?" she agreed. "Rhiannon is so deep that sometimes I have trouble understanding her."

Why did that not surprise me?

"But wait—no—that's not right," she said. "What she said is depression is *anger* turned inward."

"Oh. Right. Well, that makes more sense," I said quickly. Actually, none of it made sense, but I was desperate to get her out of my room so I could get back to figuring out what the heck had happened while I was sleeping.

"I know you need to get back to figuring out an outfit, but I just wanted to say that if you ever want to talk—you know, *really* talk—that I'm here for you," she said. "I know that technically I'm just your parents' personal assistant, but I wouldn't mind putting that psychology degree I got at Sarah Lawrence to good use."

Since when did my parents have an *assistant*? And for what? To try to recruit people to be in their videos?

"Great. I'll keep that in mind," I said.

She put out her arms. "You really look like you need a hug," she said. "Would it be okay if I gave you one?"

Before I could respond she gathered me in her arms and smothered me. For someone so little, she was really strong. "It's okay to let your heart chakra open, Zoe," she said.

I would have responded, but I was too busy holding my breath in order to block out the overwhelming scent of patchouli that was assaulting my nostrils.

"Being graced with the gift of popularity like you have is a prime opportunity to spread the message of cohesion rather than exclusion," she went on.

I knew it was wrong to make the connection that dreadlocks equals a love for Bob Marley and pot, but she had to be smoking something.

"Right. Absolutely," I agreed. I had heard that it was best when dealing with crazy people to just agree with them until you could get to safety.

She finally let go and smiled at me. I still couldn't stop staring at the hoop. "Good. I'm glad we had this talk."

"Oh, me too." I smiled back. *What* was going on here?!

As soon as she was down the stairs, I ran over to Ethan's room. Like mine, his was totally different as well. His *Star Wars* poster was still over his bed, but on the right wall there was one for a thing called *Hunger Games*. "I need to call Jonah," I announced nervously.

He looked up from the flat screen on his desk, which was similar to the one on mine. "Who's Jonah?"

"I don't have time to fool around, Ethan," I said, annoyed. "I'm in a hurry."

"Fine. But that doesn't mean I know who Jonah is."

Usually I could tell when my brother was giving me a hard time, but the look on his face made it clear that he was serious, which freaked me out even more. "Where's my phone?" I asked.

"Um, in your hand?" he said slowly, in the tone actors on TV used when dealing with some crazy person who was about to be locked up. "What's your deal, yo?"

Okay, I needed a different way to handle this. For whatever reason, these people weren't finding things to be the least bit weird around here. It was probably easier for everyone—not to mention a lot less time-consuming—if I just played along and acted like I thought everything was normal as well. "Of course it's in my hand. I just . . . can't remember his number for some reason." Lie.

"So look in your contacts."

"That's what I was planning on doing." Another lie. "But for some reason I can't find it."

"What is your problem?" he harrumphed as he grabbed the pink thing from me. I watched as he clicked on the button marked *Contacts*, and a bunch of names came up. But it wasn't just random names—it was a VIP list of all the most popular kids at Castle Heights.

Why were all the popular kids' names on there? It was as if

I had woken up a totally different person. Which, of course, was not possible.

Ethan held out the pink thing toward me. "I don't know who this Jonah dude is that you're talking about, but he's not in your phone," he said, just as it *ding*ed again, with a different sound. We looked at the screen. **Morning babe. How r ur lips today? Haha.**

At the top of the screen it said *Brad*. "Who's Brad?" I muttered.

Ethan gave me a look. "Why are you acting like you have no idea who you are?" he asked.

Um, maybe because *I didn't*?

Helllllooooo? U there? flashed across the screen.

Ethan handed me the pink thing. "Go sext with your BF in your own room."

My head started throbbing even more as I walked back to my room. Once there, I stared at it, afraid that at any second it was going to come to life and start talking or something. When nothing else happened, I began pecking at the letters that were underneath the message. At least they were in the same order as the keys on a typewriter.

Who is this? I typed. Nothing happened. Seeing a button that said *Send*, I tried that and jumped as a *whoosh* sound came from the phone.

What do you mean who is this??? It's your BOYFRIEND.

Jonah, stop kidding around. I'm completely freaked out here.

Who's Jonah? the typer typed back.

The pink thing made a weird noise as another message came through. **Hey check this out—took this selfie yesterday. We look awesome, right?**

When I saw the picture that came through, I screamed.

It was a photo of me. Not *me* me, with my asymetrical haircut—the one I had had the day before—but *this* me, the one with the long, layered hair I saw in the mirror, wearing a matchy pink dress and cardigan. But I wasn't alone in the photo. I was full-on kissing a guy tonsil hockey–style. A guy who just happened to be none other than *Brad Bundy, Andrea Manson's boyfriend!*

"Rain, I thought I told you to get the kids to stop yelling," my mother yelled downstairs before she stuck her head in my room. "Zoe, *what* is the matter?!"

I looked up. "What happened to your hair? Where's your perm?" I demanded.

"What perm?" she asked, confused. "Perms are so . . . eighties."

"And what are you doing with *cornrows*?"

"Honey, what are you talking about? I've had these ever since the first *Holla Your Way to Health* DVD."

"DV what? What happened to Discosize?

"What's Discosize?"

Even without the lines that usually appeared on her forehead and in between her eyebrows when she was confused, something told me that it was better to not get into it and instead just act like I knew what she was talking about so she could leave and I could call Jonah and he could shed some light on why my life was not my life at the moment.

"Right. I forgot," I replied. "The *Holler Your Way*—"

"*Holla*," she corrected.

"Huh?"

"Not 'holler'—*holla*." She waved her arms above her head. "*Holla!*" she said before walking over and feeling my forehead. "Sweetie, do you feel okay?"

I put my hand up to feel it as well. I hoped I was burning up. That way I could chalk this all up to delirium. Unfortunately it was ice-cold. I reached over and pulled at her braids.

"What are you doing?!" she cried, pushing my hands away. "Do you know how long it took to do these?! Your father and I have the photo shoot with Nicki Minaj tomorrow for the new DVD!"

Who?

"I don't know what's going on here, but I don't have time for this," she huffed as she turned to leave. "I have to get ready for the conference call with Drake's people to see if we can license 'HYFR' for the abs-and-butt sequence. Now get dressed."

What was it with all these abbreviations? It was one thing for Ethan to try to mess with me, and that Rain lady, whoever she was—she seemed kooky enough to believe she was living in an alternate universe—but my mother was the most rational person I knew. The kind of person who when you made a joke, looked at you blankly until you said "It's a *joke*, Mom" before she smiled and said "Oh. I see. Very funny, then." If *she* was going along with this, something seriously weird was happening.

Could I be dreaming? I decided to pinch myself, like people always did in movies, to see if I was. "*OWWW!*" I yelped. Okay, then. Definitely not a dream. After I threw on the jeans and pink (*pink?* I hated pink) T-shirt from the tufted bench in front of my bed, I grabbed the silver thing. Jonah's number may not have been in the contacts, but it didn't matter because I obviously had it memorized. I punched the numbers in and waited. Nothing. "Why aren't you ringing?!" I yelled at it, panicked, half expecting it to talk back to me. I saw a button that said *Call* and pushed it, which did the trick. "Come on, Jonah—pick up the phone!" I cried as it rang.

"Santa Palm Car Wash," a voice barked over the hissing of what sounded like jets of water.

"Is Jonah there?" I asked as a car horn tooted daintily outside my window.

A symphony of vacuums started up. "Who?" he yelled over the noise.

I walked over to the window and saw a little car that reminded me of the ones you saw clowns come out of at the circus. It was the same ugly shade of blue as the BMW convertible Andrea Manson had gotten for her sweet sixteen.

"I think I have the wrong number," I said before pushing a button that said *End*.

More like the wrong *life*.

As the car door opened and the driver stepped out, my

mouth fell open. "No way. It can't be," I said, dazed as I watched her move up the walkway to our front door.

But when the door opened and I heard her say "*Hi-i*, Brenner family!" in the same nasally voice that Jonah and I had tried on numerous occasions to imitate but failed miserably because it really was one of a kind, I realized not only could it be, but it *was*.

"Hey, Andrea," I heard my dad say.

Andrea Manson was in my house. Those were six words I never thought would be strung together in a sentence. It wasn't just that Andrea and I just weren't friends. We were *archenemies*. The only list of hers I'd be number one on would be "People I Can't Stand." I pinched myself again, just to make sure that the pinch before hadn't been part of the dream.

Ow. Yeah, definitely not a dream.

"Loved that pic you tweeted yesterday of me and Kanye," my dad went on. "It's totally waack."

Was that even English?

"Omigod, right?" Andrea agreed. "I couldn't believe how nice he was! We're totally friends on Facebook now."

Who was this Kanye person? Did he go to Castle Heights?

"Right on, yo," my dad replied.

What happened to *dynamite*? As corny as it was, I'd do anything to hear him say that right now.

"Well, I better go see how Zoe's doing on the wardrobe front," Andrea said.

"I hope for your sake she's narrowed it down to five different outfit choices." My dad laughed.

"Oh, even if she hasn't, that's okay," Andrea replied as I heard her start to come up the stairs. "I mean, what are best friends for if not to cosign your fabulous fashion sense."

Best friends?!

"*Hola, mi* BFF!" she trilled as she waltzed into my room.

Hola, I got, but the B thing was a mystery. I was so shocked, I looked over my shoulder to see if she was talking to someone else. Before peering at her hand to see if she had some sort of weapon in there.

She thrust a cup that said Starbucks toward me. "Your mochaccino awaits you, your majesty."

I wasn't even going to ask what that was. Obviously there was some . . . glitch that had happened overnight where when I woke up, I was me, but not really. The sooner I could get out of here and in touch with Jonah, the faster we could figure out what was going on. I don't know why I thought he'd be able to figure this out. It wasn't like he was all that much smarter than me, but as my best friend, we had an unspoken agreement that we were in everything together.

I took the cup from her and sniffed it. Did poison have a smell? The minute it hit my mouth I spit it out. Right on my T-shirt. So much for the no-stain thing.

"What's the matter?" she cried.

"This is—"

"—exactly the way you like it," she finished. "Not only did I tell them to use exactly one third of a Splenda and just a splash of soy milk, but I then watched as they did it.

"Zoe, what is up with you?" she asked.

From the look on her face, I knew that I needed to get it together. "And it's delicious!" I quickly said. "It's so deliciously perfect that it just surprised me with its . . . delicious perfection!" Actually, it tasted the way I thought motor oil probably did. "We should get going, don't you think?"

She looked up from her own little computer thing, which had a pink case with a picture of Hello Kitty on the back. "Well, yeah. As soon as you change."

I grabbed a tissue, dipped it into a glass of water on my nightstand, and started dabbing at the stain. "No need for that." Once I was done I flashed a smile. "Good as new."

Andrea looked horrified. "You can't wear that!"

"We have a twenty-minute drive to school," I said. "It'll be dry by then."

"No, I mean, you wore that yesterday. Not to school, but when we were FaceTiming last night."

"Right. I forgot about the FaceTiming thing," I replied. What did that mean? You timed how long you could go without blinking or something? It was obvious from the look on Andrea's face that the idea of me wearing something for longer than twelve hours in a row was not something I did on a regular basis. I walked over to my closet. The one that, once I opened the door, would have Andrea even more horrified than the idea of me wearing the same T-shirt from last night. Organization wasn't one of my strong suits. In fact, it wasn't one of my suits, period. Jonah liked to say that was because I was a left, versus a right, brain, which had something to do with the fact that I was creative rather than into math.

But when I opened the door, *I* was the one who was horrified. Not only was everything perfectly organized, in neat rows that went from light to dark, but it seemed that this version of me was a big fan of pink.

"What the—?!" Talk about organized. There wasn't an ounce of left brain to be found in these rows and shelves. I bet if I had gotten a ruler and measured, there'd be the same amount of space between each hanger on the rod.

Andrea joined me and smiled. "You have the *best* closet. Susie Shapiro was so smart to feature it on her *Closets We Love* Tumblr."

I was so freaked-out, I didn't even have it in me to ask what a tumbler was. I started to rip through the pale pink skirts, the carnation-colored cardigans, and the fuchsia sundresses. It was like a Pepto-Bismol explosion in my closet. "Where's my black New Order T-shirt with the white letters?!" I cried. "And my lime-green Lycra skirt?!"

Beside me, Andrea tried to catch the various garments as they flew off the rack. "Lycra what?" she asked. "And what new order? Omigod—did you do some online shopping without me? BFFs never let BFFs shop alone!"

"All this pink. It's like the dressing room of a ballet recital in here!"

"What are you talking about? You love pink. Pink is your *thing*."

Ew. I *hated* girls for whom pink was their thing. As far as I was concerned, they belonged on a desert island with boys like Brad Bundy, who wore sherbet-colored Izods with upturned collars.

Andrea grabbed my arm. "Okay, Zoe? You're scaring me. Do you think it was the fact that you got a large instead of medium at Red Mango at the Dell yesterday? Who knows what that extra dose of fake sugar did to your brain—"

"Huh? I'm allergic to mangoes," I replied.

She looked at the clock on the Hello Kitty thing. "We're totally going to be late for the meeting with the Go Green Biracial Gay and Lesbians group."

"The who?"

"Those dorks who asked to meet with you to talk about fining anyone who doesn't recycle."

"Oh. You mean the Recyclers."

"No. The Go Green Biracial Gay and Lesbians."

"Why would they want to talk to me?"

"Because you're class president, silly!"

"*I'm what?!*" I yelled.

Andrea looked scared. "Maybe you're having some sort of weird reaction to that new ADD medicine."

"Right. The Go Yellow Bicycle—"

"Go Green Biracial," Andrea corrected.

"—club. Them. I have to talk to them," I said, dazed.

Andrea looked at me funny. "I'm just going to chalk this up to lack of caffeine on your part," she said. She looked at the Hello

Kitty thing. "If you hurry up and change, we'll be able to stop and get you a Red Bull."

I plucked out the least offensive thing I could find from my closet: a pale pink minidress. I had hoped to pair it with my Doc Martens boots, but they were nowhere to be found. Apparently this version of me preferred heels. High heels, kitten heels, wedge heels—if it had a heel, I owned it. The problem was, I couldn't walk in them to save my life. After I barricaded myself in the bathroom, I threw the dress on. "Okay, calm down," I said to my reflection in a very uncalm whisper as I twisted my now-long hair into a very messy French twist, "you can do this. You're going to find Jonah as soon as you get to school, and he'll help you figure out what happened and how to get back to your regularly scheduled life."

And then it hit me: *not only was I popular but I was class president.*

Maybe I shouldn't be in such a hurry to get back to my regular life. Maybe I could—and *should*—use the power that went along with being popular and class president to make some of the changes I wanted to make before going back to where I belonged. I owed it to my fellow students. All I had to do in the meantime was somehow play it off that it wasn't the slightest bit strange that I owned only pink clothes and that my archenemy was now my best friend.

"Zoe?"

I opened the door and walked out. "All set." For an Easter egg hunt, that was.

Andrea smiled. "You look great. How much do you want to

bet Anthropologie sells out of that dress by the end of the day because of you?"

"I'm sure you're right," I agreed. "All because I'm me."

Whoever *that* was.

"WOW. WHO WOULD'VE THOUGHT THAT someone would come up with the idea to make an energy drink that was like having seven cups of coffee but with a delicious cherry taste?" I asked as we drove up Mulholland after stopping at 7-Eleven so we could get one of those Red Bull things. At first I didn't know what the big deal was—it tasted like cherry soda to me—but soon enough, as I started drumming my fingers on the seat to keep the beat with my escalating heart rate, I got it. I guess some people would find the feeling uncomfortable, but I kind of liked it.

"I know. Can you believe that they didn't have them back in the eighties when our parents were in school? I mean, how did they study back in the old days?" She shook her head. "I wonder if they knew it would be like this in 2016."

I choked on my drink—*2016*?! I put my hand over my heart to keep it from leaping out of my chest. *How was it 2016?!* That was impossible. It was one thing to wake up a completely different person, but a completely different person *in a different century*?!

I needed to stay calm. I couldn't let Andrea know that I wasn't really me. I couldn't confide in my worst-enemy-slash-best-friend that, actually, it *was* 1986, at least in my world. If I did that, she'd probably take me straight to the nurse, who would give me an aspirin before she called my mom and suggested she take me to some psych hospital. I ducked down and put my head between my legs and started breathing deeply, like I saw people do on TV.

"What are you *doing*?" Andrea asked.

I popped up and put on the most nonchalant look I could muster. "I was just looking for . . ." I reached down and snatched the first thing my hand landed on and held it up. "This."

"My dirty sock?" Andrea asked, confused.

I looked at it. "Yes. I didn't know if you had seen it here, and I didn't want you to lose it," I said as I quickly dropped it. I looked at my watch. Jonah would be on the air by now.

That is if Jonah still *existed* in 2016.

I reached toward the radio and turned it on and began to frantically push the buttons.

"What are you doing?" Andrea asked.

"Looking for a radio station."

"Just put Spotify on."

At least I no longer had to feel bad that I didn't know what any of these words meant. I began to turn the knob until I got to 88.1. *Please let Jonah be here*, I said to myself. *Because if he's not, I don't know—*

"And to start the morning off, we've got a classic from the Avett Brothers and their *Four Thieves Gone* album . . ." said the voice I knew as well as my own. Actually, better than my own because your own voice, when you actually heard it on a tape recorder, never sounded like you.

"Oh thank God," I breathed. "You're still here."

"Of course I'm here," Andrea said. "I'm driving."

". . . 'Famous Flower of Manhattan,'" Jonah continued. "Going out to Montana."

What was an Avett brother, and why was he dedicating a song to an entire state?

I waited for the familiar sounds of some techno organ, or a synthesizer—the hallmarks of New Wave music—but instead the airwaves were filled with the soft, slow twang of a single guitar followed by an American guy singing a folk song. *Folk music?* We made *fun* of folk music.

But at least he still existed in 2016. Once we were together I could get on him about his choice of music.

"What's the deal with all this traffic?" I said impatiently. And why were there so many giant cars that looked like small trucks?

Andrea turned the radio up. "Ooh—Katy Perry's new song."

A bouncy pop tune filled my ears. I hated bouncy pop tunes almost as much as I hated folk music.

"I totally think that when it comes time for college applications, you should submit that English paper you wrote about how she's a much better poet than that Robert Frost dude," she went on.

I cringed. The 2016 version of me considered bouncy pop tunes poetry? My silver thingy made that weird beeping noise again. I looked down to see a little cartoon character–looking thing blowing a kiss.

Andrea looked over. "You're so lucky to have a boyfriend who's man enough to use emoticons," she sighed.

I cringed at the word *boyfriend*. Apparently Jonah had been right when he said that Brad had a crush on me. But there was no way this version of me was so shallow that she would date someone like him. What could we have to talk about? Unless . . . we didn't talk and instead spent all our time making out! I shook my head as hard as I could to remove that horrible image from my mind as I made a mental note of *emoticon* so I could look it up in a dictionary later on. "Right?" I replied. "So lucky." I tried not to gag on the words.

And then it hit me: in this version of my life *I* was Andrea! And Andrea was Cheryl! I shuddered. This was definitely not good. It was, however, my chance to do some fishing. "Can you believe how long he and I have been together?"

"Omigod, I know. Two and a half years is like forever!"

At that I choked. How was it possible that I could stand being with him for two days, let alone two and a half years?

Luckily, Andrea was the kind of person who liked to talk. And talk. And talk. Which meant that I could keep quiet for the rest of the ride and not give away that when she talked about things like Tumblrs and Facebooks and Googles and Twitter followers, I was completely lost. When we pulled into the parking lot and I saw Jonah's blue Buick that I knew so well (a little more dinged than usual) in front of the casita that housed the radio station, I took it as a sign that everything was going to be okay.

I already had the door open before the car had come to a complete stop. "Okay, well, thanks for the ride, see ya!" I said as I prepared to jump out.

"Where are you going?" Andrea asked.

"I have to stop at the radio station," I replied. "I'm . . . doing some early campaigning for next election."

"But what about the Go Greeners?"

"Right. I forgot about them." I sighed. If I really was class president, I needed to tend to all my constituents, even the ones who I hadn't known existed up until a half hour ago. "Give me ten minutes, and I'll meet you in the cafeteria."

I slammed the door and tripped my way up to the front of the station before flinging open the door. "Jonah, you're never going to believe—" I started to announce. I squinted. "What is that on your face?" It looked like someone had taken a Magic Marker and made squiggles on his chin.

He reached up. "My goatee?"

Not only that, but he had a black fedora on his head. This was a whole other look for him. It wasn't a *bad* look. It was just . . . weird.

Nerdy Wayne was next to him, looking at me like I had three heads. Nerdy Wayne turned to Jonah. "That's not really . . ."

"Zoe Brenner?" Jonah continued. "Yeah. I think it is."

"But . . . why is she talking to *us*?" Wayne asked, confused.

It was then that it hit me. If this was really 2016, and I was really this version of me rather than the real version of me, then Jonah and I *weren't* best friends. We probably weren't even friends. The thought of which made my eyes start to get all teary before I bit the inside of my cheek to stop them. I cleared my throat. "I'm here to talk to you today because, uh, as class president, I'm trying to spend as much time as possible getting to know the various cliques in school, and, uh, I thought that getting to know the radio guys—"

"Radio people," Nerdy Wayne corrected. "You're forgetting about Montana."

"We live in California."

"Montana's a girl," Jonah explained. "You know her. She's the one whose haircut you're always tweeting about how much you hate."

"Montana Russo?" I asked, confused. Why would I say stuff about her hair? Her hair was normal.

"Yeah." He tried to keep his voice neutral, but his voice was frosty.

Andrea used to make fun of *my* hair. Wait—so did that mean—

"So . . . you and Montana . . . you're friends?" I asked as nonchalantly as I could. Jonah put his finger up and pointed to the On Air sign. "And now—from their debut album, we have Arcade Fire's 'Wake Up.'"

"Why aren't you playing any Echo and the Bunnymen?" I asked.

He gave me a look. "Aren't they from, like, the *eighties*?"

Oh boy. This was going to be harder than I thought.

"He and Montana aren't just friends—they're *best* friends," Nerdy Wayne replied.

The tears were threatening to come back. "Right. Well, that's great. And it's been terrific getting to know you guys a little better, but I just remembered there's somewhere I need to be," I said quickly as I made my way to the door and got out as fast as I could.

I was walking toward the main building, both surprised and a little freaked-out about the amount of greetings I was getting from people, when I heard someone calling "Babe! Babe!" And then finally "Zoe!"

I turned to see Brad, in a baby blue Izod and jeans, coming from the parking lot. How was it that everyone in 2016 was wearing different clothes except for him? Talk about a time warp. And not in a good way.

I tried not to flinch as he put his arm around me and leaned in to kiss me on the cheek. "Hey, babe."

"Well, hi . . . babe," I managed to get out. He smelled like Drakkar Noir–scented breakfast burritos. "Gag me with a spoon," I mumbled under my breath.

"Huh?" he asked, confused.

"Nothing."

As he leaned in toward me, I leaned to the side. It was one thing to pretend to be this version of me, but pretending to be Brad's girlfriend was definitely not going to be easy, especially because I had never had a boyfriend.

"You were right—this shirt does look awesome on me," he said. "I'm so glad you picked it out for me." He kissed me on the cheek. "I have the most awesome girlfriend ever."

As I got another whiff of the Drakkar Noir burrito scent, my eyes widened. I knew that smell! I had smelled it the day before, at Terri's store! All at once it came back to me—how he had walked in looking for the video game store; the way I choked on the Fun Dip stick; his offer to perform mouth to mouth. . . .

Oh my God. His mouth had been on mine! Had we kissed?! I couldn't remember. It was after that that I had passed out. So it was something about that kiss that had put me in 2016. As we got to the main building I saw Andrea standing on top of the steps, her eyes lighting up when she saw Brad.

"Hey, Zoe! Oh *hey*, Brad," she said hopefully.

"Hey," he said back.

"That shirt looks awesome on you," she went on. "It totally makes the blue of your eyes that much bluer."

Brad moved back and forth in front of a locker to try to get a glimpse of his reflection. "It does, doesn't it?"

Andrea turned to me. "They're all in the cafeteria waiting," she said. "And I just need to warn you—they seem to be on the militant side."

"Really? Cool!" I said excitedly as Andrea gave me a weird look. I turned to Brad. "Time to go effect some change!"

"Is this when you bring up your idea about heated floors in the locker rooms?" he asked.

"Now *that's* a dumb idea," I replied.

"It is? When you came up with it last week, you said, 'This might be my most brilliant idea ever.'"

Oh boy. Dealing with myself was not going to be easy. "Yeah, well, I changed my mind. I'll see you later."

As he leaned in for a kiss, I swiveled my head at the last minute so he missed my lips. With my luck, if he kissed me again, I'd end up in 1683.

As Andrea and I made our way down the hall, I found myself being treated like royalty, to the point where I could have sworn Laura Preston curtsied when I walked by.

"Okay, this is freaking me out," I muttered. I was so not used to being social that I kept hitting myself in the head with my hand as I waved at them.

"What is?" asked Andrea. "The fact that you only now realized that you wore that dress two and a half weeks ago?"

Seriously? I had that many clothes that I was able to that? "Yeah, well, this is a new me," I replied. Maybe I could keep using that whenever anyone questioned the fact that I wasn't acting like my normal self due to the fact that I wasn't actually myself.

"But why would you want to be a new you when everyone already worships the existing you?"

I looked at her to see if she was serious. She was. Wow. I had no idea how to be worshipped. "Because it's time to switch things up."

"And again I'm going to ask . . . why? You're the most popular girl in school. And I'm the second most popular. Our lives are exactly how we want them," she said as she opened the cafeteria door. Were they? Was this how it felt to have everything you wanted? Because if so, so far I wasn't impressed.

"Um, hello, can someone please tell that guy that gauchos were hip in, like, the *eighties*?" Andrea snorted as we made our way across to where a group of unsmiling students were lined up on one side of a table like an overaccessorized army. She squinted. "Wait—he's a she."

I stopped myself from telling her that back in the eighties, Andrea had been the queen of gauchos. I shrugged. "I don't know. . . . I think the way she's paired it with the rainbow belt is pretty cool."

"Oh, me too," she agreed without batting an eye.

Yup. Just like Cheryl Mancini. "Hey, where's Cheryl?" I asked. "I haven't seen her lately."

"Who?"

"Cheryl. Mancini."

She continued to look blank. "Is that someone who friended

you on Facebook? Oh wait. Isn't that her over there?" she asked, pointing to one of the girls in the line.

I squinted. It *was* Cheryl. But instead of her usual pastel-colored poufy skirts and shirts, she was dressed all in black. And her hair—which was usually so big it needed its own zip code—was short and slicked back. Whoa. Talk about a makeover.

I may not have heard of the Go Green Biracial Gay and Lesbians for Mideast Peace group before now, but I already knew a lot of the members. They were the ones who got picked last in gym class and pounded the hardest in dodgeball and slammed up against the lockers. But now there was something different about them. It wasn't just that a lot of them had different hair (the last time I had seen Patricia Simmons—the girl who Andrea had mistaken for a boy because of her short hair—she had had her long curls pulled back in a banana clip), or dressed a different way (instead of his standard uniform of baggy jeans and a Magic Johnson Lakers jersey, Terrell Sampson was wearing sharply creased chinos, a short-sleeved plaid shirt, and a bowtie). Before they had walked around folded up like origami animals. But now, they were . . . *unfurled.*

Like before, Cheryl had always been in Andrea's shadow. But no longer. Instead of trying to hide, these guys were sitting up ramrod straight, staring the world in the eye. And no one more so than Lindsy Rauch—the girl who talked out of both sides of her mouth and had sided with Andrea about my asymmetrical haircut.

"Hey, guys," I said with a smile. For as long as I could milk this popularity thing, I was going to use my powers for good and make it so people weren't intimidated by me. "I love your outfit, Terrell," I said. "The bowtie is an awesome touch."

His mouth opened so wide that his gum fell out and landed on his leg. He popped it back in. "You know my name?" he asked, amazed.

"Of course I do," I replied. "Don't you remember we were lab partners in biology? Remember how each class you'd sing a song from Michael Jackson's *Off the Wall* album?"

At the Michael Jackson reference, the group looked confused. Right. He was probably like sixty now. "What I meant was . . . would it be okay if we joined you?" I asked.

"Omigod, totally!" Lindsy cried. "Ralph, give her your chair," she ordered to a large kid wearing a T-shirt that read MILEY WAS ROBBED, almost pushing him off his seat.

"It's okay—I'll sit here," I said as I started to pull out another one.

Andrea put her hand on my arm. "What are you doing?" she whispered.

"Sitting down?"

"We can't *sit* with them!"

"Why not?"

"Well . . . because . . ."

We all watched, waiting for her to go on.

"It's just . . ." She gave me a pleading look. "You really need me to explain this?"

"Actually, yes. Yes, I do." Was I putting her on the spot

and collecting payback for all the times she made me suffer? Maybe. But it was for a good cause. I was like the Robin Hood of popularity.

"Why don't we just go up to the Ramp?" she suggested. "Where we always sit."

"I'd rather sit here," I said as I plopped down. I looked at the group. "So tell me—what I can do to help?"

They looked at each other. "*Help?*" Cheryl asked, incredulously.

Steve Frankfurt whipped out this phone thing and aimed it at me. "Can you say that last line again? I'd like to get it on tape and sample it for a song on my new *Overprivileged White Boy Blues* album."

Wow. It was cool that you could tape people with that thing. Not to mention a lot less bulky than a tape recorder, which is what I used to tape songs off the radio when I didn't want to spend the money to buy the albums. "Well, yeah. I mean, I'm the class president," I replied. "That's my job." I leaned back in my chair and crossed my legs. "Talk to me." I smiled at the group. I turned to Andrea. "I've always wanted to say that."

She shook her head. "I officially have no idea what's going on with you," she said under her breath.

I ignored her. "I understand it's got something to do with fining people for not recycling?"

Lindsy sat up straighter. "Steve was able to hack into the computers of all the surrounding private schools and we're, like, next to last in terms of our recycling record."

"It's truly abominable," Terrell interjected.

"Sounds like it," I agreed. "So what are you thinking? A quarter? Thirty cents?"

"Wait—you're *supporting* this?" Lindsy asked.

"Well, sure," I replied. "I mean, you've been all about recycling since, like, 1982." Whoops. "What I meant to say is that recycling has been a big issue since 1982, and had you been alive back then, I'm sure it would have been a major cause of yours. Like if you had been in high school then? I bet you would have been part of a club called the Recyclers." I really needed to shut up before I put my foot in my mouth any farther. I cleared my throat. "So. Getting back to the issue at hand. How much of a fine do you think is fair?"

"I don't know. I guess I was so sure you'd veto the bill that we didn't even bother thinking that far," she admitted.

"How does everyone feel about a dollar? I think a dollar is perfect," Andrea said quickly. "Okay, then! A dollar it is!" she said before anyone had a chance to answer. She took my arm and tried to haul me up. "Now, let's go."

I didn't budge. "Actually, I'd like to hear what else you're all working on."

Andrea gave up trying to corral me and flopped down on a chair and took out an emery board and began to file her nails.

"Well, we were thinking that with the fine money, we would start a garden so the cafeteria could use organic vegetables," Cheryl said.

"I love that!" I cried. "In fact, that's one of the things I was thinking of doing back when I was running for office. Don't you remember?"

No one did. Which made sense, seeing that none of them was even a speck in the universe back then.

"No," Andrea said, looking up from her nails. "I do, however, remember your promise to bring in a chair masseuse on Fridays."

I watched the Go Greener attention turn toward the door. Curious to see what they were looking at, I swiveled my head. Over near the snacks, a girl with short brown hair in a pixie cut was loading up her arms with an assortment of sugary and salty delicacies.

"I have such a girl crush on Montana Russo." Steve sighed.

She did have a very cool look. You wouldn't think the pairing of leopard flats would work with camouflage capris and a T-shirt that said THE LUMINEERS, but it did. And there was nothing wrong with her hair.

"I just have a crush on her." Cheryl sighed.

She wasn't particularly beautiful. In fact, unlike Andrea, who reapplied her lip gloss every five minutes, Montana's face was free of makeup. But something about the way she looked like she had just rolled out of bed was attractive. The fact that she didn't stand out *did* make her stand out.

"You gotta love a girl who isn't afraid of carbs," Sherri said as Montana added some Pop-Tarts to her stash. "I know I do."

Andrea wrinkled her nose. "Ew. She's like a walking advertisement for preventive stomach stapling." She turned to me. "I'm sorry, but she is."

Snacked up, Montana made her way toward us. "Hey, guys. What's going on?" she asked as she tore open a bag of SunChips with her teeth. She turned and looked me over. "Zoe," she said. I knew that clipped tone. It was the same one I used when greeting Andrea in front of teachers.

"Hey, Montana," I said. "By the way, I love your name."

She raised an eyebrow. "You hate my name."

"I do?"

"Oh, you totally do," Andrea chimed in. "You know, like how behind her back, you like to call her Dakota. And Utah. And Ohio—"

Montana's other eyebrow went up. She was ambieyebrow-ous. "Ohio. That's a new one."

I cringed. Was this version of me really that much of a jerk? That was like bullying. "Yeah, well, that was before," I said. "I'm a different person now." How many times was I going to say that today?

"Really," she said dryly.

It was refreshing to meet someone who wasn't kissing my butt. "Yes. Really," I replied. "And also? I like your pants. A lot."

She looked around. "Am I being Punk'd?"

What did that mean?

"Because you always make fun of my clothes whenever you get the chance," she went on.

"Why would I do that?" I asked. "You've got awesome style."

"Maybe because you're a walking example of what it looks like to follow soulless trends that are sold to us by advertisers and a fashion industry that feels we need to starve ourselves and show as much skin as possible so that we as women can remain objectified by the male patriarchy."

Wow. She was good. I would have voted for her as class president.

She looked at her watch. "I've got to motor. I need to get more signatures on my petition to ban the use of fetal pigs in biology."

As she walked away, Andrea rolled her eyes. "Motor. Please. Quoting *Heathers* is so old-school."

I didn't know who this Heather was, but I liked her. "I like old-school." I shrugged.

Talk about an understatement.

The thing about being best friends with someone is that you know their routine. Which meant that I knew that Jonah had a free period after second period, and spent it in the radio station DJing his *Midmorning Meltdown* show. I myself had Spanish, but decided to fake period cramps and ask to go to the nurse. Señora Fritsche was so old, I doubted she even remembered what getting her period was like, but she excused me. Most likely because my accent was so bad, her entire face scrunched up in horror when I tried to speak.

Because the On Air sign was glowing, I entered as quietly as I could. A song finished up. One I had never heard of. This one had synthesizers, but it wasn't New Wave-y. It was . . . I had no idea.

"In honor of the Castle Heights Cougars' soccer playoffs this afternoon, that was Daft Punk's 'Get Lucky,'" he said into the mike. "And now, to amp things a bit because the soda machine is broken therefore denying us some much-needed caffeine this morning, here's some TV On The Radio."

Where was New Order? He always played them between second and third period. Jonah and Nerdy Wayne looked over, surprised to see me.

"Dude, is that really her, or a hologram?" Wayne asked, freaked-out.

"It's really me," I said.

Jonah didn't look freaked-out that I was there. He just looked a little annoyed. "We usually don't allow visitors in here—"

"I know. But I'm not a visitor. I'm your best . . . fan," I vamped.

"*You* listen to our shows," he said doubtfully.

"I do. Every day." I left out the part that sometimes I'd fall asleep to them. "Can I please talk to you alone for a second?"

Jonah looked at Nerdy Wayne.

"Dude, I am *not* missing this," Wayne said.

Jonah brought a five-dollar bill out of his pocket. "Go get yourself a few doughnuts."

Wayne took the money. "Okay. But I don't have to share, right?"

Jonah opened the door so he'd leave.

"Thank you," I said when we were alone. I took a deep breath. "Now what I'm about to say is going to sound weird. Like *really* weird. But I just need you to hear me out—"

He put his finger in front of my lips to shoosh me for a second as he introduced the next song. "And now, for all of you deep in the morass of a heartache, here's a little something by the National," he said as a depressing song started up. He turned to me. "What is it?"

"What it is is that . . . I'm not who you think I am—"

"I know that."

I brightened. "You do?"

"Yeah. Don't take this the wrong way or anything, but you barely ever leave your perch on the Ramp, so for you to come here—"

"No. That's not what I mean," I said. "What I mean is that . . ." I got closer to him. "You *really* don't recognize me?"

He looked confused. "Of course I recognize you. You're the most popular girl in school."

"I'm really not."

Now he really looked baffled. "But that was your campaign slogan. 'Vote for me—Zoe Brenner. The most popular girl in school.'"

I cringed. How could this version of me stand myself? I started to pace. I needed to figure out a way to tell him who I really was without completely freaking him out. Well, I paced until I had to sit down, because my feet were killing me from the heels. I took one of my shoes off and began to rub my feet. "These things are killing me. Remember that time at the ballroom dancing class finale? Me in my heels, and you with toilet paper stuck to your loafer?"

At that, his face got pale and his eyes narrowed. "How'd you know about the toilet paper thing?"

So much for the avoiding-freaking-him-out thing. I took another deep breath. It was time to just go for it. "Because I was your partner!" I replied. "We danced to that song 'At Last' by Etta James but instead sang 'I Melt with You' by Modern English to each other!"

I watched as he started to squint, the way that he did when he was trying to remember the lyrics to the Plimsouls' "A Million Miles Away" from *Valley Girl*, a movie which although he proclaimed to think was dumb, I knew he secretly liked from the so-called allergy attack and leaky eyes that just happened to come on right at the moment when Deborah Foreman told Nicolas Cage that it was over and she never wanted to see him again. "Montana was my ballroom dancing partner," he said, confused.

"You really don't know?" I asked anxiously.

"Know what?"

I searched his face to see if he was kidding. Jonah was the only person who could get me like that. But he wasn't kidding. He was dead serious.

Just then the door opened and Nerdy Wayne walked in with a handful of doughnuts. "I know I said I wasn't going to share, but you want one?" he asked as he held his hand forward.

"I'm good, thanks," I said. I looked over at Jonah, who was still freaked-out. "I should probably go."

"Yeah. That's probably a good idea," he agreed firmly.

I nodded sadly. What did you do when the one person in the world who really got you thought you were crazy?

As I turned to go, the door opened and Montana walked in.

When she saw him, her face lit up with a smile. Even the gap between her top front teeth was cool. Like an accessory or something. But when she saw me, the smile faded. "Wow. You're really taking this fraternizing with the commoners thing seriously. Is there some special election coming up or something?"

"No. I was just . . . going," I mumbled as I made my way out before the tears that were springing to the corners of my eyes could take off. Once I got outside, I turned for one last look through the window. As I watched them, I couldn't help but notice that they fit together perfectly. Like chocolate and peanut butter. Or popcorn and Hershey's syrup. All things that Jonah liked to eat when we hung out together back when *we* were best friends instead of them.

CHAPTER
Six

I'D BE LYING IF I SAID THAT I COULDN'T WAIT to get back to being an invisible nobody in 1986. Even though all the new technology was freaking me out, and I'd probably have to add another year of high school just to learn it, it was kind of cool to be in 2016. Just like I'd also be lying if I said I had no interest in taking over Andrea Manson's title of "Most Popular" if only because it allowed me to be class president. If I played my cards right, I could effect a lot of change before I went back. That is, if I ever figured out how to get back. But if being popular in 2016 meant that I couldn't have Jonah as my best friend, then I'd trade it in an instant. I would have rather been a 1986 nobody with Jonah by my side than the most popular girl in the world without him.

I had just come out of the girls' room (apparently some things did not change—like the smell of the bathroom after Janet Wishner made her morning visit) and was examining the contents of my new locker (hair products, makeup, two mirrors) when a pair of hands grabbed my waist and Brad's face appeared next to mine in the mirror.

"Ahh!" I yelped.

"Man, we're so hot together, aren't we?" he asked.

My initial impulse was to try and slither away from him, but if I was going to be here for a while, I was going to have to do my best to act like I really was his girlfriend. "Oh totally," I agreed nervously. "Hotter than . . . a summer day in Palm Springs."

Before I knew what was happening, Brad managed to snake his leg between and around mine so that I couldn't move. What he was missing in brains, he more than made up for with coordination. "You miss me?"

"Um—"

His face fell. Poor guy. Who knew he was so sensitive?

"What I mean is how can I possibly miss you when you're always sending me texts on my iPhone," I said as I held up my pink thing. I had learned that during the ride to school with Andrea.

Brad's face fell further. "But you love how I always text you," he said. "You're always saying how lucky you are that I'm like a girl that way."

I couldn't believe it, but I actually felt bad for the guy. There he was, standing there with a totally open heart, willing to hand it over without question to his girlfriend. The problem was, I wasn't his girlfriend. But if I was having a hard time convincing Jonah of who I really was, Brad *definitely* wasn't going to get it. We had been in algebra together. I knew this.

"And I do love it," I agreed quickly. At least this version did.

"Babe, what's going on with you?" Brad asked. "You're, like, *different* today."

Talk about the understatement of the year.

He leaned in closer. "I mean, you always get a little insane after a particularly intense make-out session, and granted yesterday afternoon's was off the charts, but you're acting way weird."

Okay, I could not think about that at the moment. Just like I couldn't think about the fact that as long as I was in this life, there was a very good chance that the kissing thing would probably come up again.

Brad leaned in. "I'm thinking I need to kiss you again right now as an anecdote—"

Like, say, now. "Actually, it's antidote," I said as I leaned back. "See, an anecdote is a funny story, whereas an antidote is what you take to counteract a poison," I rambled. "How, like, if you're bitten by a snake, and you went to a doctor—well, if you were able to make it to the doctor before you died—then you'd be given—" The bell rang signaling the beginning of fourth period. "An antidote! Gotta go!" I cried as I started to bolt.

"Aren't you going to walk me to Remedial English?" he called after me.

"I wish I could, but I don't want to be late for trig," I answered over my shoulder.

"But you hate trig,"

Some things hadn't changed. "Yeah, well, this is a new me!"

I wondered if I'd ever get back to the old one.

At lunch that day, I got a new perspective on my life.

Literally.

"Wow. It's not like we're all that high up here, but it does make a person feel above everyone else, huh?" I said as I peered over the edge of the Ramp. The Ramp was an area of about 150 square feet that was raised about three feet higher than the rest of the cafeteria, with tables and chairs. Because of who I was—at least in this life—we had the best table up there: smack in the middle, right next to the edge. All the better to gaze over my kingdom at my subjects.

Brad did his inbred-cocker-spaniel head tilt again as he thought about it. "But that's, like, the point, isn't it?" he finally said.

"Omigod, that's so weird! I was going to say the *exact same thing*!" Andrea gasped.

Did she realize that she was kissing my boyfriend's butt right in front of me?

"It probably is the point," I replied, "but that doesn't mean it's right."

"It's not?" Brad asked.

"Nope. This is a democracy. Not a monarchy," I said. "Which means that we should all be on the same playing field."

Andrea leaned toward him. "I don't know what's going on with her," she whispered as she not-so-subtly yanked the front of her top down so she was showing some cleavage. "She's been like this ever since I showed up this morning to pick her up."

As I scanned the cafeteria, I saw Jonah walk out of the food bay with his tray. Even from this far I knew what was on it: a taco, which he would drown with hot sauce; no beans, because he had once farted during history after eating them and it scarred him for life; and extra tortilla chips that he had charmed out of Gladys, the lunch lady who scowled at everyone but was nice to him because he had won her over with his corny knock-knock jokes. "Jonah!" I yelled without thinking. What was I doing? He had pretty much made it clear that he wanted nothing to do with me.

He turned and scanned the cafeteria, looking for the source. When he saw me, he looked embarrassed. Maybe because I was waving my hands so he'd see me, and attracting a lot of strange looks.

I jumped up and jogged toward him. "I . . . um . . . was wondering if you wanted to come up there and check out the view," I asked. "Because, you know, you've never been up there."

He wasn't the only one who looked uncomfortable. The entire cafeteria looked freaked that I was daring to talk to a mere mortal.

"Thanks, but I think I'm good," he said warily as he walked into the sea of tables over to where we sat. And where Montana was waiting for him. With a sigh, I went back to my table and, for the rest of lunch, tried to pay attention to what Brad and Andrea were talking about (something about something called Instagram) but I found myself unable to stop looking over at Jonah and Montana. Every time I did, Jonah was in mid-laugh over something she had said. She had great style *and* she was funny? I watched as she shoved some potato chips in her mouth. And she wasn't a dainty eater like most girls? She was kind of perfect. No wonder Jonah liked her.

The hair on the back of my neck stood up. But did he *like her* like her?

And if he did, why did the idea of that make me upset? He was my best friend. I wanted him to be happy.

Right?

As I watched her make Jonah laugh yet again, I heard the sound of someone clearing her throat. I looked down toward the ground and saw Sarah Bernstein standing there, holding her phone. "Oh hey, Sarah," I said.

"Hi," she said, surprised to be recognized.

"So what's up?"

"I was wondering if I could get a picture," she said nervously.

I looked around. "I don't see any signs that say you can't."

"No. I meant . . . with you," she said.

"Why would you want a picture with me?" I asked, confused.

"Um, because you're you and she's her?" Andrea offered as Brad laughed.

To them—people who had always been *have*s versus *have-not*s—they wouldn't have noticed it. But for me—someone who knew all too well what it was like to be looked down upon—I caught the shame that flashed across Sarah's face. "It's for my little sister," Sarah went on. "It's her birthday. She's a huge fan. She follows you on Facebook and Twitter."

I didn't know what that meant, but it sounded like it carried a lot of weight. I smiled. "Of course. Come on up."

Her eyes widened, like a cat stuck in the headlights of an oncoming eighteen wheeler. "On . . . the Ramp?"

I nodded.

She looked down at her clothes. "I'm really not dressed for it today."

"Hello, understatement of the year," Andrea muttered.

I shot her a look before turning back to Sarah. "Fine. I'll come down there," I said, getting up. All this rarefied air was making me light-headed anyway. To say that the crowd parted as I made my way down wasn't a lie. I was so used to getting jostled and having to go around people because everyone ignored my *Excuse me*s that I felt like a stone a slingshot had just released. I practically tripped my way there, although part of that was probably because of the heels. After the picture, I took a deep breath. It felt good to be on solid ground again.

"Zoe, what are you doing? Come back up here," Andrea called nervously.

"I'll be back," I called over my shoulder as I started to make my way into the sea of non-Ramp-dwelling students.

"Hi, guys," I said as I slid into a seat at the table where Jonah and Montana were sitting.

"Oh no," Jonah said under his breath.

Montana was so stunned that she didn't notice the salsa that dripped off her chip onto her shirt. And when she finally did, she dabbed at it once before forgetting about it. Which—from the amount of stained T-shirts I owned—was exactly what I did.

"I don't mean this to sound rude," she said when she recovered, "but what are you doing here?"

I shrugged and reached for one of Jonah's chips. "Just saying hi." I knew I was pushing my luck, seeing that Jonah had already made it clear that he wanted nothing to do with me, but I couldn't help it. Something in me just wouldn't let it rest.

As Jonah reached his hand out, it collided with mine.

"Oh my God. Our snacking synchronicity is gone," I gasped.

He looked at me. "Our what?"

I stared at him. Jonah had one of those faces where everything showed, and yet there was nothing. It was obvious that he really didn't know what I was talking about. "You really don't know who I am, do you?" I said softly.

I looked over at Montana, who was staring at me like I was up to no good. It was exactly the kind of look I'd give someone if they were doing this to Jonah. I stood up. "Never mind. Sorry to disturb your lunch."

It looked like I was on my own with this stuff.

CHAPTER Seven

AFTER SCHOOL, WHEN ANDREA ASKED IF I wanted to go shopping on Fairfax, I got excited. Not because I liked the idea of some BFBWS (Best Friend Bonding While Shopping, according to Andrea, who was big on abbreviations), but because I could stop and see Terri. Terri was just weird enough that if I told her what had happened to me, she'd probably believe it. And even if she didn't know how to help me get back to 1986, she had enough weird friends that maybe one of them would know. And if she did think I was nuts, I could run out of there and never show my face again.

But when we got there, Terri's store was nowhere to be found. In its place was something called the Dell, a giant mall. "Where's Terri's?" I asked Andrea as we pulled into the parking structure.

"Who's Terri?"

"Terri of Terri's Totally Bitchin' Treasures."

"I have no idea what that is," she replied. "Did it just open?"

"No. It's been here since 1982."

She wrinkled her nose. "So it's old. Must be over in the Farmers Market with all those other old people. Ew. It always smells like Vicks VapoRub over there."

As she pulled up to the valet, a bunch of guys descended on the car and fawned over us like we were royalty. "Miss Zoe! So nice to see you always!" one of the men said as he opened my door.

"Thank you—" I shot Andrea a look.

José, she mouthed.

"—José," I finished.

"Those guys are so great," Andrea said as we got in the elevator. "Remember that coronation ceremony when we were granted VIP Parking status and they sang 'For She's a Jolly Good Fellow' to us in Spanish and gave us those tiaras and you wouldn't take yours off for two days?"

I cringed. First the discovery about my love of pink and now the revelation that I had dared to wear a tiara in public. If it were possible to perform a citizen's arrest on yourself for fashion faux pas–ing, I'd do it. "That sure was a great day," I lied. Maybe Terri's was now part of this Dell thing, even though Terri had sworn she'd never be part of a mall culture.

When we got out of the elevator, my eyes widened. This Dell thing wasn't a mall. It was more like a mini Disneyland complete with trolleys and a fountain that moved in time to music that just happened to have stores thrown in. As Andrea put her hand out to stop me before I got hit by a trolley, I turned to her. "What a wonderful use of our time to come here every day."

I was quickly learning that while "nonfat, nonwhip two Splenda mochaccino" may have been a large part of Andrea's vocabulary, irony was not. Which meant that my comment— like a lot of things—sailed right over her head. "Well, yeah," she agreed. "If we didn't, how else would you have won Best Accessorizer at Castle Heights three years in a row?" As we approached a place called Anthropologie, she grabbed my arm. "Time to go to worship at the altar of fabulousness," she announced, yanking me inside.

Once inside, my face flushed, my heart raced, and my stomach swirled. But not in a good way, like it did when I walked into Terri's.

"Are you okay?" Andrea asked worriedly. "You look really red."

"All this pink," I murmured. "And the floral prints. And the ruffles." I looked at her. "It's like . . . an overload of fabulous!"

From the smile on her face, I could see that she hadn't come any further along with her proficiency in irony. "Well, *yeah*."

"While you become even more fabulous, I think I'm going to sit this one out and go see if I can find a Hot Dog on a Stick."

"A what on a what?" she asked, confused.

"A Hot Dog on a Stick," I repeated. They had to have one there.

From the look on her face, apparently they did not.

"Or I'll just go . . . get some . . . frozen yogurt?" I asked. That seemed like something this version of me would like.

She smiled. "I'll meet you there."

Once I got outside, I was relieved to hear Whitney Houston's "The Greatest Love of All" blaring from the speakers as the fountain dramatically jumped in time to the lyrics. Finally. Some music from the eighties. It was good to know that you could always depend on Whitney.

"I still can't get over the fact that Whitney's gone," a middle-aged woman wearing a T-shirt that said I'M A BELIEBER said with a *tsk* to her friend as they passed me. "To die like that?! How awful."

Okay, then. You *couldn't* depend on Whitney. After buying a smoothie at a place called Jamba Juice (similar to Orange Julius, but way more flavors and way more expensive) I wandered around the mall, peeking in the various windows. Where were the wide patent leather belts? And the leg warmers? And the fingerless lace gloves?

And then I saw it.

Which was kind of a miracle, as it was all the way in the far corner of the mall, near a generator that made a lot of noise. There was no sign, but something about it captured my eye. Maybe it was the Rubik's cube in the window. Or the ripped sweatshirt à la Jennifer Beals in *Flashdance*. I almost started crying when I heard Cyndi Lauper's "Girls Just Wanna Have Fun" as I entered. I wasn't a huge fan—probably because MTV totally overplayed the video—but it was just such a relief to be surrounded by something familiar.

And when I saw Terri behind the counter sorting leg warmers, I almost started to cry. "Terri! Thank God," I cried as I ran over and hugged her.

"Wow. Aren't you a hugger?" she said, patting my back.

Just hearing her voice made me hug harder.

"Okay, I think we can stop now," she said before she untangled herself from me.

I looked at her. "You look so . . . *normal*," I sputtered. She was Terri, and yet she wasn't. Her hair was all the same color—brown—and she had only one earring in one ear instead of the usual five.

"I'm not sure if that's a compliment, but I'm gonna take it as one," she replied. "I don't mean to be rude or anything, 'cause God knows I need the business, but do we know each other?"

"You don't recognize me either?" I asked, alarmed.

"Wait a minute—yes! I do!"

My shoulders began to relax.

"You're the one who the valet guys gave the tiara to, right?"

"Terri, it's *me* . . . Zoe."

"Nice to meet you, Zoe."

"No. *Zoe.* As in your best customer? The girl who you said that if you had a younger sister, you would have wished it were me?"

Instead of jogging her memory, she was starting to look a little nervous.

I looked around the store. The clothes were the same—miniskirts; stirrup pants; poet blouses. "I was in here yesterday. Don't you remember? You were altering a dress on me, and then Brad came in?"

"Is Brad your boyfriend?"

"Yes and no," I replied. "I mean, yes, he is, at this moment, but not in real life."

"Ah. So what you're saying is he's a booty call."

"Ew. No!" I cried. "What I mean is . . ." How could I say *He's not my boyfriend back in 1986, which is where I live*? That wasn't going to fly. "Never mind" is what I went with instead.

"Look, I don't want any trouble," Terri said. "I already get enough grief as it is being the sole vintage place in a mall in a city that worships all things shiny and new. I don't know what kind of dare your little friends sent you on, but I'm just a single working gal trying to make a living, so while I could certainly use the business, it's probably better if you go on back to Anthropologie or Abercrombie or wherever else it is you buy your cute little dresses—"

I motioned to my dress. "But this isn't my style!" I cried. I held up a poet blouse. "*This* is my style!" I loved poet blouses. They were so . . . *puffy*. Which helped to hide how close to boobless I was.

Terri stared at me. "If you like it so much, why don't you go try it on?" she dared me.

"Fine. I'll do that," I said as I marched toward the dressing room. I plucked a pair of culottes off a rack. "I'll even try on these."

When I came out, Terri smiled. "Now *that* is an awesome outfit," she announced.

"I know, right?" I said as I checked myself out in the mirror.

"Let me get you some accessories," she said.

I tried to think of a way to bring up my situation without sounding completely nuts. "Hey, do you believe in past lives?" I asked as nonchalantly as possible as she rummaged through the jewelry.

"Well, yeah, sure," she replied. "You kind of have to if you live in L.A., right?"

Okay, this was good. I could work with this. "So . . . if we really had past lives, then if we met people in this life that we knew from past lives, we would know stuff about them, right?"

She shrugged as she put a triple strand of pearls around my neck. "I guess so."

"Soo . . . if I told you that you had a birthmark in the shape of a butterfly above your right ankle, that wouldn't be weird then, right?"

At that she paled. "How'd you know that?"

Finally—we were getting somewhere! If I could convince her I knew her, then hopefully when I brought up the time-travel stuff she wouldn't think I was too nuts. "I know that because—" Before I could continue, the door to the shop opened. "Zoe? Are you in here?" I heard Andrea call out. "One of the valet guys said they saw you come in here."

Unlike me, Andrea made a dainty *click-clack*ing when she

walked through the store, like a row of dominoes tap dancing. "I've been looking everywhere for you," she said. "Why didn't you answer my texts?" When she got a look at the poet blouse, she made the same face I gave my mother when she tried to get me to drink wheatgrass juice. "What *is* that?"

"A poet blouse," I replied happily. "Isn't it rad?"

I began to grab more stuff off the racks and put it on the counter near the register. Seeing that I didn't know how to get my clothes from 1986 into 2016, I needed some provisions. I even got a pair of Doc Martens boots.

"I so hope no one I know walks by," Andrea murmured as she typed away on her phone.

I only had ten dollars in my wallet, but I did have my Visa card, which I slapped down on the counter. Technically it was only to be used for emergencies, but as far as I was concerned, overdosing on pink could be potentially fatal.

Andrea grabbed the credit card. "Okay, I'm sorry, but as your BFF I need to do an intervention here," she announced. "Do you not realize what this could do to your reputation? Not to mention mine, by default? You can't wear stuff that's so . . . *eighties*!" she cried. "It's a form of a social suicide!"

"Two hundred five dollars and ninety-two cents," Terri said when she was done ringing it up.

Whoa. That inflation thing we learned about in social studies really must have been true. I turned to Andrea. "It's okay— once my parents see the charge on their credit card, they'll end up killing me anyway." At least I'd be dressed well when I went.

"If it's okay with you, I'm going to go wait outside," Andrea said. "You know I'm allergic to vintage."

"That's fine," I said.

After she left, Terri handed me the bag. "You're all set. I'd say it was nice talking to you, but really what it was was weird."

You could always count on Terri to say it like it was.

"I know it seems that way," I admitted. "But I swear to you—I'm not nuts."

"Uh-huh," she replied in the kind of tone reserved to talking to those who were nuts.

My parents have always been responsible (read: cheap) with their money. Even after Discosize started doing well, and they got so busy that it became clear that they needed to hire an assistant, they would only go for someone part-time. So the whole concept of this Rain person, who—I gathered at dinner—not only worked for them full-time, but also joined us on holidays ("I'm so lucky that one of the gifts of having a dysfunctional family that I can't stand to be within a fifty-mile radius of is that the Universe led me to all of you to adopt as my surrogate family," she mentioned during the moment of silence she made us take before we began eating something called quinoa and tempeh), was bizarre.

Rain was bizarre in general. I was fascinated with her dreadlocks and the earring in her nose. As it was the end of the day, the patchouli was now mixed with some funky body odor (I found out later she didn't believe in deodorant because, according to

her, it could cause Alzheimer's), which took away my appetite
a bit, but that also could have been because the entire meal had
zero flavor.

I wasn't wild about the way that whenever anyone in the family spoke, she reached for their hand and held it while looking
soulfully into their eyes ("Once you've learned how to be present
and *really* listen to someone, there's no going back," she'd tell me
later), but I had to admit it was a nice change from my parents,
who never really listened to anything that I said.

As I took a second piece of bread, my mother's eyebrow
went up.

"What?" I asked.

"Nothing. It's just . . . the bread's usually just out there for
show," she replied. "No one actually *eats* it."

I got up and went to the fridge for the butter. "Then why
bother buying it and putting it out?"

"Good question," said my dad.

"Maybe you'd like to work out with me to the new routine
when you're done," my mother said hopefully. "It's the one we're
doing with Drake next week."

"Who?"

"Too bad he doesn't have a younger brother for you to date,"
I heard my father mutter.

My mom swatted him on the bald spot on the back of his
head. "Larry!"

"What? Drake's half-Jewish."

"But she already has Brad," she hissed.

Whatever appetite I did have left quickly vanished.

She turned to me. "So what do you say? I could really use your input on the routine."

Not to mention it would burn off the carbs. It was sad to see that my mother was still obsessed with her weight. "I wish I could, but I have a ton of homework I need to do," I said.

"Since when do *you* do homework?" Ethan snorted.

"What are you talking about?" I asked. "I always do my homework."

"You mean you always use your power to force your minions to do it for you," Ethan whispered as my parents went back and forth about the idea of doing a special Christmas edition of *Hip-Hop Your Way to Health* that would pair rappers with country singers who were well-known for their faith. ("Like an exercise version of that show *Crossroads* on CMT!" my mom said brightly.)

I had minions? "I do not do that!" I whispered back harshly. Andrea did, I knew that, because right after she had given me grief about doing mine, she had had the nerve to ask me to do hers. For free.

"Yes, you do," he said. "I even got it on tape once, in case I needed to blackmail you down the line." He shrugged. "I think it's great. Once I'm super popular, I'm going to do the same thing."

As I watched Rain "eat mindfully" (read: chew every. single. bite nineteen times) I came up with an idea. "Actually, this homework I have to do tonight is really interesting," I announced.

No one said anything. Instead they clicked away on their

iPhones underneath the table on their laps. Everyone except Rain, that was. She reached over and squeezed my hand. "I think it's so great that you're opening up to the family like this, Zoe," she said. "Would you care to share with us what the homework is?"

I pushed the food around on my plate. "It has to do with time travel."

At that, my dad looked up and looked over at my mother. "We're paying thirty grand a year so she can study *time travel*?" he asked.

"What class is this?" my mother asked.

"Science."

"That's ridiculous," she said firmly. "There's no such thing."

I shrugged. "I don't know. It kind of sounded like there might be." I turned to Rain. "Hey Rain, what do you think? Do you believe in that kind of stuff?"

She chewed about a dozen more times before swallowing. "Oh totally."

At that, my dad sighed and went back to typing.

"Rhiannon wonders how people could *not* believe in alternate universes," she went on.

My father looked up. "Is that that psychic lady you've been trying to get me to go to?"

She nodded.

He sighed again and went back to typing some more.

Before I could push the subject any further, my parents got sidetracked by an e-mail from someone named Jay Z's manager, who from the way they started screaming and jumping up and down, seemed pretty important, and they got up from the table and left the room.

After getting Ethan to help me clear the table (which, from the look I got from him, was not something I did often) I followed him up the stairs and watched as he went straight to the computer in his room. That was what I needed to do—get onto that thing so I could do some research about how to get back to 1986. From the way people talked about those things, they could teach you how to do anything.

The problem was, just looking at all the various buttons and symbols made me start to sweat. I couldn't do this alone. As much as it pained me, because I knew it would probably end up costing me a fortune, I was going to have to ask Ethan for some help.

"Hey, can I talk to you for a second?" I asked at I stood at his door. "I need your help."

"Depends. What's in it for me?" he asked as he typed on the computer with one hand and his iPhone with the other. My brother may have had no coordination when it came to sports (see: losing to a first-grader in T-ball. Twice. Last year) but when it came to anything electronic, like video games and computers, he would have won an Olympic gold medal.

"The opportunity to help your older sister, whom you love so much," I replied as I plopped down on his bed. "The same one who happens to be a foot taller and thirty pounds heavier than you, and therefore could sit on you and cause a great deal of harm if she wanted to."

He swiveled around in his chair. "Tell me what it is first, and then I'll tell you what it'll cost you."

"Okay, but you can't tell anyone," I replied. "Not even Mom and Dad."

His eyes lit up. "So it's illegal? That's gonna *really* cost you, then."

"No, it's not illegal," I said. "It's just . . . it'll probably sound a bit strange when I tell you, but you have to promise to listen with an open mind."

"Open mind's gonna cost you more."

"Ethan. Come on. I'm serious."

He put his hands up. "Okay, okay." He reached under his messed-up covers to the foot of his bed and pulled out a bag of already-opened chips. So that's what that crunching sound was when I sat down. "What is it?" he asked before he jammed his mouth full of them.

I took a deep breath, hoping this wasn't going to sound as crazy out loud as it did in my head. "Well . . . the thing is . . ." I reached for the bag of chips. I definitely needed reinforcements for this.

"Can we get to it already?" Ethan asked impatiently. "There's a webinar about self-publishing e-books that I want to see."

"E-what?"

"E-books."

"What's an e-book?"

He gave one of his more annoyed sighs—the ones that he drew out super long. "I thought you had something important to tell me."

"I do! And that's part of it, kind of," I said.

"What is?"

"The d-book thing."

"What's a d-book?"

"The thing you just said."

"I *said* e-book."

"Right. That's what *I* said," I lied so we could get back to business. "Okay, so here's the thing . . . see . . . It's not actually 2016. It's 1986."

He rolled his eyes. "Can you leave now? Some of us have stuff to do. Like Facebook creeping."

"I'm serious," I said.

"And I'm serious, too. There's this new girl named Hedy Epstein, and she's really hot and I'm hoping her Facebook page is public so I can drop her favorite books and bands into conversation tomorrow."

"That's just great, Ethan. Pretending to be someone you're not is an awesome beginning to a relationship."

"I know. Why do you think I'm doing it?"

"I'm being serious here," I went on. "Last night when I went to bed, it was 1986. And when I woke up, I was here." I wrinkled my nose as I looked at my dress. "With a pink wardrobe."

His eyes narrowed. "Are you doing drugs? Did you not pay attention in health class about how that stuff can warp your mind and make it so you screw up on your SATs and not get into a good college, which will ruin your life forever?"

"Of course I'm not doing drugs!" I cried. "I really mean it. I . . . time traveled."

"So that's what that was about at dinner," he said. "I knew something was fishy, because you never get excited about something in school other than your approval rating going up."

"I mean it. I swear to you."

He searched my face. "Why aren't you blinking? You always blink when you lie."

"Because I'm not lying!"

He shook his head. "I don't know what's going on, but I don't have time for this."

"Fine. I'll convince you. I know—I'll give you a list of the popular bands from 1986: Psychedelic Furs, New Order, Depeche Mode, Pet Shop Boys—"

"You could've found that all out from Googling."

"I don't even know what a google is!"

He shook his head. "People don't time travel to Los Angeles," he said. "They go to interesting places, like different planets."

"It's not like I got to fill out a questionnaire before I left!" I grabbed his arm. "I know it sounds crazy—"

"Yeah. Because it *is* crazy."

"And since I can't get Jonah to believe we really are best friends and help me, I'm turning to you."

"Andrea's your best friend."

"In this version, she is, but in 1986 we're actually archenemies."

"And who the heck is Jonah?"

"I just told you—my best friend. You know him! He's great at *Donkey Kong*."

"*Donkey Kong*'s a video game from like a million years ago."

"Yeah. From 1986!" I sighed. "You don't even have to believe me. You just have to help me find information about time travel."

"I don't know anything about it. Because it doesn't exist!" he cried.

I pointed at the computer. "I bet that thing does."

He shook his head. "Fine. I'll help you do a search. But I'm only doing this to get you to leave me alone. *Not* because I believe you."

I threw my arms around him. I usually avoided it, because of his funky BO, but I was so relieved I couldn't help myself. "So what do we do?"

He swiveled his chair so he was in front of his computer screen and cracked his knuckles. "We Google it."

I pulled a chair up next to him at the computer. "What's that?" I asked as he moved something in his right hand.

He looked at me. "Seriously?"

"I told you I'm not from this century." I cringed. "Did I really say that aloud?"

"You did. And the fact that you said something so stupid makes me think that maybe you *are* telling the truth. Anyway, it's a mouse. And this is going to take forever if I have to explain technology to you."

"Okay, okay, I'll be quiet."

As he moved the mouse, an arrow moved across the screen, across little pictures of folders underneath them, down to the bottom of the screen where there was a long line of symbols, including a musical note, a calendar, and a camera. He turned to me. "And if you *do* want me to explain it, it's going to cost you extra."

I rolled my eyes as he typed in *how to time travel back in time.* After a second a bunch of things popped up on the screen.

"How about that one?" I asked, pointing to something that said *wikiHow.* "It even has pictures."

He clicked on it. "*Go faster than light,*" he read. "*Dive through a wormhole.*"

I did not do worms.

"*Reminisce to relive your past,*" he continued. "*Listen to songs you used to love.*"

"That could work. Let's try that," I said.

He clicked on a button and something called Spotify filled the screen. "What was the name of that band you like? The Psych Out Somethings?"

"Psychedelic Furs."

He clicked away until a list of their songs filled the screen. "Pick one."

"'Love My Way,'" I replied.

The song began to pour out of somewhere, even though there were no speakers to be seen. I immediately felt myself relax. In fact, I started to get a little teary. How many times had Jonah and I listened to this together? "So what happens now? Do I close my eyes and end up back in 1986?"

Ethan shrugged. "I don't know. Try it."

"Okay."

As I closed my eyes he turned the music up and we waited. Through "Love My Way" and two songs after that, but nothing happened other than my back getting stiff.

"Am I still here in 2016?" I asked with my eyes still closed once "Pretty in Pink" ended. Maybe I had gone into some sort of deep sleep without realizing it.

I heard Ethan shove some chips in his mouth. "Uh-huh," he said with his mouth full.

I opened my eyes. "So much for that." I sighed. "If I'm going to be here for a while, can you at least give me a primer on all this electronic stuff?"

"I guess. Otherwise you're just going to bother me with questions about it."

I smiled gratefully. "Thanks."

For the next hour I got a crash course on all things electronic. Or, to be more specific, all things called social media. Facebook. Tumblr. Instagram. Spotify. Foursquare. Google Plus ("No one actually uses that, but it's good to be signed up for it in case it ends up taking off one day," Ethan explained). By the end of my lesson, my head was spinning.

He looked at the clock. It was already nine. "Okay, you think you can handle it from here?" Ethan asked. "Because I'm gonna binge-watch some *Parks and Recreation* on Netflix."

"Binge-watch?" I asked, confused.

"I'll explain that one later," he said, pushing me out the door.

"Hey," he called when I was almost to my room.

I turned.

"I'm not saying I believe you or anything, but if I *did*, back in 1986, am I as cool as I am now?" he asked anxiously.

I thought about how to answer. He may have been the most annoying little brother on the planet, but he was *my* little brother. "You're even cooler," I finally said.

He smiled smugly. "That doesn't surprise me."

Back in my room, I plugged my iPhone into the speaker on my desk like he had taught me. There was a lot of stuff by someone named Justin Bieber in my iTunes library. And a band called One Direction. And that Katy Perry chick Andrea said I liked. All of it was poppy and mainstream. Exactly the kind of stuff you'd expect the most popular girl in school to listen to. There wasn't one New Wave song—not by the Cure, or the Psychedelic Furs, or Depeche Mode. Luckily I found it all on Spotify, which Ethan had showed me earlier. As I listened to some Depeche Mode, I picked up a framed photo of Brad standing behind me with his arms around me and studied it. I looked happy. But when I drew it closer, I saw that wasn't entirely correct. What I looked was proud, which was a whole different thing than happy. Andrea's social stock had risen when she started dating him, and I bet it had been the same for me.

Brad didn't seem like a bad guy. Sure, he wasn't the brightest star in the sky, but he wasn't a jerk or anything. But as my grandmother liked to say, every pot had its lid, and Brad was not my lid. I picked up the photo on the other side of the computer, of me and Andrea. Blocking myself out of both photos, I put them together so that Andrea and Brad were now the couple.

"Now *this* is a pot and a lid," I said aloud. Even their poses matched up, so that it looked like he had his arms around her and she was leaning her head back against him.

Since I couldn't find my boom box anywhere that would allow me to listen to the radio, I typed in the school radio station's call letters into the Google search bar. (I had learned from my tutorial with Ethan that when all else failed, try that.) Sure enough it came up, with something that said *Click here to listen.* When I clicked on it, Jonah's voice came out from the computer, announcing that we had just heard a song by a band called Okkervil River and were about to hear the Head and the Heart. It sounded corny, but just hearing his voice while I played around on the computer was comforting, even if he wasn't talking to me.

Somehow I managed to get onto that Facebook thing everyone was so obsessed with. When the page loaded, I was greeted with a picture of myself wearing a tiara. Andrea wasn't kidding. "Well, *that's* got to go," I said aloud. Eight hundred twenty friends?! Who were these people? I scrolled down, recognizing some of the names—of course there was Andrea and Brad and other kids from Castle Heights, like Dylan Schoenfield and Josh Rosen. Even my grandfather was on this thing, with a picture of a bagel and cream cheese above his name. The only person I seemed to not be friends with was Jonah. I typed in his name and clicked on a button that said *Add Friend.* I knew I was pushing my luck and officially entering stalker land, but if he wasn't going to talk to me in person, maybe he'd do it this way.

While I waited for something to happen (What, I wasn't sure. . . . His face to pop up on the screen? An alarm to go off?) I started scrolling down on something called a newsfeed. I quickly discovered that Facebook was as addictive as Bubble Yum gum. I tried to get off—I really did—but scrolling down a person's page, there'd be some article that looked interesting, or a video clip about dogs nursing newborn kittens, which would then lead to a quiz. Just as I was about to take one about what your clothing style says about your personality (I had a hunch mine would say I was old-fashioned and had a hard time letting go), my phone rang and Brad's photo flashed across the screen along with the word *FaceTime*.

"Hello?" I said warily after I clicked on *Accept*.

"Hey, babe."

"Ahhh!" I yelped as I jumped. This wasn't just a phone call—I could actually *see* him.

"What's the matter?"

"Nothing. I just . . . didn't know you were going to call me now." Was that how you even referred to what this was? A phone call?

He did the inbred-dog move with his head. "But I always call you to say good night."

Wow. That was *so* sweet. Too bad I wasn't the least bit attracted to him, because if I had been, I would have been a very lucky girl. "And I *love* that you do, because it's so considerate," I improvised.

He smiled. "So whatcha been doing?" he asked.

"Oh, you know. . . . This and that. . . ."

"Yeah. Me too." He yawned. "Okay I'm gonna hit the hay. I did upper and lower body at the gym, and I'm beat."

Suddenly the screen got all wonky. "I think something's wrong with your phone," I said.

He leaned back. "I was kissing you."

"Right. Because . . . you always do that when we say good night."

He smiled again. "Of course I do."

Maybe I could keep our relationship confined to the phone and we could just kiss that way.

"Aren't you going to kiss me back?" he asked.

"Oh. I . . . uh . . . of course." I took a deep breath and leaned in and gave a quick kiss to the screen.

"That's it?" he asked, disappointed.

I fake-yawned. "Yeah. I'm a little tired. Sorry."

"Okay. Well, good night, then. I'll see you in the morning."

"Wait!" I yelled as he went to hang up.

"Yeah?"

"I have a question."

"What is it?"

"I was just wondering . . . am I happy?" I blurted. I knew it was a weird question to ask, especially because mine and Brad's ideas about happiness were probably really different anyway, but it was kind of scary to not know yourself at all, which was the position I was in at the moment. And after Andrea, Brad was probably the closest person to me. A fact that was so weird, I could barely comprehend it.

"Well, sure you are," he replied. "I mean, we're together. You can't get happier than that."

"Yes, I know. But what I meant is . . . am *I* happy," I went on. "You know, with my life."

"You're the most popular girl in school. Of course you're happy."

"I know, but is that really enough?" I asked.

He thought about it. For a long time. Like so long that I was reminded of why he had been held back a year.

"What I mean is," I continued, "don't you think I should be doing more?"

"You mean like that idea you had to start a consulting business giving makeovers to people?"

"No. I meant like trying to effect change. . . . You know, bringing everyone at school together."

"I guess you could try that," he said, "but wouldn't that take you away from your goal of getting the school to hang a portrait of you near the office?"

I could tell this conversation wasn't going to be much help. "You're probably right," I said. "Thanks. Good night."

"Good night, wookie. Love ya!"

I was dating a guy who called me *wookie*? Oh boy. "See you tomorrow," I said as I clicked off. I sighed as I turned up the volume on the computer to hear what was going on on Jonah's show.

"And now *Talk to Me* is open for questions," I heard him say.

"Whether you need relationship advice, music recommendations, or want to debate what the best energy drink is out there, we're here to answer your calls."

I picked up my phone and dialed. I knew the number by heart because I always called to request songs.

"Talk to me," Nerdy Wayne barked when he answered.

"Hi. I, uh, have a question."

"What is it?" he asked.

"It's a question for Jonah."

"I'm the producer. All questions go through me," he said.

Now he was a *producer*? Geez, there was a lot of upward mobility in this millennium.

"Fine. See, I have a situation—"

"Everyone has a situation. That's why they call here."

"Can you just put me through?" I asked impatiently.

"Okay, but I'm only doing so because we've been light on the calls tonight, and I'm running out of excuses as to how to keep my mother off the air. Please hold."

I paced nervously while I waited for Jonah to pick up. I wasn't even really sure what I was going to say. I hadn't gotten that far.

"Thanks for calling in to *Talk to Me*. And you're on the air," Jonah said a second later.

Why did this suddenly feel like a really bad idea?

"And who's this?" he asked.

"This is . . . um . . . Baffled in Beverly Hills?" I replied.

"Cute. So what can I help you with, Baffled?"

"So, um, I have this situation—"

"Everyone has a situation. That's why they call here."

I rolled my eyes. "Is that like your new tagline or something?"

"No, but maybe it should be. It *is* kind of catchy. So what's your situation?"

"Well, see, I . . . there's this person . . . a guy—"

"Ah. So it's a romance question."

"Nope. It's a best friend question."

"A best friend who's a guy. So which one is it?"

"Huh?"

"You're secretly in love with him, or he's secretly in love with you?"

"Neither."

"Huh. Okay. This is a new one, then. So what's the deal, then?"

"The deal is that . . . I miss him."

"How can you miss him if he's your best friend?"

"I miss him . . . because . . . recently he acts like he doesn't know me." That was true.

"How come?" Jonah asked. "Did you guys have a fight or something?"

"Nope. It was like one morning I woke up and things were totally different." Again, not really a lie. Not the whole truth, either, but if I told the whole truth, he'd probably hang up on me.

"Well, have you tried to talk to him about this?"

"I have."

"And?"

"He doesn't seem to be all that interested in talking about it."
That was *definitely* true.

"Huh. Well, all I can say is that if he's really your best friend, then you should keep trying," he replied. "Because a good best friend is a terrible thing to waste."

Hearing him say that made me feel worse. What if I kept trying and it still didn't work? Then what? "Okay. I guess I'll do that," I said. "Thanks."

"You're welcome."

I started to hang up.

"Wait—" he said.

"Yeah?"

"Do we know each other? Your voice sounds familiar."

"No. I don't think we do," I replied sadly. That also wasn't a lie. If I were Jonah, I'd have no interest in knowing this version of me, either.

Around midnight I was just about to turn out my light and go to bed (that Internet stuff was *addicting*) when my phone *ding*ed with an e-mail telling me that Jonah had accepted my friend request on Facebook. Clicking on his page, I discovered I now had full access to see pictures that he had posted and status updates like *Wherever you go, there you are . . . unless you're not* and *Who beliebs the Biebs? Not I.* I could also scroll down through random things that he "liked," such as J. R. R. Tolkien, some TV show called *Lost*, and Mexican food.

When I saw that most of the photos on his page had been posted by Montana, I got that same feeling I had when I saw them at lunch together. Sad and left out and jealous. From the various check-ins and tags, it was clear that the two spent a lot of time together.

Like best-friend-level time together.

I don't know why I was surprised. I mean, Jonah deserved a cool best friend. One who was down to earth. And smart. And passionate about the world. Montana seemed to be everything that this version of me was not. I would have rather hung out with her than me any day. Well, this version of me. And I really needed to stop saying "this version of me," because it was driving me nuts.

Starting from when Jonah had first joined Facebook, I read everything he had ever posted. I wasn't sure what I was looking for. It was more like I was looking to feel connected to him again. At times I smiled at the corny posts that probably no one but me would find funny. Other times I got sad—especially when he tagged Montana in what were obviously private jokes. It was weird how this Facebook thing made you feel both more connected and more isolated at the same time. It was also—I realized when I looked at my clock and saw that it was one a.m.—a major timesuck.

I was just about to click off when I saw it.

A link to a YouTube video of Modern English's "I Melt with You." Our song. The one we had sang during ballroom dancing. The one we yelled at the top of our lungs when it came on in the car, even though we were both tone-deaf. The one I couldn't hear without thinking of him.

Montana wasn't tagged in the post. She didn't even "like" it. In fact, no one did. It was like this lonesome little post in the middle of this sea of information.

I moved my finger and clicked *Like*.

Saying it was a sign was a reach, I knew that. And a sign of what, I wasn't even sure. That Jonah would somehow come around to believing me when I told him what had happened? That I hadn't lost the one person who got me and made me feel less alone on the planet?

But I was going to take it as one anyway.

CHAPTER *Eight*

IT'S IRONIC THAT AS THE MOST POPULAR girl at Castle Heights, I was probably also the loneliest. As I walked the halls the next morning, smiling and saying hi as Andrea echoed me, all I could think about was how I would much rather go back to being invisible. When you were invisible, you could stare at people all you wanted like an anthropologist and not be called out on it, or be judged, or held up to some impossible standard. This popularity thing had me actually feeling bad for Andrea and the pressure she was under all the time. Maybe that's why she had been such a jerk to me before.

"I feel like Mother Teresa," I said as we made our way through the crowd. "But with better fashion sense." In my new poet blouse, leggings, and Doc Martens, I felt somewhat back to normal.

"Who?" asked Andrea. Or maybe she had been a jerk because she was frustrated that she was dumb.

Seeing that Mother Teresa had already been, like, 150 back in the eighties, she was probably dead by now, but, still, you'd think she'd be in a history book.

"Oh—I almost forgot," she said as she opened her bag and took out two typed pages and handed them to me. "Here's your presidential speech."

"*You* wrote my speech?"

"Well, yeah. I always write your speech," she replied, confused. "You love when I write it and you get to take credit for my awesome words."

I cringed. It was one thing for Jonah to write my speech. We were in sync in terms of our views. But I let Andrea do it? I couldn't even imagine what she had come up with. Yet another reason I didn't want to be *this* me but wanted to go back to being *me* me. I took the pages from her and started scanning it. "May Makeover Month?" I said. "What's that?"

"We talked about that. It's where you offer makeovers to those in need, for no charge," Andrea explained. "It would be a public-service thing."

Seriously? I could barely put on mascara without blinding myself. "*Get one of the Kardashians to speak at Career Day*," I read. I looked up. What was a Kardashian? Just the word itself didn't sound good. "Wow. That's just brilliant."

She smiled.

I folded the pages in half and stuck them in my bag. "Andrea, this is just great, and I really appreciate you taking the time to do this—"

"Really? That's so sweet. You never thank me for doing it."

"—but I think I'm going to take a crack at the speech myself this time," I finished.

"Oh. I can make any edits you have. It's no big deal—"

"That's sweet of you, but it's fine. Thanks." Who knew how many chances I'd have to stand up there and say my piece? I might as well take advantage of it and try to implement as many things as possible.

Before Andrea could argue with me anymore, we saw Brad striding down the hallway.

"Ooh, look—there's Brad," she said. She smoothed her hair and turned to me. "Do I look okay—I mean, you look great," she corrected.

"Hey, babe," Brad said when he got to us. Today's polo shirt was lilac, with—surprise!—the collar turned up.

"Hi Brad," Andrea said. "I love your shirt."

"Thanks," he replied, not even looking at her. He took in my outfit. "What are you wearing?"

"A poet blouse."

He reached over and patted the arm. "It sure is puffy."

"Isn't it?" Andrea agreed. "That's our girl—never afraid to be bold with her fashion choices!"

"Hey, Andrea?" Brad asked.

"Yes?" she said, way too hopefully.

"You think I can talk to Zoe for a second?"

"Sure," she said, not moving.

"I meant . . . alone."

"Oh. Right. Of course."

As she started to move away, I grabbed her arm. "It's okay—she can stay," I said nervously. "I mean, we *are* best friends"—why did my throat always feel like it was closing up when I said that?—"which means I just end up telling her everything anyway—"

"But I wanted to talk about Friday night," Brad said, his eyes glinting.

"Friday night," I repeated blankly.

"Yeah. You know . . . our *big date*."

I did not know about our big date, but I knew enough from the look on his face to know that whatever he had in mind didn't include board games, except for maybe naked Twister.

"Right. Your big date," Andrea said, deflated. "I'll just go to the cafeteria and binge on low-carb snacks."

As I watched her walk away, the usual cheery *click-clack*ing of her heels replaced with a sad slither, I couldn't believe how bad I felt for my archenemy.

"So Friday night," Brad said, smiling. The way the light hit his teeth reminded me of fangs.

"Friday night," I said again. I wondered if I sounded as freaked-out as I felt.

He cocked his head and squinted. "I'm thinking a walk on the beach at sunset, I'm thinking dinner, and then, after that . . ." He leaned in. "Well, *you* know. . . ."

I did not know and didn't even want to try to guess. "And then after that you drive me home so we can both get to sleep early because studies have shown that at least eight hours of sleep are necessary for the healthy development of a growing teen's brains?" I asked hopefully as I leaned away from him.

"No. And then you come over . . ." he said as he leaned in closer, "to my empty house . . ." Closer still. ". . . because my parents are in San Francisco . . ." If I leaned back any farther, I was in danger of doing a backbend. ". . . and not coming back until Saturday night . . ." I was totally losing my balance. ". . . and you've already told your parents you're sleeping at Andrea's. . . ."

That did not sound like run-of-the-mill making-out stuff. That sounded more like a sleepover. I had to believe that if I wasn't still a virgin I'd know that, and I certainly didn't have any plans to change that now or for a long time to come. Before he could go on—and I did *not* want him to—my foot gave way and I toppled backward.

Brad's phone *ding*ed with a text. "Ooh—Andrea says they're handing out tofu breakfast burritos in the caf." As if he needed yet another burrito.

"That's great. Definitely go get one and have some quality one-on-one time with Andrea," I said as I pushed him in the direction of the cafeteria. "I'll see you later, okay? Bye!" I said as I started off the other way.

And landed smack into Montana who was in yet another cool outfit. This time it was a patchwork denim miniskirt, black tights, and short motorcycle boots topped with a black tank top and a red crochet cardigan.

She took in my own outfit. "Is that a poet blouse?"

"It is."

"Huh. I have to give it to you—that's a very brave choice."

I couldn't tell if she was being sarcastic or not, but I smiled anyway. "Thanks. I like your outfit a lot."

"You do?"

"I do."

She cocked her head. "Don't take this the wrong way but the last few days, you're, like, a totally different person."

"Tell me about it."

Just then Jonah came up.

"Hey, Jonah," we said in unison, before exchanging a look.

"Hey," he said, seeming to be somewhat uneasy with the attention.

"Well, I guess I should get going," I mumbled as I started off.

Why was it that every time I was around him I got nervous? I never got nervous around Jonah. In fact, he was like the one person in the world outside of my family I *didn't* get nervous around.

By the time lunch was over, poet blouses was doing something called "trending" on Twitter which—according to my new best friend Google—meant it was really popular. Also by the time lunch was over, my face ached from the perma-smile that was attached to it. From the surprised looks I got whenever I said hello to someone, I got the sense that I was very partial about who I spoke to, which made me go out of my way to talk to even more people. As long as I was stuck here, I was going to milk my popularity power for all it was worth and make sure that no one felt less than or left out. It was strange, though. For someone who was supposedly so popular, I felt really alone. When you're up on a pedestal and people are intimidated by you, you feel just as out of sync as when you're sitting on the edge of the cafeteria.

By the time study hall came along I was excited for the chance to just be by myself for a while. According to my Twitter feed that I had read through last night in my crash course of trying to figure out who I was, I usually spent study hall surfing fashion websites, such as Piperlime and Shopbop. Not that afternoon, though, once I noticed Nerdy Wayne sitting two seats away from me.

And then it hit me—if anyone would know about time travel, it was him! Why hadn't I thought about this sooner? He was the one who had come up with the idea for Socialize, which, I now realized, was almost identical to Facebook! And then I remembered that not only did he believe the Socialize idea could work, but he had gone as far as to say that one day we'd be able to see each other on screens when we talked to each other on the phone. (Um, FaceTime anyone?) So if he was so good about forecasting the future, maybe he knew a thing or two about the past as well. Or at least getting back there.

I watched as his head bobbed over his iPad. (Turned out I had one as well. With a cover that was pink, natch.) "Hey, Wayne," I whispered loudly.

Nothing.

"Wayne?" I said louder.

At that his head raised, and I saw two white wires hanging out of his ears. As he took one of the wires out, I could hear music coming through the little circle thing at the top. They were like the headphones I used with my Walkman, but much smaller. "If I did something to offend you, I'm sorry," he said. "Even if I don't know what it is."

It was like the entire student body lived under a cloud of collective guilt. "I didn't say you did," I replied. "I just have a question. See, I was sitting over there, and I don't know why, but for some reason I started thinking about the idea of time travel. Do *you* ever find yourself thinking about the idea of time travel, Wayne?"

"Is this a trick question?" he asked suspiciously.

"Nope."

"*You* want to know about time travel."

I nodded. "It's a new interest of mine," I replied. "Much more interesting than hairstyles and accessories. So do you know anything about it?"

"Actually, I do. I just wrote a blog post about it."

"I love blogs," I ad-libbed. "I have a bunch of them. In a lot of different colors." Man, it was hard to constantly come up with things on the spot like that. It made my head hurt.

From the way he looked at me, like I was nuts, that may have not been the right thing to say, but oh well. "You can link to it through my Facebook page. Or my Tumblr. Or my Twitter," he said. "There's a lot of useful information in the post about how to do it."

"That's awesome," I said, relieved. I just had to track down the log—I meant, *blog*—and hopefully by dinner I'd know how to get back to 1986. Not that I was planning on going right away. I was going to at least wait until after I gave my presidential speech.

"Oh yeah. From the amount of hits I've gotten, it seems that a lot of people are interested in traveling to the future."

I guess I shouldn't have been surprised. This is the guy who came up with the idea for Facebook. Well, obviously not the idea for Facebook, because if he had, I bet he would've dropped out of high school and bought himself a small country somewhere. "I'm sure they are," I said, trying to keep my voice neutral. The last thing I needed was for it to get around school that I was asking about time travel. I could only imagine how that would morph as it made its way through the game of Telephone. "What about the past?"

"The past?" he asked, confused.

"Yeah. What about traveling back to the past?"

"Why would anyone do that?"

"Well, because there's a lot of great stuff back there."

"Like what?"

"Like . . . New Wave music. And John Hughes movies. And Bubblicious gum."

"But they didn't have technology."

"Sure they did. What about VCRs? And Walkmans?"

He stared at me blankly. "Anyways, if you still want to check out my blog and like it on Facebook, that would really amp up the hits, which would be awesome."

So much for getting an answer.

"You're really taking this 'down with the people' thing seriously, huh?" a voice said from behind me.

I turned around to see Montana, her boots up on the seat in front of her, even though there was a big sign forbidding it on the wall to her right.

"I was never *not* down with the people," I replied. I cocked my head. "What does that phrase even mean?"

Montana cocked hers as well as she thought about it. "You know, I have no idea."

We shared a smile for a brief second before hers went away. "Says the girl who spends her time ruling her kingdom from the Ramp."

"Okay, (a) I don't have a kingdom," I replied. "And (b) I actually have a big announcement about the Ramp coming up very soon."

"And what's that? That you're taking money from some scholarship fund to raise it so it's even higher?"

"No." I got up and walked to her row and plopped into the seat next to her. "The announcement is . . . it's coming down," I whispered.

Her eyes widened. As did mine. What was I saying?

"What are you talking about?" she demanded.

What *was* I talking about? "Well, I mean, I don't know that for sure, but after much thought"—like, say, almost thirty years' worth—"I've decided to suggest that we get rid of it entirely." I was? Really? I needed to shut up. Now.

She reached out and felt my forehead.

"What are you doing?" I asked.

"Checking to see if you're delirious," she replied.

I took a moment to check in with myself. "Nope. I'm completely in my right mind," I replied. "I mean, what kind of class president would I be if I didn't try to restore democracy to Castle Heights?"

"I hate to tell you this, but from what I've heard, I don't think there's ever been democracy here."

She wasn't wrong. "Yeah, well, there should be. And I'm going to be the one to bring it," I said. As much as I could before I went back to 1986.

As Montana stared at me, as if trying to see whether I was telling the truth, I felt my face turn red. It was nice to be seen as just a regular human again as opposed to being feared or adored. "Huh." She finally nodded. "Who knew?"

"Who knew what?"

"Who knew there was a whole other side to you," she replied. "Poet blouses . . . democracy . . . next thing you know, you're going to tell me you hate Top Forty bands."

"Oh, I do," I said.

"What do you listen to, then?"

"New Wave."

"Like . . . New Wave from the eighties?"

I nodded. "Yeah. Psychedelic Furs. Modern English—"

"Modern English," Montana said. "That sounds familiar."

"They sing that song 'I Melt with You.'"

She squinted. "Right. I think Jonah likes that song."

"He does."

Her eyebrow started to go up.

"What I mean is . . . I saw it on Facebook."

Her eyebrow went up higher. "Oh. I didn't know you were Facebook friends. When did that happen?"

Was it my imagination or did she sound the teensiest bit jealous?

"Yesterday?"

"Did he friend you?" she demanded.

When did "friend" become a verb? I shook my head. "No. I friended him."

"Oh. That's good," she said, relieved. "I mean, it's not a big deal either way. You friend him, he friends you . . . but . . . why?"

"Why what?"

"Why did you friend him?"

I shrugged. "I don't know. Because I want to be his friend?"

Her eyes narrowed. "Is this like some kind of prank?"

"No! What is it with everyone getting so freaked-out about me doing things differently?"

"You really want to know?"

"Yes."

"You're sure? Because just so you know, I tend to be kind of blunt."

I shrugged. "Blunt away."

"Okay, then. See, the thing is, Zoe, you're not really known for being . . . *nice*."

My face fell. While I guess I knew that, hearing it from another person was hard to swallow.

"In fact, you're kind of known for being a bitch."

My face fell even further. While I had gotten the feeling that I wasn't in the running to take over Mother Teresa's spot, I didn't know I was *that* bad.

"So when you do things like take the Go Green Club seriously, or friend unpopular people—"

"Jonah's not unpopular," I said defensively.

"Well, he's not popular. And neither am I. Which is why we're such good friends." Her eyebrow went up again. "Why are you defending him like this?"

I shrugged. "I don't know. He just . . . seems really nice."

"He is," she agreed. "Like, the nicest guy in the world."

"I know." Boy, did I know.

Before I could say anything more, the bell rang, and Montana was out of her seat. "It's been nice talking to you," she said. She cocked her head "Which is kind of weird. See you around."

"Yeah. See you around," I said.

Things just got more and more strange.

CHAPTER
Nine

"**Y**OU WANT TO HANG OUT BY *YOURSELF* this afternoon?" Andrea asked as we walked to the parking lot after school with Octopus Brad (I had started calling him that—at least to myself—after second period, when he always seemed to grow another hand no matter how quickly I removed one of his from my body).

"Yeah," I replied.

"But *why*?"

"I don't know. Because I want some alone time."

"But alone time makes a person feel so . . . alone," Andrea said.

"That's kind of the point," I replied. "Actually, I think I'll work on my class president speech."

"Didn't Andrea write it for you?" Brad asked as he tried to snake his arm around my hip.

"I did, but she didn't like it," Andrea pouted.

"It wasn't that I didn't *like* it," I corrected. "It's just that I'm feeling inspired to put some different ideas out there." Ideas that—once she and Brad heard them—would make them think I had gone even farther off my rocker.

"I can't believe we're not going shopping," Andrea sighed. "We always go shopping after school," she said. "It's, like, a tradition."

One that I did not need to partake in again for a long time.

"And what about me?" Brad asked. "I thought you were going to take me shopping to get new polo shirts."

Suddenly a light bulb went off. "I have an idea," I said. "Why don't you two go shopping together?"

They looked at each other. "Just the two of us?" asked Andrea. I could tell she was trying to keep the excitement out of her voice, but some of it snaked through anyway.

"Like . . . alone?" Brad asked doubtfully.

"Yeah. I mean, Andrea, you're a genius when it comes to shopping. And so good with color—"

"I am, aren't I?" she said, pleased.

"Oh yeah," I agreed. "See, I've been thinking about it and as my two favorite people in the world, I think you guys need to spend more time together. Without me."

Brad cocked his head and thought about it. "Sorry, but I'm lost."

That wasn't surprising, but you couldn't really blame the guy. It's not like I was making a ton of sense. "You know . . . in case I end up, I don't know, gone or something."

He gasped. "Is this the part where you tell us you have some sort of terminal disease and you only have a few months to live? Like in a Nicholas Sparks book?"

Where did *that* come from? I had no idea who Nicholas Sparks was. And did Brad actually read?

"Hey, do you think Channing Tatum could play me in the movie?" he asked excitedly. "I know he's a lot older than me, but I think our pecs are the same size."

I had no idea who Channing Tatum was, but I sure hoped for his sake that he was smarter than Brad.

"I'm not going to die," I said.

"Oh good," he said. "Wait—you mean like if aliens came and abducted you?" he said excitedly.

"Actually, I meant more along the lines that I . . . I don't know . . . moved or something."

His face fell. "You're moving? How could you not have told me?"

I sighed. "I said 'or something.' It's, like, a hypothetical thing." Man, I'd hate to be his teacher. "I'm not moving." I turned to Andrea. "I would hope that as my BF—"

They looked confused. "I'm your BF," Brad said.

"And I'm your BFF," Andrea added.

I needed to write all those abbreviations on the bottom of my shoe so I didn't keep screwing them up. "That's what I said. I just said the second F at very low volume. Anyway, as my BF*F*, I hope that if at any time I could not fulfill my girlfriendly responsibility of making sure my boyfriend looks good, that you would fill in for me."

"Oh, well, sure," she said, again trying to hide her excitement and, again, barely succeeding. "I'd be happy to." She grabbed Brad's arm and dragged him toward her car. "Let's take my car and leave yours here so we don't waste any time apart."

"Hey, what about me?" I called after them. "I need a ride home!"

Andrea was already peeling out of the parking lot before all the words were out of my mouth.

"I guess I could drop you off," a voice behind me said.

The hair on the back of my neck stood up. I turned around. "Really? You wouldn't mind?" I said to Jonah. Even if he didn't know it was me—his *real* Montana—just seeing his face made me feel better.

He shrugged. "It's okay. I have to go over Coldwater anyway."

I smiled. "Thanks. I'd really appreciate it." I stopped walking. "Wait—you know I live on Coldwater?"

He stopped as well, looking confused. "No. I have no idea why I said that. That's weird."

He knew! He didn't *know* that he *knew* knew, but he did! On some level, he recognized me as well!

He started walking toward his car and pointed to the passenger door. "You have to—"

Before he could finish I was already giving it a couple of bangs with my hip.

"How'd you know that's what you have to do to open the door?" he asked, clearly weirded out.

I tried to appear as confused as he had earlier. "I have no idea." I wanted so badly to tell him what was going on, but I didn't know how without coming off as a complete nut.

The first few minutes of the ride were painful. Literally—because one of the springs was sticking out of the seat—and figuratively, because neither of us said anything. How did you go backward with someone, and talk to them like they were some stranger rather than the one who knew everything about you?

"Thanks for being my friend on Facebook," I finally said.

"Oh. You're welcome."

We went back to being silent, save for the radio. "This is a good song. Who is it?" I asked.

"Local Natives?"

"Of course. Right. Local Natives. I love them," I lied. They were okay, but they were no Psychedelic Furs. "I, uh, liked the photos on your Facebook page." It was weird to feel nervous around Jonah.

"Thanks," he replied.

I wondered if he was nervous around me. Seeing that, you know, I was the most popular girl in school. And how weird was that for those words to be strung together in that order in a sentence?

"And you have cool taste in books," I went on. "*From the Mixed-up Files of Mrs. Basil E. Frankweiler* is one of my favorite books, too."

He looked at me. "Really?"

I nodded. That was one of the things we had bonded over when I was at his house for the first time. "I say you can tell everything—"

"—about a person by their bookshelves and music collection," we finished together.

"Okay, that was bizarre." He laughed nervously.

The thing was, it *wasn't* weird. That was what we did. We finished each other's sentences and read each other's minds and did all other sorts of Wonder Twins–like things. In fact, Jonah was always saying that if one of us ever got a monkey, we'd have to name it Gleek because that was the name of the Wonder Twins' pet monkey in the Saturday morning cartoon.

I shrugged. "I don't know. Is it?"

"Well, yeah. I mean, we don't even know each other."

"Right. But don't you think that sometimes people can *know* each other even if they don't *know* each other?"

"You mean, like they knew each other in a past life or something?"

Was 1986 a past life? With all the computer gadgets and the apps and the social networks, it sure seemed like that. "Kind of. Something like that. Past life . . . time travel . . . that kind of thing."

"*You* believe in time travel?" he asked, amused.

"Oh yeah. Sure I do."

He laughed.

"What?"

"Nothing. I just didn't take you for a time travel kind of girl."

"Oh, I am. You have no idea," I said ruefully.

"My buddy Wayne—"

"—just wrote a log post about it," I finished. "I mean a blog post."

"How'd you know?" he asked, surprised.

I shrugged. "We were talking about it in study hall," I said nonchalantly.

As he reached over to the dash and pushed the buttons, "Melt with You" came on.

"I love this song," we said at the same time.

We looked at each other. I smiled. Obviously I wasn't surprised—I knew Jonah loved the song. He, on the other hand, looked freaked-out again.

"Why do you keep looking so freaked-out?" I asked.

"I don't know. I guess because we have so much in common."

"And you think that's weird because we're in different social circles?"

"'Different social circles'?" He laughed. "That's one way of putting it."

"We're really not," I insisted. "At the end of the day, we're all the same. Just trying to make sense of life." That was pretty good. I was going to have to remember that for my speech.

He laughed. "Okay, changing the subject. So you like New Wave?"

"I do."

"I wouldn't have expected that."

"See? You're doing it again," I said. "What, you think I like people like Justin Bieber and One Direction and Katy Perry?"

"Well, yeah," he admitted. "I mean, they're listed on your Facebook page."

Huh. So he had taken the time to study my Facebook page. Probably not to the extent that I had studied his, given the fact that mine had so many posts that I gave up reading my own page after getting through only a week. But still—that meant something.

"Well, it's a mistake," I said. "Who I really meant to put was the Psychedelic Furs and New Order and Echo and the Bunnymen and Depeche Mode—"

His nose wrinkled.

"You don't like eighties stuff?"

He shook his head.

That made me sad. I motioned to the radio. "You like this song enough to have put it on your Facebook page." The minute the words left my mouth, I cringed. That made me sound like a class A stalker. Especially because he had posted it, like, a year before. Maybe he wouldn't notice. He was a guy. Guys didn't analyze things like girls did.

"That was a long time ago," he said. "You went that far back in my Facebook history?"

Of course he noticed. The reason I loved Jonah was *because* he noticed things and wasn't a typical *guy* guy.

"Huh," was all he said.

What did *that* mean? I'd be dissecting that one for at least an hour. And since when did I spend time dissecting anything that

Jonah said? That was the kind of thing you did with guys you *liked* liked.

Luckily, we were almost to my house. "Hey, you missed the turn," I said as he sped right past it.

"Sorry. I didn't know."

"How could you—" I stopped myself. "—know where it was?" I said as a save. "Unless, you know, you were some creepy stalker or something. It's the Spanish one with the red roof."

After he pulled into the driveway, I turned to him. "Well, here we are."

"Yup."

"Yup," I echoed as I continued to sit there.

"So . . . did you need something else?" he asked.

Yeah. I needed to tell him what was going on, and I needed him to believe I wasn't nuts, and I needed to feel like everything was the same it had always been between the two of us. "Just . . . thanks for the ride."

"You're welcome."

What was my problem? I had gotten what I wanted: I was alone with Jonah and could spill my guts about everything that was going on. And because his car was so old and it took a while to open the doors, he'd be a captive audience for at least as long as it took me to tell the whole story and maybe, just maybe, he'd help me solve my problem. Because as my best friend, that's what Jonah did—helped me solve my problems. Everything from where to hang my posters in my room to how to tell my parents that the more I thought about it, college felt like a waste of time when what I really wanted to do with my life was direct music videos. Jonah was the one who was always there for me; the one who had my back; the one who I knew I could tell anything to, no matter how crazy, and he'd understand.

But telling someone you had time traveled thirty years, and you were now someone else on the outside, but on the inside you were still the person you had always been? That seriously pushed the bounds of normalness.

I took a deep breath. "And there's one other thing I need to tell you—" Apparently I was going to push it.

"What?"

"I need to tell you that . . . I really need to get going because I have to go work on my presidential speech."

"Okay. I have to get going, too. On Tuesdays I—"

"—go to the nursing home to see your grandfather, I know."

He looked confused. "How do you know that?"

"I . . . saw it on Facebook?" I said hopefully.

"Why would I put that on Facebook?"

"Maybe it wasn't Facebook. Maybe it was . . . Twitter. Or Insta—?"

"Insta*gram*?"

"Yeah." The reason I knew was that he went every Tuesday and had for years. Sometimes I went with him. Especially if it was around the high holidays or Hanukkah, when all the relatives dropped off tons of pastries for the residents because they felt guilty they had shoved them in the nursing home to begin with. "I think I saw it there."

"You follow me on Instagram, too?" he asked suspiciously. "I didn't see a notification about that."

That was because I was lying. I could barely figure out Facebook, let alone conquer another one of those things. "Yeah, don't know what to tell you," I said quickly as I reached for the door handle.

"To open it you have to—"

"Jiggle it three times and then push. I know." Whoops. "At least that's how it works on mine." I jumped out. "See you tomorrow!"

I ran into the house and saw Rain sitting on the couch with her legs crossed in a way that looked super uncomfortable. Her eyes were closed and some Indian-like music was coming out of her iPhone. I tried to tiptoe as quietly as possible toward the stairs.

"Greetings, Zoe!" she chirped.

"Oh hey, Rain. I didn't want to disturb you."

"It's okay. I'm done anyway. I was just doing my afternoon gratitude-to-the-goddess meditation."

"That's good. Those are very important."

"I meant what I said last week—anytime you want me to teach you how to meditate, just let me know. I know you think it's all weird and airy-fairy, but I'm telling you—it'll totally change your life."

"You know, I think I'm good for now, but thanks for the offer."

"So how was school?"

"Fine." I shrugged.

"That doesn't sound so convincing."

Was that what meditation did? Made it so you could tell when someone was lying? "You don't seem to be yourself these last few days," she went on. "Is there anything you want to talk about?"

I flopped down on the couch next to her. I don't know why I felt like I could be honest with her, but I did. "If I tell you something, do you promise not to tell my parents?"

"Of course," she replied. "You know that everything we discuss is sacred and just between us goddesses. You know, like how you enlisted my help to cover for you on Friday when you spend the night at Brad's."

I had *told* her about that?

She patted my arm. "I'm assuming that you've thought long and hard about taking this next step and that you're prepared— mentally, emotionally, *and* prophylactic-wise—for the ramifications of it." She sighed. "You only get your first time once. I remember with mine—"

"Can we talk about something else?!" I said, freaked-out.

"Of course." She squeezed my hand. "The last thing I want to do is make you uncomfortable."

Yeah, well, we were way past that.

"What is it that you'd like to discuss?"

"I'd like to discuss..." Could I trust her? Apparently, from the way I had confided in her, I thought I could, but scheming about lying to your parents about sleeping over at your boyfriend's, and confiding in someone that you had inadvertently ended up in a different millennium due to a kiss gone bad were two different things. ". . . that psychic lady you mentioned."

"Rhiannon?"

"Yeah. Her. I was wondering if you could make me an appointment with her."

She reached over and hugged me, once again covering me with patchouli. "Omigoddess, of *course* I can! I'd love to. And not just because that means I'll get twenty-five percent off on my next reading. When would you like to go?" she asked, picking up her iPhone and starting to type.

"I don't know. Maybe on—"

"Her assistant told me last week she's totally booked until the fall—that appearance she made on the E! Oscar Pre-show really helped business—but because it's me, she might be willing to fit you in sometime sooner." A second later her phone *ding*ed. "Yup. She can fit you in."

Wow. These people were *fast*.

"Okay, then," I replied. I felt both relieved and scared at the same time. On one hand, I didn't believe that this Rhiannon person could actually help me with my problem, but . . . what if she could? Was I ready to go back? Granted I wasn't used to this popularity business by any means, and if I stayed, I was going to have to get some new friends, not to mention a whole new wardrobe, but it was kind of nice not being invisible anymore. It felt good to be seen, and to have people feel like my ideas were worth listening to. If I could get them to listen to the really bad ones (see: Mani/Pedi Monday), then I'd have no problem getting them to listen to the good ones.

Right?

Before parking myself at the Farmers Market to work on my speech, I decided to stop by Terri's again. Maybe this time would somehow jog her memory and she'd remember me. Or maybe I could just get a pair of those cute silver hoops I had been eyeing last time I was in there.

When I arrived, I saw that Andrea wasn't kidding about how much pull I had when it came to fashion. "I guess I have you to thank for this," Terri said as she motioned to an empty rack. "I sold out of all my poet's blouses within an hour of school letting out." She nodded appreciatively. "You've gotta lotta cred in the fashion department. Nice."

I shrugged. "I guess."

"A queen bee who's *modest*? Wow. You don't see that very often."

"I'm really not all that special. Believe me." I laughed ruefully.

Just then I saw Montana walking by outside, alone. The swagger that I had found so intimidating was gone. In fact, she looked pretty lonely. I ran to the door and pushed it open. "Montana!"

She turned. "Oh hey." She walked over and came in. "Wow. How retro."

"Are you by yourself?" I asked.

She shrugged. "Yeah. So? There's nothing wrong with hanging out by yourself," she said defensively.

"I agree. I just asked because I'm by myself, too, and if you were, too, I was going to say that maybe we could go to the Farmers Market and, I don't know, get something to eat." I really needed to work on my speech, but I usually looked for at least three ways to distract myself before actually settling down and getting to work on something anyway.

Montana looked around the store.

"What are you doing?" I asked.

"Looking for cameras."

"Huh?"

"I'm obviously being Punk'd."

Thanks to Google, I now knew what that word meant. "Why is it so weird that I would want to hang out with you?"

"How about because . . . I'm me and you're you?"

Terri nodded. "I don't even know you guys, but even I can tell there's a massive class difference going on here."

Even Terri—who at thirty-five was a grown woman complete with gray hair that she was so vain about that she kept a bottle of hair color in her purse at all times—was part of the problem. "Why is everyone so stuck on trying to keep everyone all Us and Them?" I demanded.

Terri and Montana looked at each other. "You wanna take this one or should I?" Terri asked her.

"Go for it."

Terri turned to me. "Here's the thing: the Us and Them thing is the entire basis for all movies, TV, and music that are set in high school. If everyone was created equal and got along, there'd be no angst. You can't be a teenager and not have angst. That would be like ..."

"Popcorn without Sriracha sauce?" Montana suggested.

"Actually, I was gonna say Red Bull without vodka but then stopped myself because you guys are underage and I should be setting a good example. But you're right—that is a good combination."

As she reached into her pocket and started feeling around for something, I reached into my pocket and pulled out some gum. "Here," I said, as I held it out to her.

"How'd you know I was looking for my gum?" she asked suspiciously.

I shrugged. "Lucky guess?"

"So. As I was saying," she went on as she shoved two pieces of Trident cinnamon in her mouth. "Artists build entire careers on teenage angst."

"Yes, but it doesn't have to be that way!" I cried. "We *can* all get along!" From the looks on their faces, I could tell they didn't agree. "Okay, fine, maybe not, like, *everyone* can get along." I was thinking specifically of this kid Kurt Cotner who still ate paste. "But a lot of people could. But they won't get to know that unless they stop with the Us and Them thing." I turned to Montana. "So do you want to get something to eat or not?" I demanded. Whoops. I was so high up on my soapbox that that came out a lot more forceful than I intended it to.

She shrunk back. "Okay?" she said meekly.

"Great. Come on," I ordered as I whisked her out the door.

In order to get to the Farmers Market, we had to walk through the mall. And maybe because we were girls, we had to take a few detours and stop and look at store windows in case there was something we desperately needed to have. As we did, I was all too aware of how weird it was to be with a friend who didn't know you inside and out. Who didn't know that, because of an unfortunate experience at Zuma Beach during your eighth-grade field day, where a giant wave took your bikini top straight off your body, you had a phobia about setting foot in bathing suit stores. (Which had been just fine with Jonah because there was no way he was going in one, even if I wanted to.) Who was unaware of the fact that you were afraid of balloons. Who had no idea that before you bought something, you needed to let an hour go by, and if you were still thinking about it, then you could buy it.

I was so used to Jonah being able to read my mind just from reading my face that while I wouldn't have traded my friendship with him for anything, it was evident that my conversation skills had evaporated over the years due to having no other friends. Not like Montana was that much better. She wasn't talking, either. Finally, after not being able to take the silence between us or the instrumental version of what I now knew to be a Katy Perry song because it was my ringtone for Brad, I cleared my throat and turned to her. "What a mall. Huh?"

She shrugged. "I guess. I mean, if you're into getting run over by trolleys and the threat of epileptic fits because of singing fountains." She cringed. "Sorry. I probably shouldn't have said that."

"Why not?"

She shrugged. "I don't know. Because you're, like, queen of this place."

I shrugged back. "Yeah. But that doesn't mean that I actually like it."

She looked surprised. "You don't?"

I shook my head as I motioned to a group of middle-aged women teetering by in stilettos and full makeup. "A place where you have to go shopping to buy something to wear *before* you actually go shopping? No thanks."

"Omigod! I said the exact same thing to Jonah last week when we came here to go to the movies!" she gasped.

"You did?"

She nodded. "That's so weird."

It both was and wasn't. "Yeah."

We went back to being silent. As we passed a clothing store whose window was filled with clothes so tiny they looked like doll's clothes, Montana turned to me. "Sorry I'm not more talkative. I guess spending all my time with Jonah has made it so that I have no idea how to be social," she said wryly.

I paled. Okay, now this was getting *really* weird. We were like the same person. Not to mention it made me sad. And . . . a little bit jealous. "Yeah. I know what you mean."

She looked over at me. "That spending all my time with Jonah has made me socially awkward?"

"No. I mean, I know what it's like to spend all your time with someone who, even when you're not talking, you're still talking with. Because you don't have to talk because they already know what you're going to say."

I was pretty sure I sounded like a complete idiot until she smiled. And not just a regular smile, but one that was full of relief, like she finally felt understood.

"You have a really pretty smile," I said. "You should do it more often."

The smile went away. "Why?"

I shrugged. "I don't know. It makes you look . . . softer. More . . . approachable."

"Who says I want to be approached?" she asked defensively.

"No one. I'm just saying, it's a whole other look for you."

She looked down at the ground. "Sorry for being so defensive. It's a bad habit." She sighed. "Jonah says the same thing."

"What? That you have a pretty smile?" Did I sound as jealous as I felt? The jealousy wasn't *jealousy* jealousy. It was more about the idea that she was the one he chose to know better than anyone.

"No. That when I smile, I look more approachable." She shook her head. "I'm sorry. I'm just . . . not used to being around girls, I guess. I don't have a lot of experience with it."

I nodded. "I know what you mean."

Soon enough we had made our way over to the Farmers Market. With its old-school bakery stands and fudge shops and L.A. T-shirts and souvenirs, it didn't have the cool factor of the Dell—in fact, it was downright cheesy. But I had a soft spot for the place. Especially Bob's Coffee and Doughnuts.

"I'm totally craving—" Montana started to say.

"—a doughnut from Bob's," I finished.

She looked surprised. "Exactly."

"*Glazed*," we said at the same time.

This time we both smiled.

"I don't know what's weirder," she said. "The fact that you've even been to the Farmers Market or that you eat carbs," she said as we sat at a table watching the senior citizens with their walkers and black socks and sandals go by. I was so relaxed that I wasn't even self-conscious about the fact that I ordered not one but two doughnuts.

"Yeah, everyone seems to be surprised by the carbs thing," I said. We sat there in comfortable silence for a bit. There was something I wanted to bring up, but I wasn't sure how.

"So you've never really thought of going out with Jonah?" I blurted out.

I guess that was how to bring it up.

Montana wrinkled her nose. "Ew. No way."

"How come?"

"Because he's my best friend!"

I slurped away at my mochaccino (over the last few days they had grown on me). "Right. Which is exactly why he'd be the best possible boyfriend. What could be better than kissing your best friend?"

She took a sip of something called a venti half-caf Americano (you could write an entire book made up of just names of drinks at this Starbucks place) and looked at me for a moment. "If I tell you something, do you swear not to tell anyone?"

I nodded.

"I mean it. Seriously. Like *no one*."

"I promise."

"Okay. Well . . . we actually . . . have kissed."

I felt my stomach fall to somewhere around my knees. "Oh yeah?" I tried to keep my voice neutral. Why was I upset? I was the one who had suggested it!

"Yeah."

"And?"

"And . . . it was a disaster."

My stomach shot back up to its original setting. "How come?"

"Because it was like kissing my *brother*."

"Well, first kisses are always weird," I said. "Did you try again?"

She shook her head. "No. We were both too traumatized by how wrong it felt."

It was weird to feel such relief and have no idea *why* I was relieved. It wasn't like *I* wanted to kiss Jonah.

She finished off her doughnut and sighed. "Jonah's awesome. He's my best friend. He's just not . . . my person."

I nodded. "It's tough to find your person."

"But you have."

"No, I haven't."

Her eyebrow went up. "Brad isn't your person?"

"Who?" I asked, distracted, too busy wondering whether I'd ever find my person.

"Brad. Your boyfriend."

And with that, I was slammed back into reality. If that was what this was. "Oh, *Brad*. Right. Yup. He's my person." Something told me that I could have told Montana that Brad was not my person, but I stopped myself.

"He really seems to like you," she said.

"Yeah. He does." I sighed. What was I going to do? Why couldn't I just like him already? So what if your boyfriend didn't get your jokes. Or have similar interests. Maybe it was enough that he texted you all the time and talked about how much he wanted to make out with you. Maybe wanting your boyfriend to also be your best friend was asking too much. But in my heart of hearts, I knew that wasn't true. That, in fact, being your best friend was part of what made you love someone: the idea that you didn't want to just kiss them—you wanted to tell them your secrets and fears and hear theirs in return.

Montana's iPhone beeped with a text. "I've got to go pick up my little brother." She rolled her eyes. "A car full of fourteen-year-old gamers. Do you have any idea how long it's going to take me to get the smell of BO out of there?"

I laughed. Of course she had a fourteen-year-old brother.

She smiled again. "This was fun," she said.

"It was."

"I'd say let's do it again, but I know that's probably pushing it."

"No, it's not," I replied. "I was going to say the same thing."

She looked surprised. Pleasantly so.

"I'll find you on Instagram," I said. That day I had learned—from eavesdropping on Michelle Sawyer and Lora Levitt while changing in gym class—that Instagram was way cooler than Facebook.

"Awesome sauce," she said with another smile before walking away.

I smiled. For the first time since waking up as the most popular girl in the world, I suddenly didn't feel so lonely.

CHAPTER
Ten

I HAD JUST GOTTEN MY PEN AND PAPER OUT to start working on my speech when my phone rang and Rain's name flashed across the screen.

"Hey, Rain," I said when I answered.

"Zoe?"

"Yeah?"

"It's Rain. Your family's personal assistant."

Maybe all that patchouli she wore had caused some brain damage. "What's going on?" I asked.

"I just got a call from Rhiannon's assistant, and her five o'clock just canceled, so I went ahead and booked it for you."

"Five o'clock *today*?"

"Yeah."

"Oh. Um, okay," I said nervously. While it had been my idea to go to the psychic, now that it was actually going to happen, I was having second thoughts. What if she told me something I didn't want to know? Like that I would never fall in love. And I'd end up like my great aunt Florence, alone in a condo in Florida with a yippy Maltese, with the only thing to look forward to my weekly mah-jongg game.

"Great. Why don't you come home and get me and I'll take you there?" she asked. "Rhiannon is *very* careful about who she gives her address to. I don't want to text it and risk having some hacker get hold of it."

"Got it," I said.

I was that much closer to getting an answer to how to get back to my regularly scheduled life. So why wasn't I more excited?

Rhiannon lived in Laurel Canyon, which, according to Rain, had been ground zero for the music scene in the seventies. "You know, Joni Mitchell; Crosby, Stills, and Nash . . . everyone who was anyone lived up here," she said as we rounded a particularly sharp corner. "Her spirit guides told her to move there when she got off the bus from Minnesota."

"Good thing she listened to them," I replied. *What* was I getting myself into?

"Hello, hello, come in, come in," said the woman with the jet-black bob and ruby-red lipstick who opened the door. Dressed in a crisp black suit with high heels, she towered over us. Definitely not what I thought a psychic would look like.

I smiled. "Hi, Rhiannon. Thanks for fitting me in—"

The woman laughed. "Oh, I'm not Rhiannon. I'm Barb."

"Barb is Rhiannon's publicist," Rain explained.

"Psychics have publicists?" I asked, confused.

Which from the way her smile disappeared, probably wasn't the right thing to say. "Only the ones who think big-picture," Barb sniffed as she moved out of the way so we could enter.

I was about four steps in when I stopped short. In addition to the wall-to-wall green shag carpet, there were smoked-glass mirrored walls and macramé plant hangers. It was like something out of the later seasons of *The Brady Bunch*, when Greg started looked all hippy-like and had the love beads in his bedroom. *Whoa*, I said to myself. I may have been stuck in the eighties, but Rhiannon's house was stuck in the seventies.

"I sense that you, too, are a fan of the art of macramé, am I right?" said a voice that sounded like the product of way too many packs of cigarettes a day.

I turned to see a woman wearing a black crushed velvet dress with flowy sleeves and red suede lace-up boots lying on a purple velvet tufted couch. Her hair was long and blonde and feathered, and even from as far away as I was standing, I could tell that it had been fried to death over the years.

"Actually, other than my grandmother's house, I don't know if I've actually seen macramé in person," I replied.

"Well, the spirit guides tell me that you *are*, and you just don't know it yet," she shot back.

"Okay." I shrugged.

The woman hauled herself off the couch and made her way

over, jangling as she did due to the many bangles that she wore on both arms. She thrust a hand out, and I took it. "I'm Rhiannon," she announced, her fuchsia Lee Press-On Nails digging into my hand.

"I'm Zoe," I replied.

"I already know that. What kind of psychic would I be if I didn't?"

"Not a very good one, I guess," I replied.

She dug her nails in harder and marched me back over to where she had been lying and pushed me into a very uncomfortable black leather chair while she stretched back out onto the chaise. "Sorry to cut the small talk, but I'm due to meet with a major reality-television star who shall remained unnamed, so we have to get this show on the road." She took one hand and put it around my wrist as if taking my pulse while taking her other hand and putting it across her forehead and shutting her eyes. She looked like a character in a Charles Dickens novel who had just learned she was about to die because she had tuberculosis.

"So . . . how does this work?" I asked after we sat there in silence for a bit, with Rain and Barb hovering over us. "Am I supposed to ask you questions or . . ."

"Shhhh," Barb hissed. "She's getting in touch with them."

"In touch with who?"

"The spirit guides," Rain whispered.

"Oh. Sorry."

We waited a while longer. To the point where I wondered if

Rhiannon wasn't just getting in a nap. "Sometimes the barometric pressure affects the frequency," Barb explained.

Before I could ask if it might be better if I came back another day—like, say, one with less humidity—Rhiannon took a deep breath. Her eyes popped open. "I'm ready!" she said breathlessly.

Rain clapped her hands and gave a little squeal. "Ooh, goody!"

We all looked at her.

"Sorry," she whispered.

"You're here today because you want to talk about love," she announced.

"Actually, no."

For a second she looked lost. "But that's what everyone who comes to me wants to know about."

"Yeah, well, not me," I replied.

"Career, then?"

"I'm in high school."

"How to hide your money from the IRS?" She shook her head. "Sorry. That was just that Silicon Valley guy."

"I'm here to find out about time travel."

She relaxed. "Time travel? Oh, that's easy." She grabbed my wrist again and closed her eyes. A moment later she opened them. "The spirit guides are saying you belong in 2043."

"Oh, I don't want to go *forward*. I want to go back to the past."

She smiled. "Right on, sister."

Finally! Someone who understood that there was value to the past, even if you couldn't post or tweet or text about it!

"I was totally picking up on that seventies vibe when you walked in," she continued. She closed her eyes again. "Oh yeah. I'm getting . . . Linda Ronstadt."

"Who?" I asked, confused.

"No! Wait!" she said putting up her hand. "Oh wow. . . . I'm getting . . . Can it be . . . ? Yes, yes it is. . . . I'm getting Stevie's little sister."

"Who's Stevie?" I asked.

Her eyes snapped open. "*Who's Stevie?*" she asked incredulously.

"Uh-oh," I heard Rain say quietly.

"Stevie? As in Stevie Nicks? As in only the most talented songstress *ever*?" She pointed to a framed record album cover that had a man and woman on it dressed in really dorky clothes, like they belonged at one of those Renaissance fairs. It said *Fleetwood Mac—Rumours* on it. "'Dreams'? 'The Chain'? '*Gold Dust Woman*'?"

"Don't forget 'Rhiannon,'" Rain piped up.

I nodded. "Oh, her. I think my mom likes her."

"I knew there was a reason I felt an affinity with you when you walked in," Rhiannon said. "And that's because we're sisters. Not just in the figurative sense, but in the cosmic sense."

"Soooo . . . you're, like, the reincarnation of this Stevie woman?" I asked.

"Not exactly, because Stevie is still alive and well and living in Malibu," she replied. "But I do feel that we share the same stardust. And I think you might be of the same crop."

This chick was nuts. "That's great," I said. "But I don't actually want to go back to the seventies. I want to go back to the eighties. To 1986, to be specific."

She wrinkled her nose. "Spandex and neon colors? Why would you want to do that?"

I thought about my options. I could either cut my losses and get up and leave right then and there. Or I could take the risk and come clean and tell her my story. It was obvious that she was loony tunes, so how crazy could waking up thirty years into the future sound to her? I was already here, and, according to Rain, the hour was already setting me back a hundred and fifty bucks. ("Her normal rate is three fifty an hour, but because you're a friend, she's doing me a favor," Rain said as we stopped at the bank machine.) So what was there to lose?

I took a deep breath and told her everything, starting with Brad coming into Terri's shop, and the Fun Dip stick, and waking up to find my hair had grown out, all the way up through realizing Montana was this millennium's me. The way she kept nodding and saying "Uh-huh, uh-huh" made me relax, as if maybe what had happened to me wasn't all that crazy.

When I was done, she took hold of my wrist again and closed her eyes. After a few moments she opened them. "And this Montana—does *she* resemble Stevie in any way?"

I sighed as I took my hand back. So much for this helping. "No. She doesn't," I replied.

She shrugged. "Oh well. Can't win them all!"

What did this woman *want*? A land full of Stevie clones? This was a colossal waste of time. "So do you have any suggestions as to how I might be able to get back to 1986?"

"I might, but let me ask you first: Why would you want to?"

"Because that's where I'm from. That's where my life is."

"Yes, but from everything you're telling me, it wasn't all that great," she replied. "I mean, you're *popular* now. Isn't that what everyone wants?"

From the corner of my eye, I could see Rain nodding. I turned to her and she stopped. "Sorry," she said.

I shrugged. "I don't know," I said honestly. "I mean, I'd be lying if I said that popularity sucked, but . . ."

"But what?" Rhiannon asked.

I felt my face turn red. "I miss Jonah." It felt stupid to admit I missed someone who didn't want anything to do with me.

She nodded. "Of course you do. We always miss our twin flame when we're not united."

"Twin flame?" I asked.

She nodded. "Twin flame, soul mate . . ."

I laughed. "Jonah's not my soul mate. He's my best friend. He's the person who knows me better than anyone. He's the one I'd want to be stuck on a desert island with. But soul mate?" I shook my head. "No way."

The way Rhiannon looked at me was making me uncomfortable. "And anyways, I already have a boyfriend," I said nervously.

"Brad." And all I could say was that if that was what a soul mate felt like, we were all in big trouble.

From the way Barb was tapping her watch and mouthing *It's time to go*, I could tell it was time to wrap up. Rhiannon shrugged. "Okay. Well, I'm only here to share what the spirit guides tell me. Not force you in any sort of direction that doesn't feel right for you. Especially if I want the repeat business and a good review on Yelp. So what is it you'd like to know?"

"Well, I'd like to know . . . how to get back to 1986 . . . if that's what I end up choosing to do. . . ." I said. I wished I could have sounded a little more sure of myself, but the truth was I was nervous. Maybe Rhiannon was right—maybe being here wasn't all that bad. Maybe I should have looked at it like moving. Lots of kids moved when they were growing up. I had just moved years instead of states.

She took hold of my wrist again and closed her eyes. Well, closed them until her phone beeped with a text, and she opened one eye to check it. Finally she opened them. "The spirit guides are telling me that you need to kiss this Brad guy again." She nodded for a few moments. "Yes. Kiss him, and it will bring you back to 1986."

My stomach started to clench. "Did they give you any other suggestions?" I asked hopefully.

She shook her head. "Nope."

"But what if it doesn't bring me back to 1986?" I asked. "What if it brings me back to . . . 1786?"

She closed her eyes a moment and then opened them. "They said they can't guarantee what will happen, but it's worth a shot."

Great.

"Wait—they say they want to tell me one more thing." She closed her eyes again and then opened them. "They said . . . you should twirl."

"Twirl what?" I asked, confused.

"You know—*twirl*. Like Stevie." With that, Rhiannon stood up and began to twirl around. First slow, and then faster, so that her sleeves made her look like some sort of earthbound butterfly. Finally she stopped and stumbled a bit.

"And that will help me get back to where I came from," I said doubtfully.

She shrugged. "I don't know, but I really have to get going," she said as she stood up and gave me that *okay, you can get going now too, thanks* look.

I stood up as well. "Thanks," I said, starting to rustle in my bag for the money.

"Barb will take care of my fee," she said. "The spirit guides don't like me to get involved with the money thing. They think it dilutes the gift." She picked up her phone and began to walk away. "And remember—*twirl*."

I had never thought I was psychic before, but I was psychic enough to know that this was a complete waste of time.

"You didn't mention it was Flashback Friday!" my mother exclaimed as I walked into the kitchen the next morning wearing my new leggings, shirt, and belt. "Do you want me to take a picture of you? Or did you do a selfie?"

"Yup. I did a selfie," I replied, making a mental note to look up the word.

In keeping with her multitasking personality, she was alternating between painting her nails, making an egg-white omelette, and doing squats while some rap music blared. Every few moments she'd stop and try out some sort of move that ended with her crossing her arms in front of her and smirking before making a notation in the little notebook she carried around all the time. "Where'd you find that? In the attic?"

"It's not Flashback Friday, and, no, I bought it yesterday," I replied as I grabbed a muffin and sat down at the table.

"You should have worn that yesterday for Throwback Thursday," Ethan said as he made his way out the door after grabbing half my muffin in one fell swoop.

When she looked at me she stopped her multitasking and joined me. "Honey, I know now isn't the time because you have to get to school and I have a conference call with Rihanna's people, but I have to tell you—I'm worried about you."

"How come?" I asked with my mouth full. What muffins had lost in taste over the years, they had gained in size. This one was the size of a small country.

She pointed to the muffin and moved it to the side as I went to grab another piece. "Because of the muffin, honey. You know we don't actually eat those."

"Let me guess—they're just for appearances," I said wryly. "Like the bread."

She grabbed my arm and gave me a serious look. I had noticed that the wrinkles that used to appear on her forehead when that happened were no longer there. According to the women on a TV show called *The Real Housewives of Atlanta* that I had come across last night while channel surfing (it's hard to fall asleep after twirling) this had to do with something called Botox. "Are you depressed?"

"No. I'm just hungry," I said, grabbing the muffin back.

She took in my new outfit. It looked awesome, if I did say so myself. "Zoe, in an attempt to honor your individuality, I let the poet blouse go yesterday. And obviously being popular gives you a lot of leeway in the fashion department, but don't you think you might be pushing it a bit with what you're wearing today?"

I shrugged. "If people decide I'm no longer cool because of what I wear, then oh well," I said as I turned on my phone. I had turned it off when I started to write my speech because I couldn't deal with all the various *ding*s and *dong*s from Facebook and Twitter.

She put her hand to my forehead. "Do you have a fever?"

Before I could answer, a stream of beeps sounded. Twenty-two texts. How did I manage to get anything done if I was this popular? One was from Andrea, asking me to please not wear my brown Frye motorcycle boots because she wanted to wear hers to school, and it would look dumb if we were all "twinsie," but if I really wanted to wear mine, that was fine, she'd just wear hers another day but to just let her know at my earliest convenience so that she'd have enough time to re-strategize. The other twenty-one were from Brad, ranging from things like **Hey babe** to **Whassup** to **I'm bored** to **I just had a burrito.** Most girls complained that their boyfriends didn't pay enough attention to them. Mine, however, seemed to have nothing better to do than to report his every move to me.

Can't wait til 2nite ;) came through.

"Uh-oh. A wink is not good," I murmured. I knew that's what it was from the emoticon dictionary app I had downloaded the night before. A wink was a gateway to all sorts of things. I needed to get out of this. "Mom?"

"What, sweetheart?" she replied, in the middle of trying to untangle a very large gold chain with a pendant that said HOME-GIRL.

"I was thinking maybe we could do something tonight. You know, as a family."

She looked up from the pendant, confused. "But you never want to spend time with us. You're always saying we embarrass you."

She wasn't wrong. I had said that a few times. Or maybe more than a few. But to my defense, they *were* embarrassing. But it was different now. I mean, I was in another *century*. With no instruction book. "Well, maybe I haven't wanted to in the *past*, but I've been thinking about it recently, and I feel bad about that," I replied. "And now seems like the perfect time to change that. So how about game night or something?" What was I saying? I hated games.

"Honey, you hate games," she replied.

"Yes, but I'm trying to be more open-minded," I replied. "Maybe we could just go to dinner or something."

"Sweetie, you father and I have plans," she said. "We'll go for dinner on Sunday night." Her face brightened. "Ooh—I know—we'll go to that place in Koreatown that has karaoke!"

Oh boy. I had seen some video on YouTube with a woman doing that karaoke thing. It was painful to watch her, and she didn't look half as embarrassing as my parents did. I stood up and leaned down to kiss her cheek. "Maybe. Let's talk about it later. I have to go. I have my speech this morning."

"What'd you decide to go with for the speech?" she asked. "May Makeovers or the Kardashians for Career Day?"

"Something completely different," I replied.

I wasn't a great public speaker. I hadn't always hated it, but ever since the time I had done an oral book report on Judy Blume's *Forever* in eighth grade and Andrea had used the Q&A section to ask me whether the pages I had dog-eared were the sex scenes and how many times I had read them, it had been hard for me to stand in front of groups. But I was willing to walk through my fear for my country. Or at least my classmates. Plus, I had practiced my speech until one a.m., and then a few times that morning in my room using the note cards I had made for myself, so I was feeling pretty good about it.

That is, until I was in the auditorium and realized I had forgotten them on my dresser.

"You did? Really? That's too bad," said Andrea in a tone that made it seem that not only was it not too bad but it was actually awesome. She reached into her purse and whipped out another copy of the speech she had written. "Omigod—how weird is this? I just happen to have another copy of *my* speech right in here! I must have forgotten to take it out before." She thrust it toward me. "Why don't you just use this one?"

In that moment, I felt like I saw Andrea in a whole different light. As she looked at me—eager, hopeful, pleadingly—I no longer saw the bitchy girl who had tormented me for so many years. In her place was a girl who had so little sense of her own self, so little idea who she was, that she was content to just copy and live through me—a person who she thought had it all together and all figured out. (If she only knew . . .) I realized at that moment that unlike some situations where the second-in-command was planning and plotting and scheming about how she could take over and be the alpha dog, this wasn't Andrea. She was happy to continue being the runner-up.

I may have felt bad for her, but that didn't mean I was going to cave to her. "Thanks, but I think I'll just wing it," I said pushing the speech back toward her.

"Are you sure?" she asked.

Before I could answer her, Dr. Carlson, the principal, had finished introducing me, and the applause from my classmates startled me back into the moment. I stood up. Wow. Talk about a complete 180 from the last time I did this.

"Yeah. I'm sure," I said before making my way toward the stage. As I faced everyone, I could feel my palms start to sweat. "Good morning, fellow students," I said. "So, um, I've got some exciting new developments to share with you in this month's State of the Class address." Out of the corner of my eye I saw my neighbor Erica Mandell, who had recently been sent away to one of those wilderness camps. "Erica! Hey! You're back!" I exclaimed. "I love the new look," I went on. "You can really see how pretty your eyes are without all that black eyeliner."

"You know who I am?" she asked, amazed.

"Well, yeah. Of course I do."

I watched as Brad leaned over to Andrea in the first row. "Why is she talking to yet another unpopular person?" he whispered loudly.

There it was—my entrée into my speech. "That's a very interesting question you bring up, Brad," I said.

"It is?" he asked, surprised.

"It is." Grabbing the microphone from the stand, I stepped out from behind the podium and walked to the edge of the stage. "Over the last week, it's come to my attention that there's a real divide between social classes here at Castle Heights. Take the Ramp, for instance—"

"*Please* don't take the Ramp," Andrea moaned. "Please just leave the Ramp to us, like it's always been, and let's move on—"

"Who here thinks the Ramp is just as dangerous as the Berlin Wall?" I asked.

"What is she talking about?" Mitch Foster asked. "The Berlin Wall came down in 1989."

It had? Huh. Seeing that Mitch considered the *Encyclopedia Britannica* light reading, there was no reason to doubt him.

"Exactly! It did," I said. "But before it came down, it was an ugly reminder of the way that we keep ourselves separate from one another so we can continue to make judgments about each other. Just like the Ramp allows us to do."

At that, the crowd began to buzz. Buzzing was good, right? It meant that I had hit a nerve. In fact, I was so sure it was good that I was ready to take the plunge.

"Which is why I've decided that our only hope for solidarity and equality is for it to be demolished."

I waited for the applause that I was sure was going to follow. Instead, I got crickets. It was like 1986 all over again.

I tapped the microphone. "Hello? Is this thing on?"

At that, the room went crazy. Phew. It *wasn't* like 1986. Obviously they were all so stunned, it just took a moment to compute. In fact, the response was even better than I had expected. I loved knowing that my administration would really be leaving a legacy. A huge smile came over my face. "I can't tell you how happy I am about your response to this. I had a feeling you'd be excited, but I hadn't expected all this," I yelled. "So let's vote on it—who here thinks the Ramp should be demolished?" I asked.

At that, all the noise stopped, and it was back to crickets.

I tapped on the mike again. "Hello?"

This time it didn't work. Not one hand went up. I scanned the auditorium looking for Alan Sharp—the guy whose hand had gone up when I gave my last speech, back in 1986, because he had earwax buildup and couldn't hear me, but this time even his stayed down. Maybe I was just so ahead of the curve that it was going to take a minute for everyone to catch up. "Okay, listen—I know this is a lot to take in right now," I said. "It would be a huge change for everyone involved—popular or not. Which is why I'm not going to ask that we vote on this right now. All I'm going to ask is that someone seconds the motion I'm putting forth, that we vote on the demolition of the Ramp. Can I at least get that?"

Still nothing.

I looked around before zeroing in on Matt Wondriak and Russell Pogach, the founders—and only members—of the Anarchists for World Peace Club. "What about you guys? You'll second it, right?"

"Dude, the Ramp is like . . . an *institution*," Matt said.

"Totally," Russell agreed.

"Yeah, but as anarchists, you're *against* institutions, remember?"

They looked at each other, confused. I shook my head. "I'll ask again. Who here will second my motion?"

Rachel Sidar's hand shot up. I smiled. "I knew I could count on you, Rachel." Any form of injustice—an animal about to go extinct, an ocean being polluted, a kid being discriminated against—Rachel was on the front lines, leading the charge.

"Actually, I could care less about the Ramp thing," she replied. "I just had a question. Is that outfit you're wearing vintage, or did you buy it new?"

I sighed. "It's new." Here I had gotten what I thought I wanted—the opportunity to be in power so I could make a difference—and it wasn't working. "Fine. So much for promoting tolerance and equality and all those other things that admissions counselors look for on college applications. I guess we'll move on to something you guys really care about. Like . . . I don't know . . . a vote about whether the vending machines should include 5-Hour Energy drinks—"

Andrea turned to Brad. "I know how much you like them."

Okay, maybe Andrea wasn't evil like I thought she was, but that didn't mean she wasn't in love with my boyfriend.

And then Jonah's hand went up.

"Really? But you're so sensitive to caffeine," I said, confused, before catching myself. "What I mean is lots of people are sensitive to caffeine—"

"I'm not talking about the energy drinks. I'm seconding your motion."

"You are?"

He nodded.

I smiled at him as we locked eyes. "Well, thanks for speaking up," I said softly.

Montana's arm shot up as well. "I think it should go, too," she said firmly. As I looked at the two of them—looking like one of those cool couples that I had seen on a Tumblr page about Brooklyn hipsters—the spell was broken. Maybe she thought kissing him was like kissing her brother, but they looked good together. "Thanks," I said. I should have been happy to get another supporter, but suddenly I felt empty. "Anyone else?" I asked.

No one bit.

"Okay, then. We'll table this until the next meeting."

"Thank God," I heard Andrea say to Brad. "Hopefully by then we'll have talked some sense into her. Hey, do you know if there's any sort of studies that show that lots of carbs can make you crazy?"

"I can't believe you actually want us to eat down there," Andrea said as we sat on the Ramp at lunch later.

"Yeah, well, it doesn't look like that's something that you'll have to be worrying about any time in the near future," I said. I was still bummed about what had happened that morning. It sounded so stuck up to admit it, but I had really thought that my popularity would have gotten me a bunch of supporters.

She and Brad looked at each other before Andrea cleared her throat. "Zoe?"

I looked up from my phone. I couldn't believe it—in the few hours that had passed since my speech I had actually *lost* some Facebook friends! "Yeah?"

"Brad and I were talking, and we think it's time for an intervention."

"Yeah. Like that show on TV," Brad added. "But not because you do drugs or anything."

"For what?"

"Because of the Ramp thing," Andrea said. "We're worried about you."

"That's sweet, but I'm fine. Better than fine, in fact." I took a picture of myself. Whoa. Fake smiling hurt. My first selfie. I posted it on Instagram and waited for the likes to start piling up.

Who *was* I? This wasn't me. I didn't care about this stuff. I stood up. "I've got to go."

"Where?" Andrea asked.

"I'm going to take a walk. I'll see you guys later," I said as I started to leave.

"Wait—what about tonight?" Brad called after me.

Oh right. Tonight. Our big date.

"Have you given any more thought to that walk on the beach at sunset thing?" he went on. "When I Googled *romantic things chicks dig*, that was the first thing that came up."

Andrea sighed. "I love walks at sunset. Those are always my favorite scenes in Nicholas Sparks movies. Especially when there's a Top Forty ballad playing over it."

"Yeah, I'm not really a walk in the sunset kind of girl," I said.

I didn't know what kind of girl I was anymore.

As I made my way toward the exit, I saw Jonah bussing his tray, so I took a detour. "Thanks for supporting me," I said as he put his tray on the belt.

He turned, startled. "Oh, you're welcome." He shrugged. "It wasn't a big deal."

"It was a huge deal," I replied.

Was his face turning red? "I have to say—I was surprised you did that," he replied. "I didn't peg you for someone who was so . . . I don't know . . . *radical*."

I laughed. "Is that a compliment?"

Now he was definitely turning red. "I don't know. I guess."

"Well, I guess I'll see you around," I said, suddenly wanting to get out of there. What was wrong with me? First I tried everything I could to get Jonah to talk to me, and now that he was, I felt all awkward and wanted to bolt.

Things just got weirder and weirder.

Maybe it was because my ego was out of whack because of the reaction, or lack thereof, to the Ramp idea. But later that day, in study hall, instead of flipping through magazines, or reading my favorite celebrities' tweets (I didn't know who this Seth Rogen guy was, but he was hysterical), I decided to try to gain some more support for the ideas I wanted to push forward in my administration. Today's debacle had shown me that bringing them up during a speech and expecting instant support just wasn't going to happen. Panning the room, I saw a bunch of members of the Cultural Exchange Club huddled together on the stage. Back in 1986, they had liked to dress in clothes of the country they represented. Like Monique Brower (her real name was Susan, but she had changed it because there really wasn't a way to make Susan sound French), who had a different beret for every day of the week. And Kunta Solomon (né Michael, an African American kid who was adopted by a Jewish couple), who favored colorful dashiki shirts. Monique and Kunta were still wearing their respective odes to the countries they loved, but today they didn't look out of place at all. Neither did Russia-loving Aaron Kavorsky, with his T-shirt that read TOLSTOY WAS RIGHT. (Despite the fact that L.A. pretty much never got cold, it didn't stop him from wearing a fur hat in the winter months.)

As I watched them attempt to surreptitiously divvy up a baguette and spread it with Brie, I got an idea.

"Hey, guys," I said after I made my way over to them. "Mind if I join you?"

From the way their eyes widened (wide eyes plus full mouths equals a trio of moon pies) this was not how they thought they'd be spending their Friday afternoon. They looked at each other and shrugged. "I guess?" Kunta finally said.

I plopped down on the stage next to them, and smiled as if this was exactly how I thought I'd be spending my Friday.

"Do you . . . want some?" Monique said, motioning to the bread and cheese.

"I thought you'd never ask," I said, grabbing a hunk of bread and smearing some Brie on it. I took a bite. "Man, if this isn't an advertisement for spending a semester abroad, I don't know what is."

Aaron—who was a little on the nervous side to begin with—was starting to get a little sweaty. "Why are you here?" he finally blurted out.

Obviously he was now *a lot* on the nervous side. "Okay. I'll just get to the point," I said.

"Sorry. I didn't mean—it's just that . . ."

"Whenever you talk to us it's to make fun of us," Kunta finished.

"I do?"

"Singing 'It's a Small World After All' whenever you pass us?" Monique said.

I cringed. That was just stupid. "I'm sorry about that. I

haven't been myself for a while." I reached for another piece of bread. "May I?"

They shrugged and nodded.

I added some Brie and popped it in my mouth. "It's just so *good*."

"It would probably be wildly inappropriate for me to ask if I could take a picture of this, right?" Kunta asked.

I nodded.

"I thought so," he said.

"I want to run an idea by you," I said. "It's something I haven't discussed with anyone yet."

They looked intrigued.

I looked around to make sure no one else could hear, and then leaned in. "Cultural Kidnapping Day."

No response.

"What do you think?" I asked excitedly. "Do you like it?"

"Maybe if we knew what it was, we could answer that," Monique replied.

"Okay, well, in order to address the fact that we're way too segregated as a student body, I'm thinking of proposing a program where everyone would adopt a friend for a day," I explained. "Someone from a totally different social group than them."

Instead of looking at me like I was a genius and that they had just been waiting for someone to come up with such a brilliant idea, they continued to look blank.

"That way, we'll all get to see that no matter where we sit in the cafeteria, at the end of the day, we're all just doing our best to figure this life thing out," I went on. "We all have the same hopes, the same dreams, the same fears—"

"You're afraid of clowns, too?" Aaron asked excitedly.

"Not exactly. I meant it in, you know, a general way. So what do you think?"

Kunta shook his head. "I don't know."

"You don't like it?" I asked, disappointed. "I thought that you guys, out of everyone, would really go for this."

"How come?" Monique asked.

I shrugged. "I don't know. Because you're all about trying to make people aware of new cultures."

"Yeah, but that's different," said Kunta.

"How so?"

"Well, because ... it's just ... the thing is ..." He looked at the other two. "Help a brother out, guys."

"*Si ce n'est pas casse ne le repare pas*," Monique said.

"I take Spanish," I said.

"If it ain't broke, don't fix it," she translated. "Look, between wanting to take the Ramp down, and now this Adopt-A-Friend idea—"

"Cultural Kidnapping," I correct. "I mean, it's basically the same thing, but that sounds cuter."

"—but why go ahead and shake things up?" she continued. "It's not like it's not working the way it is."

I waited for the *Just kidding!* that I was sure would follow a statement like that, but none came. "Really? You think the way we're all so divided and so judgey is *working*?"

"This is high school—that's the way it's supposed to be," Kunta explained. "Haven't you ever seen a John Hughes movie?"

If he only knew. Not only had I seen them, but I had seen them on the big screen. Whereas he had probably only watched them on his computer. "Sure, but that doesn't mean it's right."

"Like I said, it's really admirable of you—in fact, if I were you, I'd find some way to work that into your college essays—but I don't think anyone's going to really go for it."

"Yeah," Kunta agreed. "If anything, it sounds like a lot of work."

It was amazing. Everyone may have thought of me as being elitist and stuck up, but weren't they just as bad? Didn't they keep to themselves and not want to branch out, either?

Before I could tell them that that's what they were doing (which probably wasn't a great idea when I was trying to look for support) there was a tap on my shoulder.

"Nerdy Wayne. Sorry—I meant Wayne—" I corrected.

"It's okay. I know everyone calls me Nerdy Wayne. I'm down with it."

"Okay, well, that's good," I said awkwardly. "So what's up?"

"Can I talk to you?"

"Sure."

"*Alone?*" he asked, pointedly.

There it was again—yet another example of people not wanting to mix.

"Sure." I turned to the Cultural Crew. "Well, thanks for hearing me out."

"You're not going to, like, curse us out for not backing you?" Aaron asked, confused.

"Of course not. What good would that do?"

"It wouldn't do any good, but that's, like, *you*," Monique said. "It's what you do."

I sighed. "Like I said—this is a new me." How many times was I going to have to say that? "See you around," I said before following Wayne over to his seat in the way, way back.

"What's up?" I asked.

"I asked around and I know a guy who knows a guy who knows someone who might have some intel about that thing you were asking about," he whispered.

He was talking so low and fast I could barely understand what he was saying. "Huh?"

He looked around to make sure no one was listening. "The time travel thing."

"You found someone who knows about going backward?"

The bell rang. "Yeah. My contact's going to put me in touch with him tonight. It's not a sure thing, but it might be something."

As I reached over to hug him, he jumped. "Sorry. I'm not used to people touching me. Especially girls."

"Got it," I said as I moved back.

"I'll let you know tomorrow what the deal is," he yelled over the noise as he started to walk away.

"But you don't have my number!" I yelled after him.

He stopped. "Oh right." He headed back and handed me his iPhone. "Put it in here."

As I started to punch in the numbers, he stopped me. "Can you hold on just a second?"

"Okay. For what?"

"I'd like to wait until Devon Patel walks by so he sees you giving me your number. If that's okay."

"Sure. It's fine."

"Great."

The thing was, Devon was rather chatty, which left us standing there awkwardly not saying anything.

"He shouldn't be that much longer."

"Not a problem," I said. Yes, I was being used to impress some guy under complete bogus circumstances. But time travelers couldn't be choosers.

Devon finally started to make his way over. "Okay, now! Do it now!" Wayne hissed.

As I began punching in my number, he moved closer to me. I looked up. "Are you looking down my shirt?" I asked.

"No."

My eyes narrowed.

"Maybe." He moved away. "Sorry." His timing was perfect. "Hey, Devon," he said as Devon got closer.

Devon looked over and didn't even try to hide his amazement. "What are you doing so close to Zoe Brenner?"

"Oh, nothing. Just, you know, getting her number," he said as nonchalantly as possible as I tried not to roll my eyes.

Devon's buggy eyes got even buggier. "Dude, that's . . . *epic*." He looked at me. "Are you going to ask him for help with chemistry? Because if so, I'm really your guy. I placed out of the AP class in eighth grade."

"Nope. Not asking anyone for any help with my classes," I replied. "We're just friends, and I find him super funny and smart and want to get to know him better."

His eyes bugged out even more as I turned to Nerdy Wayne. "Okay, so text me tomorrow and we'll figure out when to get together."

"Totes," he replied. Whatever that meant.

I nodded and walked toward the door.

I really hoped that whatever he came back with worked, because staying here in 2016 wasn't feeling like it would be all that much fun anymore.

I was on my way to the parking lot when in the distance I saw Jonah making his way there from the other direction. This time, instead of shouting his name, or running toward him, I hung back for a second. It was freaking me out that every time I saw him nowadays, my mouth got dry and my palms got sweaty. I had no idea what that was about.

Maybe I could just stand there and continue my examination of the stain I had just found on my sleeve for as long as it took him to get in his car and drive away. That seemed like a perfectly normal thing to do. And I would have, except a few seconds later, there he was, waving at me.

I waved back. I had to. There was no one else in the parking lot.

And he didn't just wave. He passed his car and walked toward me.

"Hey," he said when we were face-to-face.

"Hey," I mumbled. When did his eyes get so blue?

We stood there awkwardly for a moment. Finally I cleared my throat. "Thanks for helping me today during the assembly," I finally said.

"It's cool. You already thanked me. In the cafeteria."

"Oh right." And had he been working out? Because I totally didn't remember him having such well-defined arms. The way his Arcade Fire T-shirt hugged his biceps was not how his New Order T-shirt had looked back in 1986. And why was the idea of that making me blush? "Glad you verified that. Okay, then—I should get going. Have a good weekend." And why couldn't I look him in the eye?

"You too," he said as I started to walk toward my car. Was that disappointment I heard in his voice? It couldn't be. Why would he be disappointed? As far as he knew, I was the most popular girl in school, dating the most popular boy, and I had way better things to do than chat with him in a parking lot.

But still, I swore it sounded that way.

CHAPTER *Eleven*

IF MY DATE WITH BRAD SHOWED ME ONE thing, it was that I was just as guilty as everyone else in terms of putting people in boxes and thinking I knew who they were. Not only did Brad not show up late like I was sure he would, but he turned up early, dressed in a fresh pair of chinos (you could still see the marks from where they had been pressed) and a yellow Izod, holding a bouquet of peonies.

"These are for me?" I asked as he handed them to me in the foyer.

"Well, yeah. They're your favorite, right?" he asked anxiously. "Or is it *pansies* that are your favorite?"

Were pansies actually someone's favorite flower? "They are my favorite," I replied. "They're also really hard to find."

"Tell me about it." He laughed. "I went to four different florists before finally tracking them down at Trader Joe's. I even stopped at a gas station."

I smiled as I leaned over and kissed him on the cheek. "That was really sweet of you," I said. "Let me just go put them in some water." When I came back, I found Brad mid–breath spray.

"Whoops," he said, embarrassed. "You weren't supposed to see that."

Not that I wanted to make out with him, but I had to hand it to him—the guy was a sweetheart. Too bad he wasn't *my* sweetheart. I mean, he was. Technically. But as much as it would have been great to will myself to like him in a potential *you know*-ing kind of way, I just couldn't.

"I won't tell anyone," I said as I grabbed my purse. "Ready?"

"Sure."

He looked around. "Is anyone here?"

"No. They're at temple." My parents had dragged Ethan because his bar mitzvah was coming up and they thought their attendance at Friday-night services would help make up for the fact that he was horrible at reading Hebrew.

His face lit up. "You want to make out for a while before we go eat?"

He may have been a sweetheart, but he was still a guy. "I'm actually kind of hungry."

He nodded. "Got it. Let's go, then."

As we walked out to his car—something called an Escalade, which resembled a small truck—he ran ahead so he could open my door for me, but it wouldn't budge. "I know this is a dumb question, but is it unlocked?" I finally asked after watching him try a few more times.

He pointed his keys at the truck and clicked on the little clicker thing. The sound of the lock opening could be heard. "It is now," he said with a smile.

Oh, Brad. Once we were settled in the car, he moved his head toward me and closed his eyes and puckered up.

I moved back. "What are you doing?"

He opened his eyes. "Waiting for our Last Kiss."

"Our what?"

"You know, our Last Kiss. In case we die in a fiery car crash as we're driving."

I moved backed even farther. "Are you *planning* for us to die in a fiery car crash?"

"No! But you always make us do this."

I did? Wow. I was kind of a drama queen. "Right. Of course I do," I vamped. "Because it's a really good idea." But what if Rhiannon was right, and kissing him would take me back to 1986? Was I ready to go? I didn't see why not. At the rate I was going, any sort of change of the new world social order was going to take forever. Like a few more decades.

I leaned in. "Okay. I'm ready." I screwed my eyes shut and puckered up. But what if something went wrong, and there was a screwup and I ended up as Andrea Manson?

I leaned back again. "You know? I just realized that I'm really *really* hungry," I said quickly. "Can we skip the kiss and go to dinner? That way I'll be more energized for the kissing portion of the evening later on."

He put the car in drive and pulled out. "Sure."

I leaned back and exhaled. This was going to be a long evening. "So where are we going?" I asked once my heart rate had returned to normal.

"You'll see. I made reservations at somewhere super special."

Soon enough we were pulling up in front of a Mexican place called El Gato Negro. I went to open the door but he stopped me. "Hold on." He jumped out of the truck and ran around to the side to open it for me. Except he couldn't. I let him try a bunch of times before I opened it myself and got out.

"I always forget that I lock it when I start to drive," he said sheepishly.

I looked at the peeling paint on the building and tried not to cringe. "This place looks . . . interesting."

"Their guac is off the charts," he said. "But that's not why I brought you here."

He brought me here because he wanted me to get food poisoning? "Oh yeah?"

He grabbed my hand and dragged me toward the entrance. "You'll see why in a second."

After we were seated, I didn't just see why he had brought me there. I also heard it. Over and over and over and over.

"A real live mariachi band," I yelled over the music. I had lost count, but I was pretty sure they were on their fifth or sixth rendition of "Cielito lindo." And it wasn't like that came in between other songs—it was the *only* song they played. "What a great touch."

He smiled. "I thought you'd like it," he yelled back.

By the time we left, my cheeks hurt from smiling so much at the musicians, and my skirt was stained from when the guitar player knocked over a bowl of salsa onto my lap.

"You ready for what's next?" Brad asked as we got back into the car.

"I guess so?" I said. I only hoped it didn't include noise and was near a drugstore so I could get some aspirin.

"Awesome."

A few minutes later we were driving down Ocean Avenue. After he parked, we walked across the street toward the water. I stopped. "Are we taking a walk on the beach?" I asked. If we were, I wasn't sure how I would get out of kissing him, then.

"No. You said you didn't like that stuff," he replied. "Plus, it's past sunset." He pulled me toward the Santa Monica Pier. "We're doing something else."

"Are we going up in the Ferris wheel?" I asked nervously. If you didn't get kissed in a Ferris wheel, I didn't know where you got kissed. "Because I'm feeling a little full from dinner."

"Nope," he said as we moved toward the arcade games. When we got to the one where you shoot water into the clown's mouth and wait for the balloon to fill up and pop, he stopped. "I'm going to win you a prize. So you have a whatsitmacallit—Nintendo—of the night."

"Do you mean *memento*?"

He cocked his head and thought about it. "Yeah. I think that's it."

Oh, Brad. I really hoped he wasn't spending his Sundays trying to do crossword puzzles.

He slammed a ten-dollar bill down on the counter. "Hit me, dude!" he said to the bored pimply-faced kid slouched on a stool, playing some game on his iPhone. He turned to me. "I'm not going to use all of this money. I just don't have any ones."

I nodded as I made myself comfortable. I didn't mind if it took a while. It would give me time to come up with an excuse as to why all kissing was off-limits that night. Like, say, I was afraid that I had suddenly come down with mono.

But an hour later, after Brad had blown through not just all ten dollars, but twenty more, I was ready to go. "It's really nice of you to do this," I yelled over the heavy metal that was blasting from the kid's speaker attached to his iPhone, "but it's okay. I don't need a stuffed animal. Believe me—I won't be forgetting this night any time soon."

Brad was concentrating so hard on trying to shoot the water into the clown's mouth that not only did he not hear me, but he was *drooling*. After he lost (again) he turned to me. "Did you say something?"

"Yeah. Let's go. You don't have to keep doing this."

"But I want to get you a—what'd you call it?"

"Memento."

"Yeah. That."

I shook my head. "It's okay." I broke out a fake yawn. "Plus I'm getting kind of tired."

"Are you sure it's okay?"

"I'm sure."

"Oh good. Because I'm a little dizzy from only having one eye open for so long," he said as we started to make our way back to the parking lot. As we got back to the car, he turned to me. "You sure you don't want to stop at Toys 'R' Us or something and I can just buy you one?"

I shook my head. "Thanks, but I'm good."

As we drove toward his house, I started fiddling with the radio. It said Sirius and had a bunch of stations. When I got to something called Totally '80s I smiled. "I Melt with You" was on.

"I love this song," I said, relaxing a bit. It had to be a good omen, right? Like, say, an omen that I'd be able to get out of any sort of physical contact with Brad.

We drove in silence for a bit. Brad turned to me. "So is this song about people who are in a fire together?"

"What? *No.* Why would you say that?"

He shrugged. "Because of the melting thing."

Brad. Brad. Brad.

My phone *ding*ed with a text. It was from Nerdy Wayne. **Meet me at Insomnia Cafe tomorrow at 11. I have info on the thing we talked about. Please delete this text now.**

Brad glanced over. "Who's that from? Andrea?"

"Ah, no," I said as I pushed *Delete.* "Wrong number. Hey, can I ask you something?"

"Sure."

"Was what Andrea said at lunch true? That you're worried about the way I'm acting?"

He shrugged. "I wouldn't say I'm *worried*," he replied. "But it does seem kind of weird."

"How come?"

"I don't know. It's just not like you."

"Yeah, but who says I have to be me all the time?" I asked.

I watched his face as he tried to do the math on what that meant. It wasn't happening.

"You know how I play soccer?" he asked.

"Yeah."

"And I'm always a forward?"

"Yeah," I lied. I was assuming that was a position in soccer, but as someone who had attempted to get out of gym class most of her life, I wasn't entirely sure.

"That's because I'm good at it."

I waited for him to go on, but he didn't. "And the point of this story is . . . ?" I finally said.

"The point is that people like things to stay the same," he replied. "It makes them, I don't know . . . feel safe."

Huh. That was an interesting way to look at things. Maybe Brad wasn't so dumb after all.

"Zoe, you're good at being popular," he went on. "If we were all the same, you wouldn't be popular anymore. You'd just be . . . normal."

"What's wrong with normal?"

"Nothing. But you're not normal."

He had no idea.

"You're *popular*. And even for the people who don't like you because you *are* popular, they like you being popular because then they can keep not liking you because you're popular, and everything will stay the same." He stopped. "That probably doesn't make sense."

"Actually, it does," I said, somewhat surprised.

"Jeez, mister, give it a rest," he said as the guy behind us gave up on honking politely and had moved on to just keeping his hand on the horn. "It's not like I'm speeding."

"I think he's doing it because you're way under the speed limit," I said as we inched forward. I took a look at the speedometer. He was doing thirty in a fifty-mile-an-hour zone.

"Well, I can't be too safe with you in the car," he replied, patting me on the leg. "Especially tonight. The night we finally—"

"Let's see what else is on the radio!" I yelled as I punched some more buttons. A girl warbled about how "we are never ever getting back together."

"*But we are never ever ever ever . . .*" Brad sang along. He turned to me. "Not to toot my own horn or anything, but I love that I'm man enough to admit that I think Taylor Swift is one of the geniuses of our generation." He took my hand. "I'm so glad you turned me on to her."

As he went on about how he totally related to her lyrics, and that when he listened to her albums, they allowed him to get in touch with that soft, sensitive part of himself—the part that never came out on the soccer and lacrosse fields—I started to feel guilty. He wasn't the sharpest knife in the drawer (Who was I kidding? He wasn't even a spoon), but he was cute—if you preferred the whole Ken doll look. (Which I didn't.) And he cared a great deal about fashion—granted it was a sherbet-colored palette from thirty years earlier. (Yes, I was trying to bring back fashion from back then, but some things were meant to stay in the past.) And unlike a lot of guys, he liked to be in constant contact. (Even though he had *nothing* interesting to say.) He was the most popular guy at Castle Heights. Any girl would love to go out with him. Things could be worse.

Like, say, if I never figured out to get back to 1986 and I was stuck here in this life. It wasn't like it was a horrible existence. I was incredibly popular. I had a very large walk-in closet full of clothes and purses and shoes and accessories. These were things girls *wanted*. So what if I had horrible taste in music and wore tiaras? And, according to one of my Facebook posts, thought the reason gays should be allowed to marry was because their weddings would be sure to have great food and beautiful flower arrangements?

I was the girl everyone wanted to be.

Well, everyone but me.

Brad leaned over the enormous gap between our seats and snaked his arm around me.

"What's that smell?" I sniffed.

"Axe body spray. You love this stuff. You say it makes you all animalistic."

I wrinkled my nose. It smelled like wet dog mixed with cat urine. Maybe what I meant was that it made him *smell* like an animal. "Right. Of course. Who wouldn't love it?"

Finally we got to Brad's house which was a fancy NOM one. NOM—aka North of Montana—was an area of Santa Monica. Like many of the houses in L.A., it took whatever style the owners had decided upon (in this case English manor) and just went for it.

"So how about a tour," I said as I turned away from the life-sized statue of a silver knight in the front hall that was creeping me out.

"Of the house?"

I nodded. One of the perks of having to suffer through Brad's monologue about the genius of a band called One Direction and how, if his nose hadn't been broken by a soccer ball when he was eight, he could've been in a boy band as well, was that it had given me time to compile a list of time-wasting activities to avoid getting down to the business at hand.

"But you've been here a million times."

"Yes, but in light of how *special* tonight is going to be, I want to have everything committed to memory." As in e*special*ly awkward if I had to fight him off.

He shrugged. "Okay."

As he led me through the house—with his mother's Shih Tzu trotting behind us—I was glad that Brad came from a rich family. Not because I cared about money, but because it made for a longer tour. "And this, as you know," he said with a glint in his eye as he opened up the door to yet another room, "is my bedroom...."

I poked my head in. "Huh. Look at that." It looked like something out of a catalog, if that catalog specialized in English manors. Lots of heavy dark wood and tartan plaid. Even if I were interested in *you know*-ing, I sure wouldn't want to do it in here.

He grabbed my hand and started to pull me in. "And that concludes the end of our tour—"

"You know what? I suddenly got really, really hungry again!" I said, panicked. "Like low-blood-sugar-type hungry. Can I have a snack?"

He looked disappointed before he mustered a smile. "Sure."

Once in the kitchen, I tried to waste more time by naming everything in the refrigerator and cabinets. ("Wow—you guys have pickles? That's so cool. And Saltines! I love Saltines!") At one point I looked over at Brad, who was sitting on a stool in front of the island, and found him dozing off. "Are you tired? Do you think I should go home?" I asked. "Because I don't want to keep you up."

He walked over and took me in his arms. "I'm a little tired. But I know what would wake me up—" he said as he went in for the kiss kill.

I pulled back. This was getting ridiculous. I needed to suck it up and put a stop to this now. "Brad, there's something I need to tell you," I said.

He put his hand in front of his mouth and breathed into it. "It's the onions, isn't it?" He took the breath spray out of his pocket again and uncapped it.

I pushed his hand down. "No. It's not the onions." Well, I

could smell the onions, but that was the least of my problems. "I just . . ." I took a deep breath. "I'm not ready for this."

"For what?"

"For . . . you know . . . any sort of *you know*-ing."

He did the inbred-cocker-spaniel thing with his head. "Ohhhh . . . I get it," he finally said.

Thank God. Because on a scale of one to ten of uncomfortable conversations, this was a 252. "You really get it?" I asked doubtfully. "You're sure?"

"Yeah. You're not ready to have sex."

I exhaled. Thank God he wasn't as dumb as he acted. "Yes. Right. That's exactly it." I looked at him. "How do you feel about that?"

"I'm cool with that."

"You are?"

He shrugged. "Yeah. I mean, you only get to have your first time once. I'm not the kind of guy who would force a girl into doing something she doesn't want to do. That's gross."

I smiled. It was gross. And Brad—I had discovered—was far from gross. Brad was actually a total prince of a guy and deserved a princess of a girl in return. Unfortunately, I was not that princess. And it was unfair to have him keep thinking I was.

"Okay, well, while we're on the topic of hard conversations to be having, I have something else to bring up."

He breathed into his hand again. "It really is the onions, huh?"

I pushed his hand away, but instead of letting go, I kept holding it. "Brad . . . you're an awesome, awesome boyfriend. Like, beyond awesome—"

He smiled. "Thanks, Zoe," he said as he went in for a kiss.

I pulled back. "—and you deserve an equally awesome girlfriend."

"Good thing I have one," he said as he leaned in again. You had to give the guy points for persistence.

"But that's the thing: you don't."

"I don't?"

I shook my head. "You did. But the thing is . . . you're right—I *am* different," I said. "This week, something's happened that I can't really explain, and I'm able to see things in a whole new light—"

His face was starting to fall. "Maybe you can just go back to seeing them in the *old* light."

"That's the thing—I can't," I said sadly. "Brad, you deserve someone who really, really wants to be with you. And right now . . . I don't think I want to be with anyone. I think I need to be alone for a while, and get to know myself better. The new version of me."

By now he looked like he was going to cry. "Are you breaking up with me?"

Oh man. I had no idea this was going to be so hard. "Breaking up sounds so harsh," I said. "Think of it more like . . . I'm releasing you to find your soul mate."

He thought about it and began to nod. "Huh. I like that." He stopped. "But I thought *you* were my soul mate."

"I think I was . . . but now I'm not," I replied. "There's someone a lot more soul-matey for you out there. But I'll never forget what we had." I couldn't forget it, because I didn't *know* what we had had.

He sighed. "Maybe this is for the best. I mean, I've never really ran down the field."

"Do you mean 'played the field'?"

"Yeah. That," he agreed. "So it's probably a good thing."

"Thanks for being so understanding," I said, squeezing his hand.

"You're welcome." He squeezed back before giving a giant yawn. "So if we're not going to . . . you know . . . do you think we can go to sleep? I'm *beat*."

"Actually, I think I want to sleep at home," I replied. "So as your final act of boyfriendness, do you think you could drive me home?"

When I got home, I let myself in to my house as quietly as possible, relieved to see that none of the lights was on downstairs. Sometimes my father had insomnia, which resulted in him wandering around for hours, which he didn't mind so much because he said he was his most creative and came up with some of his best Discocize moves then. My mother, however, did mind, because the next morning she'd come down to find a bunch of dirty dishes in the sink and wrappers from the Hostess cupcakes he hid from her on the table.

Somewhat hungry myself, I made my way into the kitchen.

"Ahhh!" I screamed when I saw my father, earbuds in his

ears, doing some sort of weird lunge-slash-squat move while eating from a very large bowl of ice cream.

"Ahhh!" he screamed back and almost dropped the bowl. As he took the earbuds out, I could hear some guy singing about hoes and hookas. That was definitely not disco. It had to be that rap thing they had been talking about. "Why aren't you at Andrea's? Is everything all right?"

"Everything's fine," I replied. Grabbing one of the chairs, I dragged it to the pantry and reached up onto the top shelf where I found some peanut butter, graham crackers, and M&M's. It was good to know that while this version of me may have only eaten low-calorie things in public, she also kept a stash of junk food hidden away. After getting another carton of ice cream out of the freezer and a bowl, I joined him at the table and placed it between us.

"Some excellent choices here, Zoe," he said.

"Thanks," I replied as I scooped some mint chocolate chip and butter pecan into my bowl and sprinkled some graham crackers on top. I had definitely inherited my love of strange food combinations from my father.

Before he started assembling his own sundae, he glanced over at the stairs to make sure he wasn't about to get busted by my mother. All his junk food eating took place strictly late at night. During the day it was wheatgrass and vegetables. "So what happened?" he asked as he added some M&M's to his ice cream. "Did you guys have a fight?"

"No." I added some M&M's to mine as well. "I just wanted

to be back in my own bed in my own room." Actually, I wanted to be in my own bed in my own room in a different millennium, but that was a whole other story.

He went to the pantry and grabbed a bottle of honey and squirted some in his bowl.

"Good call," I said as I held my bowl out for some as well.

"Thanks. Yeah, I've noticed you haven't seemed like yourself the last few days," he said as he squirted just the right amount on my ice cream.

Talk about the understatement of the year.

"You want to talk about it?"

"Everything's fine," I lied.

And, unlike my mother, who once she noticed something was wrong, wouldn't let it go and interrogated me like she was a detective in a TV show until I broke down and told her, my dad took a different approach. The approach where he didn't badger you. He just nodded and went on eating. Maybe it was a guy thing. "I heard what happened with your speech today," he finally said.

I looked up from my sundae. "You did? How?"

"I follow the Castle Heights Collective on Twitter."

It was kind of creepy how everything you did could be broadcast for everyone to know about. Including parents.

"I'm very proud of you," he went on. "Not to mention surprised. Don't take this the wrong way, but it was very . . . not like you."

"Yeah, well, that's the thing," I said. "Everyone seems to have this idea of what I'm *supposed* to be like and doesn't want me to change."

He nodded as he added some peanut butter to his sundae. "I can understand that. It's scary for people when someone who they think has it all starts to act out of character. People like routine." Huh. Apparently Brad wasn't as dumb as I had thought. "They like knowing what to expect." He took a bite.

"Dad?"

"Yes, honey?"

"I just broke up with Brad."

"Really? That's too bad," he said, relief all over his face. There was a reason my father hadn't gotten a role in his high-school performance of *Grease*. Because he sucked as an actor. "Did something happen?"

"Nothing *specific*," I replied. "It's more like my feelings for him had changed." As in, I didn't have any.

He nodded. "Well, that happens." He took another bite. "Is it because you're interested in someone else?"

I looked at the floor. "No." I wasn't, and yet when I said it, it somehow sounded untrue.

He nodded. "Well, if you know he's not the right guy for you, it's better to be alone until you do find the right one. How'd he take it?"

"He was awesome about it."

He smiled. "That's great. That kid may not be too bright, but he's got a good heart."

"Yeah."

He looked at the clock and stood up. "I should get back to bed in case your mother wakes up." He walked over and kissed me on the top of the head. "I'm proud of you. There's nothing more rewarding than being true to yourself. Remember that."

Why'd it have to be so complicated, though?

CHAPTER Twelve

THE NEXT MORNING I WAS GOING THROUGH my closet, hunting for something non-pink to wear when Andrea FaceTimed me. As I clicked *Accept*, her fully-made-up-even-though-it-was-only-eight-a.m. face filled the screen.

"Omigod, I can't believe I got you," she whispered. "I totally thought you'd be . . . you *know* . . ."

I shook my head. "Nope. No *you know*-ing took place last night."

"It didn't?" The thing about this FaceTime thing was that because you could see the person's face, there was no way for them to pretend they weren't completely relieved to hear something, like Andrea was at that moment. "What happened?"

"We went to dinner, and then he tried to win me a prize at the Pier, and then we went back to his house, and I broke up with him," I replied as I held up a pink crochet cardigan. I had actually paid money for this thing? Ew.

"Okay, (a) you know that's my favorite article of clothing you own," Andrea said. "And (b) *what?!*"

"I broke up with him," I said nonchalantly.

"But . . . he's *Brad* . . ." she sputtered, "and you're . . . *you* . . . and together you guys are . . . *Broe.*"

I plopped down on my bed. "You know how one day you look at something you've looked at a million times and suddenly it just looks different?"

"No. Not really," she replied.

"Well, anyway, that's what happened," I went on. "The other day I woke up, and Brad just looked different to me. And I realized I wasn't in love with him anymore." It felt weird to say that, seeing that I couldn't see being in love with him to begin with.

"I can't believe it. How'd he take it?"

"He was great about it, actually."

"That's not surprising. I mean, he's *Brad.* He's great about everything." She sighed. "Wow. I'm *so* sorry to hear this," she said, sounding not sorry at all.

"Oh, I knew you would be," I said wryly.

"So . . . is he going to look for a new girlfriend right away?" she asked. "I mean—are *you* going to look for a new boyfriend?"

"Nope."

"Wow. You *are* different," she said. "So what should we do to help you through your grieving? Go to the Dell? My source tells me that they added an entire new sale rack at Anthropologie."

"Sounds great, but I can't. I have other plans."

"But it's Saturday," she said. "We've never not hung out together on a Saturday. What are these plans?"

"You know that guy Nerdy Wayne?"

She wrinkled her nose. "Why would I know anyone with the word *nerdy* before his name?"

"You're right. You wouldn't. Silly me. Anyways, he's . . . going to help me with my science homework."

"On a *Saturday*?"

I nodded. "I have a test on Monday. A really big one."

"You're going to do homework on a *weekend*?"

"Yup. It's one of my New Year's resolutions."

"But it's April."

"I know. But I've been so busy, I only just got around to making some. Anyways, I should get going," I said. "Maybe you want to give Brad a call and see what he's doing today. He could probably use some cheering up?"

She brightened. "Really? You'd be okay with that?"

"Sure. It's the least I can do for him. Offering up my best friend to make him feel better. Maybe you two can go shopping. I know he was super impressed with the shirts you picked out for him the other day. So maybe today you could . . . I don't know . . . go pick out . . . socks."

She nodded. "Socks are an integral part of one's fashion statement."

"I couldn't agree more."

"I guess I could help out," she said, attempting to sound somewhat hesitant but failing miserably as she ran to her own closet and threw open the door. "Gotta go! Text me later!" she cried before the screen went dark.

Thanks to Google Maps and the robotic-sounding lady giving directions, I was able to find Insomnia Cafe over in Hollywood on Beverly Boulevard without a problem. It was packed with people typing away on laptops, and from the abundance of furrowed brows and distressed looks on their faces, I decided they had to be screenwriters (the coffee shops of L.A. were filled with them). I scanned the crowd looking for Nerdy Wayne and saw him in the corner, tilted back in his chair, dangerously close to falling over. As I made my way over and got a better look, I stopped short.

He wasn't alone. Jonah was with him.

"Hey," I said when I got to the table. Why was my mouth so dry? So what if Jonah was there.

"Oh wow. It's Zoe Brenner. Here at Insomnia. At eleven a.m.," Nerdy Wayne announced in a stilted voice. It was a good thing he was into computers rather than the Drama Club. "What a coincidence."

Jonah put his hand up. "Hey."

"Hey," I said back.

"So I came here to *get some work done*," Nerdy Wayne went

on. "Because that's what I like to do on Saturdays—*get work done*—and I look up, and Jonah here is standing right in front of me. *Completely out of the blue*."

"Wow. That's weird," I said, playing along.

"*Unplanned*," he went on.

I nodded. "Got it."

"But since he took the liberty of sitting down at my table, maybe you'd like to sit with us, too."

"Sure," I said, pulling out a chair.

The three of us sat there smiling awkwardly at each other for a bit. "You know what I've been thinking a lot about lately?" Nerdy Wayne finally said.

"Why you're acting so weird?" Jonah suggested.

"No. I've been thinking about time travel." He turned to me. "Do *you* ever think about time travel, Zoe?"

"You know, that's totally weird you just brought that up," I replied. "Because just yesterday I thought to myself 'I wonder if there's a way to travel back in time.'"

"Really? What a coincidence!" Wayne exclaimed. "Because *I* was thinking *the same thing*. And then I thought: you know, I should *look up some movies about time travel and see if it gave me some ideas about how to do it*."

This last part he said really loud, obviously code for "this is what my contact came up with."

"That's all it takes?" I asked doubtfully. "Watching a movie about it?"

"Apparently so," Wayne replied.

It seemed like a long shot, but it wasn't like I had any better ideas, so I shrugged and made myself comfortable while Wayne clicked on something called Netflix.

"*Back to the Future,*" I read. "*Hot Tub Time Machine.*" From the poster, that looked like the kind of thing that would only be funny if you were really overtired or whacked out on serious amounts of sugar. "*Looper. Peggy Sue Got Married.* How about this one?" I asked, pointing at something called *The Time Traveler's Wife.*

Nerdy Wayne cringed. "I had a feeling you'd pick that one."

"Why?"

He rolled his eyes. "It looks girly."

"Well, I *am* a girl."

"Okay, okay." He clicked on the computer. "*The Time Traveler's Wife* it is."

Jonah had pulled his computer out and was trying to work (he was writing an essay for his application to a summer internship at KCRW, a radio station in town), but soon enough he got sucked into the movie and watched with us.

It was about a librarian with this weird disorder that made him time travel. A cool ability to have, except for the fact that made it close to impossible for him to have a relationship with the woman he loved. I didn't usually go for super sappy movies, but I found myself wiping my eyes more than a few times. Unfortunately, by the time the movie was over, I wasn't any closer to knowing how to time travel.

"Did you just wipe away a tear?" Jonah asked Wayne as the credits rolled.

"What? *No*," he said, wiping away another one.

"You totally did."

"I did not. Why would I cry about some cheesy movie that has absolutely no basis in reality?"

"*Star Wars* has no basis in reality, and you love that," Jonah replied.

"Well, neither does *Harry Potter*, but that's different."

Who was this Harry Potter guy? It wasn't the first time I had heard his name over the last few days.

As Jonah's phone rang, I saw Montana's picture flash on the screen. He grabbed it and stood up. "Be back in a second."

"So that's it?" I asked Nerdy Wayne as I watched Jonah walk outside. Usually I thought guys who wore hats looked lame, but he could definitely rock a fedora. "That's what your contact had for you?"

"Yeah."

And it had gotten me nowhere. I suddenly wondered whether before breaking up with Brad I should have taken Rhiannon's suggestion to kiss him. I mean, I knew why I hadn't—because as much as I wanted to go back to my old life, I was also scared that there'd be some sort of malfunction; or maybe after getting a taste of this popularity thing I wasn't quite ready to give it up—but now I was left with nothing.

"So would I be right to assume that at the moment, I'm kind of stuck here?"

He thought about it. "Yep. I think that would be an accurate assumption."

Before we could talk more, Jonah came back in.

"You going to hang with Montana?" Nerdy Wayne asked.

"No. She promised her mother she'd help her get ready for her brother's birthday party."

Nerdy Wayne started packing up. "Well, I need to get going. I need to work on my costume for Comic Con." He looked at me. "I'm going as Deadpool."

"Wow. That's awesome. I love Deadpool. Their last album was awesome." I hoped that was the right thing to say, but from the looks on the guys' faces it was not.

"He's a character from a *comic book*," he said. As he stood up to leave, Jonah and I looked at each other a little panicked.

"I guess I should get going, too," I said, making no move whatsoever to get up.

"Yeah. Me too," he agreed, also not moving.

I glanced up at Nerdy Wayne to see his eyebrow go up. "Okay, then. Well, see you guys later," he said before walking off.

We stared at the table for a bit while I searched my brain for possible topics of conversation (the weather, music, whether he'd think I was nuts if I told him what was going on). "So. That movie. I kind of liked it," I finally said. That seemed like a good way into . . . I had no idea what.

"What'd you like about it?" he asked as he took a bag of trail mix out of his knapsack and put it between us.

I grabbed a handful without thinking. "I don't know. The whole person thing I guess." I glanced at him.

"Person?"

"Yeah. You know—your *person*. Your soul mate." I looked up from the table. "Do you believe in soul mates?"

He thought about it as he went to grab some. Yet again we were synchronized in our snacking. Thank God. "I guess. But I don't think they necessarily have to be *romantic*."

"Totally," I agreed as I grabbed for more trail mix. "A soul mate can be non-romantic. Like . . . a really good friend."

He grabbed after me. "Right. It's just someone you feel comfortable around."

Was he talking about Montana? Probably. "Yeah. Like someone you feel you've known forever."

"Even if you've basically just met them," he said.

I felt my face get warm. Okay, then. He was *not* talking about Montana. This time as I put my hand in, it bumped his. We were both so startled, the nuts went flying all over the floor. Jonah reached into his knapsack and took out a white paper bag and opened it to reveal a black-and-white cookie.

I smiled. "Is that from Diamond Bakery?"

He looked surprised. "Yeah. You know that place?"

"Know it? They've got the best—"

"—black-and-whites in town," we said in stereo.

We smiled at each other. "Huh. I wouldn't have pegged you as a black-and-white kind of girl," he said. "In fact, I wouldn't have pegged you as a cookie kind of girl, period." He placed it in between us. "Feel free to have some."

This was good. The subject had been changed. Instead of

talking about soul mates, we could stick to safe subjects. Like cookies. Knowing he liked to eat the chocolate part first, I reached for a piece of the white. "So what *is* the deal with you and Montana?" I blurted.

This was not talk about cookies. This was me hanging myself.

He looked confused. "Huh?"

"I mean . . . you guys spend a lot of time together."

He popped a piece of the chocolate part into his mouth and shrugged. "Yeah. She's my best friend."

"So you have no feelings for her whatsoever?"

"You mean . . . *feelings* feelings?"

Were boys really this clueless? "Yes, Jonah. *Feelings* feelings."

He thought about it. "No."

I felt relief ripple through my body. But why? Hadn't I told Montana just a few days ago that they should date? "You know, if you were to have feelings for someone, she'd be a good person to have them for," I went on, unable to stop myself.

"Yeah, I know, but we're just friends. Can we stop talking about this now?"

"Of course we can," I replied. "It's not like it's any of my business or anything."

"Great," he said, his face red as he picked up his iPhone and focused on it.

"But I'm just going to say this one last thing. Which is this."

He put down his phone.

"See, the thing is . . . you just never know what's going to happen," I went on. "I mean, you could wake up one morning and find yourself thirty years into the future. And if that happens, you don't want to feel like 'I wonder what would have happened if I had done something different back then.'"

Was I saying this for his benefit . . . or for mine?

He gave me a weird look. "What's your fascination with this time travel stuff?"

I looked at him. It was now or never. I had him alone, and he still had half his coffee drink left, and some cookie (although with my stress level escalating the way it was, that cookie was disappearing pretty quickly), so he was a captive audience. But even more than that, it felt like that by not telling him what was going on, I was lying. I hated lying to Jonah. I wanted him to know everything about me.

"Okay, I need to tell you something," I said quietly, "and at first, you're probably going to think I'm nuts, but you've got to hear me out—"

"Okay. . . ."

I took a deep breath. "See, I'm Zoe Brenner, but I'm not the Zoe Brenner who's the most popular girl in school. The one that you—and everyone else—thinks I am. I'm actually from 1986."

"What?" he said confused.

"Yeah. See, I live back in 1986, and I like New Wave music and John Hughes movies and my hair is lopsided—well, asymmetrical—and I'm actually very unpopular—not, like, complete *Social Siberia* unpopular, but on the fringe of it—and you and I are best friends and—"

By this time he was leaning back so far I thought he was going to do a backbend. "What are you *talking* about?! I wasn't even alive in 1986—"

"But you were!" I insisted. "I mean, you are!" This stuff was giving me a headache. "And you were you! Except not as well dressed as you are now. And you didn't wear hats. Oh, and Nerdy Wayne? He was always going on about this thing called Socialize that he was going to invent that would allow people from all over the world to communicate. Which I now realize is exactly like Facebook!"

"You're saying Nerdy Wayne had the idea for Facebook."

I nodded.

"No he didn't, Mark Zuckerberg had the idea. There's even a movie about the whole thing!" He scrambled to stand up. "I've got to go—"

"Wait!" I cried, grabbing his arm tightly. Wow. There was actually a muscle there. When had that happened? "Just give me five minutes to prove to you that I'm telling the truth. If you don't believe me after that, you never have to talk to me again."

"Right. Because you'll probably be locked up."

I clutched harder. "Please?" I pleaded.

He stared at me for what felt like an eternity. "I'll give you three."

"I'll talk fast," I said. "Your birthday is June twenty-fourth—"

"That's right there on my Facebook page—"

"—your favorite color is purple, but you don't like to admit it because you feel that purple is a girl color."

"I'm in touch enough with my feminine side to admit that I'm a fan," he said defensively as he broke off another piece from the chocolate side of the cookie.

I pointed at it. "You always eat the chocolate part of your black-and-whites first, and then the vanilla."

"A lot of people eat black-and-whites that way."

"Your father's name is Edward. He's an orthodontist—"

"He's listed on Facebook as my father." He shook his head. "It's so embarrassing to have your parents on Facebook. Especially my mother. Everything she writes is in caps with exclamation points."

"Her name is Janet," I went on. "She likes to dress your cat Miranda up in costumes and take pictures of her. Your father has said that if she doesn't stop doing this he might have to divorce her."

"She started a Tumblr for them," he moaned. "But how'd you know that?" he demanded, freaked-out.

"Because I was there when he said it, the night your mother made those Waikiki meatballs with the grape jelly."

"Those meatballs were disgusting." His eyes narrowed. "Wait a minute—Montana was there that night."

"Yeah, because Montana is the new me. Or rather, the 2016 version of me."

He looked doubtful.

"You still don't believe me."

"Of course I don't believe you!" he yelped. "Because you're insane!"

"Fine. I'll tell you what else I know. I know that your pig-out food of choice would be something in the sweet *and* salty category, such as Reese's peanut butter cups or kettle corn, but if forced to choose, you'd choose salty. I know that every time E.T. puts out his finger toward Elliott at the end you start to cry but blame it on allergies. I know that your right pinkie is a millimeter shorter than the other one because you got it stuck in a blender when you were seven." I could tell from the way he was mouth breathing like he did whenever he got caught up in a particularly dramatic episode of *Charlie's Angels* that I was getting somewhere. I took a breath. "I know that while you know you should think that what I'm saying is crazy, there's a tiny part of you—the part that loves *Lord of the Rings* and who stops to listen to the guy at the corner of Beverly Drive and Olympic who's always going on about how the world is going to end when the Mayan calendar does in 2012—"

"Yeah, well, obviously he was wrong."

"—I know that part of you . . . the part that kind of sort of wants to believe in magic . . . might kind of sort of believe me," I finished.

Just then we both grabbed for the cookie—him for the chocolate part, me for the vanilla part. "Oh, and we're synchronized snackers."

He shook his head. "Maybe you should go see the guidance counselor or something."

I searched his face for something—anything—to let me know that he might change his mind, but there was nothing. "So you still don't believe me," I said quietly.

"How could I?! You're nuts!" he cried.

"Right. Okay, well, thanks for listening," I mumbled as I stood up and started to make my way toward the door. Before I pushed it open, I turned to see if he had followed me, but he was still sitting there.

They say your worst fears rarely come true, but mine had. I had finally gotten the guts to tell my best friend what was going on, and he thought I was crazy.

I was really on my own now.

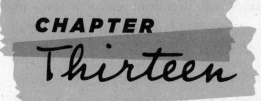

CHAPTER Thirteen

I HADN'T EVEN MADE IT INSIDE THE BUILDING on Monday morning when it became clear that the news about me and Brad breaking up had traveled faster than paparazzi pictures of Beyoncé in a bathing suit.

"Omigod, Zoe—I'm *so* sorry about you and Brad," said Arden Marshall, one of the biggest mouths in school. "You're probably in mourning right now, but when you come out of it, I'd love to have you do a guest post about it on my blog."

"Thanks," I said as I pushed the door open and sailed past her. "I'll think about it."

"Zoe. Right on," Sage Milstein said, holding up her fist for a bump. Sage was the president of the hard-core feminist Fish Don't Need Bicycles Club. Well, the president, vice president, and secretary because she was also the only member. "Way to put forth the idea that we don't need guys to complete us."

"Right. Exactly," I said as I bumped her. The good news was that I was so worried about the vote this afternoon about the Ramp that I didn't care about the fact that people were using the breakup as an opportunity to talk about me and roll around in my misfortune.

While Andrea wasn't downright ignoring me, she had taken my suggestion to comfort Brad very seriously. Like, so seriously that before the assembly I was on my own, without her offering me a pep talk, because she was too busy practically crawling into his lap. *Okay. I can do this*, I said to myself backstage as I waited for the principal to get everyone quieted down. "And even if the vote doesn't pass, at least I know I did all I could to try to make things different around here."

Finally it was time to go onstage. As I made my way across, I bumped into a metal suit of armor left over from the Drama Club's *King Artie: The Musical!* and watched as it came crashing down.

"Those hours at the gym must really be paying off," I said as the crowd laughed. I looked at them. "Isn't that what we all do?" I asked, pointing at the armor. "Walk around with a suit of armor on, giving off different messages to everyone we come into contact with?"

The laughter died as the crowd got quiet. They looked confused. Castle Heights was not used to such depth so early in the week.

"*Do not disturb. I own this 'It' bag, so now you'll think I'm cool,*" I continued. "*I'm going to dress like I don't care what you think of me, but, really, I totally do. If I manage to stay invisible, maybe you'll just leave me alone and not tease me.* Any of that sound familiar?

No one said a word. By this time you could hear a pin drop.

"This past week I had the opportunity to hang out with someone completely outside my social circle," I went on. "Someone who doesn't sit on the Ramp." I looked around and caught Montana's eye. She looked back at me warily, unsure of what I was about to say. "And what I discovered is that while we may look different, and dress different, we're way more alike than I would have thought. To me, she's a girl who looks like she has it all together. Someone who, even though she's not quote-unquote popular, is okay with that and okay with herself and has no use for someone like me in her life. And although none of you will probably believe this, if she hadn't talked to me first, I would have been too intimidated to reach out to her and try to get to know her."

Some buzzing began in the crowd.

"I would have just stayed in my own little corner of my own little world—on the Ramp—trying to come off as just as together and just as okay with myself, even though I'm about as far as having this life thing figured out as you guys are," I continued

The buzzing got louder.

"If there's one thing I'm grateful to my popularity for, it's that it gives me the opportunity to get to see past people's outsides, if only because they're too intimidated to keep me out," I preached. "I'm not invisible, and because I'm not, I get to go up to people who are and let them know they're seen." I looked around the auditorium for Terrell from the Go Greeners. "Hey, Terrell—stand up for a second."

"Me?"

I nodded. "Yeah."

He stood up slowly and looked around, like he was afraid of what was going to happen next.

"Look at this ensemble," I said. "Jeans with a seersucker jacket and a denim shirt with a bowtie. How amazingly cool is that? Now, I bet a lot of you guys have never noticed that Terrell has amazing fashion sense, but now that I've pointed it out, you won't miss it."

Terrell smiled, pleased with the attention, before he sat back down.

"Ashima Patel. Where are you?" I called out.

Over in the back corner, an arm slowly went up.

"Do you have your sketchbook?" In study hall the week before, I had walked by to find her sketching an amazing portrait of the Golden Gate Bridge in San Francisco.

She nodded.

"Open it and show everyone one of your sketches."

Shyly, she did, and the crowd began to murmur in amazement at her portrait of the Eiffel Tower.

"Isn't she amazing?"

The crowd began to clap.

"Yeah. I think so, too," I agreed. "So next time you see her, remember that even though she's quiet, there's a lot going on there. Here's the thing: whether you guys believe it or not, we're all the same. No matter where we sit in the cafeteria, or what kind of music we listen to, or how many Facebook friends we have, we all want the same thing. To be seen. And it's my belief that by getting rid of the Ramp, we're that much closer to that eventually happening."

It was hard to gauge the crowd's reaction to my speech. "I know that I probably just wasted my breath, and that none of what I said is going to change your mind about getting rid of the Ramp, but even if it doesn't, I'm glad I said all of it. Because it's important and it's true. So it's time to vote. Those in favor of the Ramp coming down, raise your hand."

I couldn't believe what I was seeing. It started slowly—a few hands here, a few there, but soon they started going up faster. And faster. Until at the end, the only holdovers were Andrea, Brad, and a few other Ramp dwellers. And then Brad's hand went up as well.

Thank you, I mouthed.

"What'd you say?" he yelled back. "I have a hard time reading lips."

"I said thanks." I looked out at the crowd. "Thanks to all of you. You have no idea how much I appreciate it."

The only thing I would have appreciated more was having someone to share this moment of victory with.

Later that afternoon, as I passed the building where the radio station was, I kept my head down. As much as I tried to get myself to stop, I couldn't help replaying the look Jonah had given me on Saturday right before I ran out of Insomnia. I couldn't believe I had taken the risk to tell him the truth. Of course he thought I was nuts.

And of course the door to the building had to open just as I crossed by.

"Zoe!" Jonah called after me.

I walked faster.

"Zoe!" he called again.

I began to run toward the parking lot, and could hear from his footsteps behind me that he was running after me. Huh. 2016 had given him a lot more stamina. "Zoe. Wait. Please," I heard Jonah say.

He had to pick *now* to start paying attention to me? I stopped. "What?" I asked.

He caught up with me. "Okay, listen," he said when he was by my side. "If I *did* happen to be the kind of person who believed in time travel—which I'm not saying I am—but if I *were*, then, maybe I would believe that what you told me on Saturday wasn't completely out of the realm of possibility."

"Really?"

He nodded.

"You don't know how much that means to me that you said that," I said as tears began to sprout in my eyes.

"Why don't we go somewhere so you can tell me the whole story?"

An hour later, fueled by a mochaccino and a chocolate chip cookie, I had run through the whole thing. The mouth to mouth from Brad. Waking up the next morning. Having no idea what an iPhone was, let alone Twitter. I told him about Rhiannon, and how she had said that I just needed to kiss Brad again, but that I hadn't done that before we broke up—

"I heard you guys broke up."

"You did?" Of course he had. The entire school had.

"Yeah. How come?"

I shrugged. "I don't know. Because he wasn't my boyfriend. I mean, he *was*, but he wasn't," I said nervously. "He wasn't . . . my person."

"That's too bad," he replied.

I searched his face for something, but nothing showed. "Yeah. I guess." I cleared my throat. "And then Nerdy Wayne said he knew a guy who knew a guy who had some ideas, but the idea was watching that movie, and that didn't help, so now I don't know what to do."

He thought about it for a second. "Well, I think I might have one, too."

"Your family pays a guy who lives all the way in India to do everything from schedule your dentist appointments here in L.A. to make homemade baked goods for you to send as thank-you gifts?" I asked as Jonah turned on his laptop. "And his name is Hank? That's not a very Indian name."

"It's actually Argjun," Jonah replied. "Hank is his customer service call center name. He chose it because of Hank Williams.

He's a big country music fan. Right now he's really into Miranda Lambert and Blake Shelton."

"And you know all this how?"

"We're Facebook friends."

"Isn't the stuff stale when it gets here?"

"Huh?"

"The homemade baked goods."

"Oh. No. He outsources that part. To another outsourcing company in the Valley."

Now I was really confused. "Let me get this straight. So you hire someone in India to hire someone here to make something homemade for you."

"*I* don't. My mom does," he said. He clicked away on the keyboard until a dialing sound was heard, like when you made a phone call. A few seconds later I saw a dark-haired guy wearing a T-shirt that said OCCUPY WALL STREET fill the screen.

"Jonah!" Long time no see," said the guy who I was guessing was Hank. "What's the haps?" His English was perfect, with barely any accent.

"Hey, Hank. How are you? How's P!nk?" Jonah replied. He turned to me. "P!nk's Hank's girlfriend. Her real name is Ashima but P!nk is her American name."

I couldn't get over the fact that neither of them seemed the least bit weirded out that they were having a conversation from different continents. "Pink's a name?" I asked, confused.

"Yeah. She's a famous singer."

"P!nk is wonderful, thank you for asking," Hank replied.

Jonah pulled me closer to him so I was in line with the camera. "Hank, this is Zoe."

"Hey, Hank." I waved. "Nice to meet you."

"You too, Zoe." He looked at Jonah. "I did not see a relationship status change on your Facebook page, Jonah."

"She's not my girlfriend," Jonah said, turning red.

"Definitely not," I agreed. "We're just friends. Not to mention I just broke up with someone."

Hank nodded. "Ah. My bad. Forgive me. P!nk and I were friends for many years before we became a Facebook-official couple."

"Okay. Moving on," Jonah said. "So we need a little help today."

"That is what I am here for."

"Now, what I'm about to explain to you might sound really weird—"

"Oh, do not worry about that," Hank said. "I recently did some work for a major celebrity who has starred in numerous high-grossing box office action films, and while I am not at liberty to discuss what he asked me to help him with because of our strict confidentiality rules, I can assure you that it was very high on the weirdness factor."

Was that supposed to make me feel better?

"So what we're wondering about is time travel," Jonah said.

"Time travel." Hank nodded. "An oft-requested subject," he replied, as if there was nothing weird about it whatsoever.

"It is?" I asked.

"Oh yes. I would say I get about five calls about it a month."

Huh. Suddenly I didn't feel so weird anymore.

"Now, are you interested in how to travel forward in time, or back?"

"Back," I replied, still not over the fact that I was talking to a computer. Or a person in a computer. Or whatever this was. That, to me, was stranger than time travel.

"Give me one moment, please," Hank said as he turned toward a bank of video monitors and began typing on a keyboard. We watched as the screens filled with information. After a bit, he turned back to us. "Okay. I ran various programs, with logarithms and other math-related things that are very boring to those who are not interested in math, so I will spare you the details," he said. "But essentially the idea is this. It is to do something very similar to the 1993 movie *Groundhog Day*, which starred Bill Murray. Are you familiar with that movie?"

"Unfortunately I am not," I replied.

"Oh. That's too bad. Because it's a very entertaining movie. If you would like, I can do a search on Dish TV to see if it will be airing anytime in the next week and I can record it for you. And if it is not, I can arrange for it to be added into Jonah's Netflix queue. And if Netflix does not offer it for instant streaming, I can purchase it for you through iTunes. And if—"

Jonah turned to me. "It really is an awesome movie. If you have the time, you definitely should try to watch—"

"Thanks for the tip. I'll definitely watch it at some point," I interrupted. "Now, if you could just explain the idea."

"Yes. Very good. Sure, I can do that," Hank said. "So the idea is very simple. It involves the person retracing their steps of the last few days leading up to the time when he or she time traveled."

"And then what?" Jonah asked.

"And then the person would get to the point where whatever it was that caused them to time travel could be done differently."

We waited for him to go on, but he just continued smiling.

"So that's it? Just go back and retrace my steps? It's not more scientific than that?" I asked. "You know, like with worm holes or black holes or logarithms?"

Hank shook his head. "I am not a PBS special."

I shrugged. "Okay. If you say so."

"Was there a certain event that spurred on this time travel incident?" he asked.

Starting with the fiasco at Hot Dog on a Stick, I told him the whole story up until Brad gave me mouth to mouth and kissed me.

"Ah. So it was a kiss from your boyfriend that did this," Hank said.

"Yes. I mean no. I mean, Brad wasn't . . . isn't . . . my boyfriend back in 1986," I replied. "He was in 2016. But he's not now. I broke up with him the other day."

"Ah. So you think you were kissed by the wrong person?"

I nodded. "*Definitely* the wrong person."

"Then it sounds like you need to be kissed by the right one!" Hank exclaimed.

Huh. Rhiannon hadn't brought up that part. "I guess so," I said.

"Do you know who the right person might be?" Hank asked.

I shook my head. "I have no clue."

"Hm. Well, do you think you might be able to figure it out?"

"Probably not. I don't really date. . . . I mean, it's not like I've never been kissed before, because I have. . . . Not like *a lot*, but enough. . . ." I was babbling. This was getting awkward. "What if I just start retracing my steps and go from there?" I asked.

Hank nodded. "That sounds like a plan, Stan."

It wasn't like we had others.

CHAPTER
Fourteen

"SO NONE OF THIS FEELS THE LEAST BIT familiar?" I asked Jonah as we stood in my kitchen the next afternoon. We were about to embark on Operation Groundhog Day (I did end up watching the movie the night before, and it was indeed awesome). Because he had been with me the day during the Hot Dog on a Stick Incident-with-a-capital-*I* (he came up with the capital *I* thing, and he was right—it was capital-*I*-worthy), I had convinced him to come with me again.

He took it in and then shook his head. "Nope. Sorry."

"It wasn't a fair question anyway," I said. "My mother's constantly remodeling." Still, now that Jonah believed me (after regurgitating about a hundred facts to him about himself that there was no way I could know unless we were close, I had finally convinced him that I was telling the truth), I was hoping that being at my house would jog his memory even more.

"So tell me again what happened in the few days leading up to the kiss," he said as we chowed down on gluten-free/taste-free crackers. Some things never changed—like the lack of good snacks available in my house.

I felt like I was on one of those crime shows that I had gotten addicted to in the past week. "We've been over this, like, ten times already," I said.

"I know, I know. But I just want to be clear. So we don't end up screwing it up." He took another cracker. "I don't want to be known as the guy who sent you back to the 1500s."

"Fine. So after school, we went to the mall to work—" I began.

He smiled. "I can't get over the fact that you had a job," he said, amused.

"Oh, not just a job, but a *good* job."

"What was it?"

"I'm not going to tell you," I sniffed. "You'll just have to wait and see."

"Did *I* have a job?"

"You did. You worked at a record store called Vinnie's Vinyl."

He nodded. "That makes sense. Wait—I didn't have a Mohawk, did I?"

"No."

"Phew."

"But you also didn't wear this," I said, pulling at his fedora.

"I'll have you know that they don't let you into Williamsburg, Brooklyn, without one of these," he said.

"What's in Williamsburg?"

"It's where I plan to live after college."

"Is that where all those hipster people live?" I teased.

"Hipster has such a negative connotation," he said. "I prefer . . . culture-forward."

"But what about London?" I asked.

"Huh?"

I shook my head. "Never mind."

"What?"

I felt my cheeks get red. "Nothing. It's just . . . we used to talk about living in New York or London or Berlin when we grew up."

"I could never live in Berlin. German food—"

"—gives you gas. I know," I finished.

Now he was the one who looked embarrassed. "I guess you *do* know me." He grabbed his keys. "Let's go."

As we turned to leave, my mother came bouncing into the kitchen and began to do some squats. "Oh. Hello," she said when she saw Jonah.

"Mom, this is Jonah," I said. "From school. We're . . . lab partners in science class. Working on an experiment."

"How nice," she said. "Odd, but nice." She did a few more moves that consisted of her shaking her cornrows and then stopped. "I have an idea—how about you two take a break and come be part of our new video!"

I felt the hair on the back of my neck stand up. It was déjà vu. I turned to Jonah who looked just as spooked.

"Okay, that's just *weird*," he whispered.

She turned to Jonah. "Zoe's father and I have a line of videos called Hip-Hop Your Way to Health. Maybe you've heard of them?"

"Ah, no. I don't think I have."

"Really? Do you follow Nas on Twitter? Because he tweeted about us just last week."

"Nope. Sorry."

"Oh. Well, we have a Facebook page, so you can learn more about us there," she said. "This new video, it's with Nicki Minaj, but we're populating the crowd with extras who are very non-hip-hoppy, if you feel me, which is why you two would be great."

We looked at each other. "You know, Mom, that sounds great, especially because I'm a huge Nicki fan and have been wanting to meet him—"

"Her," Jonah said quietly.

"—her," I said without missing a beat, "but we really need to keep working on our experiment."

"It's a timely one," Jonah added.

"You can say that again," I murmured as I grabbed Jonah's arm and dragged him toward the front door. "So we'll see you later!"

When we got outside, we looked at each other. "This is getting weirder by the minute," he said.

"I know." What if Hank was right? What if this worked? Was I ready to go back? I turned to him. "I think you should drive. You dropped me off at work the day that all this started, and I think we should stick to how it happened."

"But my car has a tendency—"

"—to get stuck in park at red lights when going uphill, I know."

He looked surprised. "Yeah, and sometimes—"

"—you have to put it in neutral and get out and push while I steer from the passenger side."

He shook his head. "I'm done being freaked-out by this stuff."

I pounded the door three times with my fist before lifting the handle up and out so that it opened. Once in, he turned to me. "So where to?"

"The Galleria."

He looked blank.

"The big mall over in the Valley?"

"You worked in the *Valley*?"

"I did. And so did you."

"Are you sure it's still around?"

"I have no idea. But I can at least tell you how to get there."

"I just realized we haven't said a word since we got in the car," he said a few minutes later as we crawled up Coldwater Canyon. "We should be talking, right?"

I shrugged. "Sometimes we go hours without talking."

He looked at me. "We do?"

I nodded. Jonah was the only person with whom I could sit

quietly without saying a word and not feel the urge to have to blab on and on just to fill the silence.

"Huh. Interesting." He was quiet for a second. "So . . . what kind of music do you like? Wait—we already covered this subject. What about TV shows? We haven't talked about that—"

The kind of blabbing that he was doing right then. "Jonah," I said cutting him off. "It's okay to not talk."

He sighed. "Got it." We rode in silence for about a minute before he reached for the radio. "Let's listen to the radio." He punched some buttons until "I Melt with You" came on.

We looked at each other, freaked-out.

What were the chances of that happening two times in a row?

But then again, by now, nothing should have surprised me.

And then—in stereo—we began to sing together at the top of our lungs.

"I'm telling you, this place was way different back in the day," I said as we walked through the almost-empty mall. "Back then, it was mobbed."

"Uh-huh," he said disbelievingly as we moved out of the way for a pack of elderly speed-walkers.

"It was. This was *the* place. They used it not only in the movie *Fast Times at Ridgemont High*, but also for *Valley Girl*."

He looked blank.

"You bought me the soundtrack for my fifteenth birthday."

"I did?"

I nodded. "On cassette tape." As we got on the up escalator,

I pointed. "Right over there is Express. That's my second favorite store after Terri's place," I explained. Except that once we got off the escalator it was no longer there. "Color Me Mine. What's that?" I asked, reading the sign.

"It's this place where you paint pottery," Jonah explained. "My mom loves it."

"I can't believe Express has been replaced by a *mom* place," I moaned. My stomach began to rumble. "Okay, time to show you where I worked." I wondered if Wally still worked there and had made his way up to manager yet. And how I was going to ask him for my job back. As we turned the corner I stopped short. "Hot Dog on a Stick is now a *cupcake* store?"

"What's a Hot Dog on a Stick?"

"The place where I worked."

He laughed. "*You* worked at a hot dog place. That's genius."

"I was very good at my job," I replied. "At least until the last day."

Jonah did that thing he did whenever he was thinking hard, which was where he scrunched up his face and squinted. The one time I snapped a picture of it with the Polaroid camera that I had gotten for my fifteenth birthday he had torn it up because he thought he looked like a crazy person, but I loved it. "Wait a minute—there's a Vegan Dog at the Dell. And since that's like the Galleria of today, maybe we should try there?"

I smiled. "See? I knew I couldn't do this without you."

Maybe it was the crash after the sugar rush of the cupcakes and the Charleston Chew and the Laffy Taffy and the Mounds and the Kit Kat that I bought in the candy-by-the-pound store that we passed on our way back to the parking garage (the only decent store in the mall now, in my opinion). Or the way a person can't help but be lulled into relaxation by the chorus in Human League's "Don't You Want Me," which was playing on Sirius's Totally '80s station. Whatever it was, during the drive back over the hill to the Dell, I felt like Jonah and I were finally me and Jonah again. Not only did I feel comfortable singing in front of him to Falco's "Rock Me Amadeus" (seeing that I was somewhat challenged when it came to my vocal talent, I tended to be a mouther), but soon enough we were finishing each other's sentences.

And yet as comfortable as it all was, something was off. And not just because the roads were filled with something called Toyota Priuses, which were supposed to burn less gas, and giant SUVs, which made up for the gas that the Priuses saved. It was more like, for the first time, the fact that we were so comfortable made me *un*comfortable. As in this was the kind of comfortable you wanted to be not just with your best friend, but with a boyfriend, too.

"You're really easy to talk to," Jonah said, surprised, as we came over Coldwater Canyon.

"So are you," I said. But I couldn't date Jonah. He was *Jonah*.

We were quiet for a bit. "So you're really not interested in Montana, huh?" I asked, breaking the silence. What was I doing bringing this up again?! He had already said he didn't want to discuss it. In an attempt to keep quiet, I rummaged in my bag for some Dentyne Fire and shoved four pieces in my mouth.

(One of the things I was most disappointed to discover over the past few days was that Bubble Yum, Bubbalicious, and Hubba Bubba seemed impossible to find.) The gum worked . . . for all of a minute. "Seriously," I said, my mouth on fire, "she's great, you're great—if you got together, you'd be great to the second degree." Seeing that I hated math so much, I wasn't even sure that was correct. But it sounded good.

"She *is* great," he said, "but . . . I don't know. I just . . ." As we stopped at a red light he turned to me. "This is going to sound really stupid. But I guess if anyone would be crazy enough to believe something really stupid, it would be you."

"Thanks. I think."

"You know what I mean."

That was the thing. I *did* know what he meant. I *always* knew what he meant. And while in the past I had always taken that for granted, now the idea of that left me feeling . . . sad . . . somehow. Because the ability to get someone and be gotten by them—that didn't happen very often. In fact, I had a sense it happened, like, a few times in your life, if you were lucky. "So what is it?"

He stared straight ahead. "It's just . . . I feel like there's someone out there," he said quietly. "And when I meet her, it'll be like I've known her forever."

"I feel the same way," I whispered. I felt my face get hot.

I began to feel that if I didn't stop talking about this, I was going to do the scarf and barf thing. "So. Changing the subject. Can you please tell me what the deal is with those Kardashian chicks? I mean, why exactly are they famous?"

From the way the color came back into his cheeks and he stopped gripping the steering wheel, I could tell he was glad for the change of subject as well. For the rest of the drive, he filled me in about this thing called reality TV and the fact that really stupid, untalented people were paid lots of money to let cameras record their every move, which resulted in them becoming famous and doing ads for energy drinks.

Jonah was still going on about it as we walked into the Dell, shouting over the sound of the fountain and the ballad by Beyoncé, according to the electronic *Now Playing* that was flashing next to it.

There had been a bunch of people there the other day, but today it was packed. Like Galleria-level packed back when the Galleria was the Galleria. "So where's the food court?" I yelled over the music. "I'm starving."

"This way," he said as he led me through the crowd. "But I'm telling you—I don't think you're going to like it."

"Hey, I've never met a food court I haven't liked." As another group of elderly speed-walkers came barreling toward us (much better dressed), Jonah grabbed my hand and pulled me aside before I was mowed over. The minute his fingers touched mine I felt a shock go up my arm. He seemed to feel it as well, because he let go as fast as he did the day that his hand landed on the stove we forgot to turn off after melting chocolate to put on our popcorn before we watched the very special episode of *Family Ties* where Tom Hanks plays Alex P. Keaton's drunk uncle.

"Thanks," I said to the fountain.

"You're welcome," he said to the cart that sold sparkly iPhone covers.

We kept walking, weaving our way through the double strollers (according to Jonah, the reason for so many twins was because lots of women nowadays had to go on drugs to get pregnant that apparently worked better than expected), while that Katy Perry chick warbled about being someone's teenage dream (from the response of the crowd, she was a big hit with the tween crowd). When we finally got to the food court, I cringed. "Okay, maybe I need to amend my statement about the food court thing," I announced. Out of the seven different stands, there was not *one* unhealthy choice among them. Nothing deep-fried. Nothing smothered in sauce. Nothing with signs that said *jumbo-sized* or *loaded* or *all you can eat*. Instead it was stuff like green juice, and brown rice, and tofu, and signs that said MACROBIOTIC and GLUTEN-FREE and DR. OZ-APPROVED.

"This is the most depressing thing I've ever seen," I announced.

"Tell me about it," Jonah replied.

And then I saw it. In the corner.

"Vegan Dogs," Jonah and I said at the same time.

There wasn't as big a crowd as there was at the sugar-free, gluten-free frozen soy yogurt place. In fact, there wasn't a crowd at all. There was just one guy, Wally's height, Wally's scrawniness, with a similar pattern of pimples, standing behind the counter. "Look at the hat!" I gasped.

"Whoa. That's weird," Jonah replied. "It's almost exactly like the one in the picture."

While Hot Dog on a Stick wasn't at the Galleria, I had been able to Google a photo of the uniforms so Jonah could see just how ridiculous they were. I felt the hairs on the back of my neck stand up. The guy was wearing a hat almost identical to the Hot Dog on a Stick one, except this one had a hot dog (well, a vegan dog) perched on top of it.

As I marched over to the stand, the guy drew himself up to his full height, which, at about five-three, was still three inches shorter than me. "Welcome to Vegan Dog. Can I interest you in a delicious organic, hormone-free, no-cruelty vegan dog today?" he asked. "Perhaps with a side of air-baked sweet potato fries?"

"Actually, I'd like a job, please," I replied.

The guy behind the counter—whose name, I now saw on the tag that was in the shape of a smiling vegan dog, was Larry (I knew I'd be pushing it if I said that both names having an *A* followed by double consonants was evidence that he was the modern-day version of Wally, but it *was* strange)—looked confused. "*You* want to work *here*?" he asked.

I nodded and flashed what I hoped was an excellent-customer-service-level smile. "Very much so. In fact, it's been a dream of mine ever since it opened." I turned to Jonah. "Hasn't it been?"

He nodded. "It has. It's pretty much all she talks about."

Larry stood up even taller. "Yeah, well, I can understand that," he said. "It was mine, too, and even though it took a while for me to convince Corporate that the fact that I failed the spatial reasoning test was just a fluke and had nothing to do with my ADHD, which, for some reason, tested off the charts that day, I achieved it," he said proudly. "The twenty-one dollars and ninety-five cents I spent on that prayer request from that website in Bali I found may have helped as well." He stood up even taller, which, when I glanced over the counter, was due to the fact that he was on his tiptoes. "What kind of experience do you have?" he demanded.

"Oh, I have lots of experience."

"Like what?"

"Like—" I looked at Jonah for help.

"She's president of the junior class."

"Really," Larry said as he stroked his chin. "Well, that could come in handy. Leadership ability can be helpful when dealing with customers who are having trouble deciding which of our organic, sulfite-free, fruit-based relishes to enjoy with our delicious organic, hormone-free, no-cruelty vegan dogs," he said. "Not to mention you're not too hard on the eyes. *Heh-heh.*" He turned to Jonah. "Sorry, dude. Not cool of me to say about your girlfriend."

"She's not my girlfriend," Jonah said over my "I'm not his girlfriend."

"Do you have a résumé?" Larry asked.

"A résumé to get a job at a hot dog stand?" I asked.

"Okay—first of all, according to the e-book I just read about how to succeed in business, the number two commandment after making sure you brush your teeth before a job interview is that you should have your résumé on you at all times," he said. "And second of all, these are not hot dogs. They're not even vegan dogs. They're—"

"Delicious, organic, hormone-free, no-cruelty vegan dogs?" I suggested. "Which taste even better when topped with one of our organic, sulfite-free, fruit-based relishes?"

"Very good," he said, impressed. "When can you start?"

I hopped over the counter. "Right now."

Of all the things that had been phased out since 1986, you'd think that polyester would be at the top of the list, but not in Vegan Dog's case.

"Wouldn't organic cotton be a more appropriate way to go?" I asked Larry as I scratched at my neck, which, only five minutes into wearing my uniform, was already turning red.

"Feel free to put something in the suggestion box about that," Larry said, motioning to a metal box that had both a padlock and a combination lock on it. "Might win you some points with Corporate, the fact that you're thinking in such a PC way. But just so you know, they're never going to lose the polyester."

"How come?" I asked as I tried to balance my hat on my head. The weight of the smiling vegan dog made it that much more difficult.

"Because the owner of Vegan Dog, Shalom—his real name was Asher, but he had a religious experience at a Lil Boosie concert and changed it—his grandfather used to own this place back in the eighties called Hot Dog on a Stick, where I guess the uniforms were made of polyester. So I guess it's kind of in his honor."

The hairs on the back of my neck stood up again. I couldn't

wait to tell Jonah when he got back from the Apple store about this new twist. "You know, I'd love you to go over the different relishes with me again before we get a customer," I said.

Larry smiled proudly. "I *knew* that twenty-four ninety-five I spent on that download on iTunes about how to trust your gut in business would pay off. I could tell from the minute you walked up that you were the kind of person who's very conscientious." He looked around to make sure no one was listening—which they were not, seeing that they were all in line for frozen yogurt from Red Mango. "I don't want to get your hopes up or anything, but if you continue showing this kind of commitment, you have a good shot of becoming assistant manager when they promote me to manager. You're already much better than Waheel, my other employee. He spends his entire time working on his Twitter novel."

"Wow. That would be just great," I replied.

I was waiting for Larry to finish writing up the cheat sheet of the menu (as the only item on the menu was the Vegan Dog and the sweet potato fries, I didn't need one, but I kept quiet, since it was a good way to waste time), when I looked up and happened to see Brad and Andrea loaded down with shopping bags, laughing and looking very much like a couple.

Déjà vu all over again.

"Brad! Andrea!"

As they looked over and saw me, they immediately moved about three feet apart. But the guilty looks on their faces were quickly replaced by horror, as if I were standing there in my bra and underwear rather than a polyester uniform and a majorette hat with a smiling Vegan Dog on top of it. It was 1986 once more, except this time Andrea wasn't snarling at me.

They came closer slowly, kind of like the way you're supposed to approach a feral cat. "Hi, you guys! It looks like you're having so much fun together," I said with a smile. At that, they went back to looking guilty. I motioned to their shopping bags. "Looks like you did some serious damage, huh?"

"Why is there a *hot dog* on your head?" Brad asked, confused.

Out of the corner of my eye I could see Larry waiting to see how I answered. "It's not a hot dog," I corrected, "it's a delicious, organic, hormone-free, no-cruelty vegan dog."

He nodded approvingly.

Andrea leaned in to get a better look at me. "Is that . . . *polyester*?

I could tell from the way Larry was trying to make himself taller, he was thirty seconds away from telling me that socializing with friends while on the clock was not acceptable. "May I interest you in one? They're extra delicious when topped with one of our organic, sulfite-free, fruit-based relishes?"

"Tell them about the two-for-one special," Larry hissed.

"It seems to be your lucky day," I said. "Because this week only we're having a two-for-one special!"

Brad turned to Andrea. "Do you think that, like, she's got some sort of brain tumor?" he asked in a loud whisper. "'Cause I saw a movie once where this girl started acting really weird and it was because of that."

"Tell them about the air-baked sweet potato fries!" Larry whispered.

"Our air-baked sweet potato fries are a wonderful complement to our Vegan Dogs," I said mechanically. "And studies have shown that together, they actually help to facilitate weight loss." That one I didn't believe, and had been thinking of asking Larry if it was possible to see these so-called studies, but I didn't want to get fired for nothing. I wanted to get fired for getting into a fight with a customer.

Andrea and Brad looked at each other. "I think I'm going to pass," Andrea said.

"Oh. Okay," I said, disappointed.

"But I'll take one," Brad said.

This wasn't going exactly the way it had on that day thirty years before, but it was close. Hopefully it would help get me back to 1986. Suddenly I froze. What if it worked *too* well and got me back there before I could say good-bye to Jonah? I was pretty sure he'd be there when I got back there, but what if there was some sort of glitch and he wasn't? If the last few days had showed me anything, it's that I didn't want to live in a place where Jonah didn't exist. And when did I start sounding like a song by that Taylor Swift chick?

I slapped some mango relish on the dog and handed it to him.

"Zoe? Is there . . . a reason you're working here?" Andrea asked tentatively. "Is it, like, something you're planning on working into your next State of the Class address? You know, kind of like how sometimes the president goes and spends the day with coal miners or steel workers?"

"Nope. I've just always wanted to work here," I replied.

"Since when?" Brad asked.

"Like I just said—since always." Wow. Good luck to him when it came to reading-comprehension tests.

Right then Jonah came running over. "Hey, look what I found over at the Farmers Market!"

My face lit up when I saw the package of Fun Dip. "Excellent. Thank you."

"The weirdness just keeps on coming," Andrea said.

"What's that?" Brad asked with his mouth full, pointing at the candy.

Okay, I'm sorry, but I was right to break up with him. How could I possibly date a guy who didn't know what Fun Dip was? Just then a woman with two kids started to approach. Jonah and I looked at each other, amazed.

"That's just too weird," he murmured. As much as it had pained me to remember the whole thing, I had told him about what happened with the mean woman that led to me getting fired.

"Okay, well, great seeing you guys!" I said as I reached over and pushed Brad and Andrea out of the way. "Time for me to get back to work!" I turned to the woman and flashed a big smile. "Welcome to Vegan Dog. Can I take your order?"

"Hiiii!" she said with an equally big smile. "Omigod, that is *such* a cute hat."

This time when Jonah and I looked at each other, it was with alarm. She wasn't supposed to be nice! She turned to the kids, who instead of trying to climb in the fountain were standing there well-behaved, as if kid actors in a commercial. "Kids, isn't that hat just adorable?"

They nodded in unison, but kept quiet.

What was going on here? "Wait a minute—you're supposed to—" I stopped. What was I going to say . . . *You're supposed to be a total jerk and treat me rudely because I'm working at a hot dog stand and being paid to be polite to you?*

"I think we're going to go," Andrea said gently and carefully, in the tone that people used in the movies when they were trying to convince someone who was about to jump off a building to come inside.

"Good, good," I replied. "Go. Bond. Please. Have a *great* time." I turned back to the customer. "Sorry about that. What can I get you?"

"Would it be possible to get two Vegan Dogs and an order of those sweet potato fries?" she asked politely.

"Sure," I said, disappointed as I watched Brad and Andrea turn around and start to walk away. I assembled her order and held the tray out to her.

"Tell her she needs to pay first," whispered Jonah.

"Right. I forgot," I whispered back. This was why Jonah and I needed to be together—we were a team. I pulled the tray back toward me. "You have to pay me first." Here it was. The moment she'd make a big stink and things would happen like they did back then.

She laughed. "Of course! What am I thinking? Sorry about that," she said as she took out her wallet and handed me a twenty.

Jonah and I looked at each other. So much for that.

"Keep the change as a tip," she said with a smile as I went to hand her her change. "And have a fantastic day," she added as she took her smiling, well-behaved children and walked away.

"Okay, *that* didn't go as planned." I sighed as I turned to Jonah. "Now what?"

"What did you say came after the part when you and the woman starting fighting?"

"The corn dog flew out of my hand and landed in Andrea's hair."

He searched the crowd. "Look—there they are! Do it now!"

"You want me to throw a corn dog at my best friend?" I asked. "That's not very nice."

"I thought you said she wasn't your best friend."

"She's not! But still." What was I saying? "But I'll lose my job."

"Exactly!" he cried. "That's what you're here to do, remember?!"

"I know, but when you say it out loud, it just sounds . . . *wrong*."

He rolled his eyes. "You don't even live here!"

He did have a point.

"If you're going to do it, you need to do it now, before they get away."

"Okay, okay," I said nervously. I looked over at the crowd and spotted them. Next to a very large bald man with a tribal tattoo on half of his unsmiling face and a giant silver ring in his left nostril. Who did not look like he'd be too understanding about my lack of coordination if I hit him instead. With a deep breath, I picked up a vegan dog and took aim. Grabbing Jonah's hand for moral support, I held my breath as it sailed through the air, coming dangerously close to taking out a Hasidic man's eye. Finally a high-pitched scream could be heard over the music.

"Omigod, my hair!" Andrea cried as she swatted at the back of her blonde hair.

Jonah and I looked at each other and high-fived. "Nice shot," he said, impressed.

"Thanks." I smiled.

We watched as she turned to Brad. "What's in my hair?!"

Brad leaned in. "I'm not sure. It's kind of long and skinny. Maybe it's an eel."

I rolled my eyes. I may have been from another century, but this guy was from another planet.

Andrea screamed again. *"Omigod, I hate eels! Get it out!"*

Brad grabbed it and looked at it. "It's not an eel. It's a hot dog."

"It's not a hot dog!" Larry yelled. "It's a vegan dog." He turned to me. "You do realize that—"

I took my hat off and placed it on the counter. "—I'm fired. Yeah, I figured," I said. I looked at Jonah. "Now what?"

"We run," he said.

We didn't stop until we got to the passageway that went

toward Terri's, where we finally skidded to a halt, out of breath but unable to stop laughing.

"Did you see the look on her face when Brad held the hot dog up to her?" Jonah gasped.

"Vegan dog," I managed to get out through my giggles. "And the way it got stuck in her hair again as she started batting it away?!"

"I wish I had filmed that with my camera. If I put that on YouTube, it would've gone viral in hours."

"Viral? What does that mean?"

"Forget it." He laughed. "But I should probably give you a primer on all the stuff you've missed at some point."

I felt my heart beat as if I had drunk two Red Bulls in a row. (They were definitely one of the most important inventions of the last few decades.) "That would be great, but if we pull this thing off, then I won't be here anymore," I said quietly.

"Oh. Yeah. I forgot," he replied. Was that disappointment on his face? He looked down at the ground and then back at me. "You have really great teeth," he blurted nervously. "They're very straight."

"I had braces," I replied just as nervously. In fact, after watching a rerun of *The Partridge Family* episode where Laurie Partridge's braces acted as a radio he and I had spent hours trying to get mine to do the same thing, with no success. "Thank you."

"You're welcome."

We stood there for a second, very close. Like, so close that if we were different people or characters in a John Hughes movie, we probably would've leaned in and kissed each other.

"So, uh, I guess you should go try on that dress," he said, just as I started to lean in.

I stopped on the balls on my feet and sort of swung there for a second like a cartoon character before pulling myself back. "You're probably right."

"So. I guess this is it," he said. "I mean, if things keep going the way they've been going, and Brad shows up at the shop, then you can get him to kiss you and go back to where you came from."

I searched his face, trying to see what he really meant, but I got nothing. "I guess so."

He put out his hand. "Well, it's been nice getting to know you."

Really? *This* was how it was going to end? I felt like crying. That is, until I got mad. I wasn't even sure who I was mad at. Him, for acting like all this meant nothing? Or me for not having the guts to tell him how I really felt?

"We already know each other," I reminded him.

"Right. I keep forgetting that."

I took his hand and shook it. "But, yeah. Thanks for your help. I appreciate it. I'll see you around, I guess."

"Right. Back in 1986."

"Exactly," I said. I just wanted to get away from him so I could cry somewhere private. "I should go."

He nodded as I turned and began to walk toward Terri's. I

wasn't sure how I did it, but I managed not to turn around to see if he was still watching.

"Hey, look who it is. . . ." Terri said as I walked in.

"You wouldn't happen to have a robin's-egg-blue Lycra mini-dress by any chance, would you?" I asked. Now that it was obvious that Jonah wanted nothing to do with me, I couldn't wait to get back to 1986.

She shook her head. "I don't think so." She walked over to a rack and started flipping through some dresses. "But I have this," she said, holding up a canary-yellow one.

Great. Yellow was not my color. In fact, I didn't think it was anyone's color. I had gotten this far, only to hit a brick wall. Now what?

"Whoa. I guess I do," Terri said, holding up the same blue dress from 1986. "I don't even remember getting this."

I felt the hair on my neck stick up again. That was just weird. Not that I was complaining.

"Please tell me you do alterations."

"Well, yeah, of course. We're a classy operation here," she replied. She handed me the dress. "Get changed."

I took it into the dressing room. "Hey, so I hope you don't think this is weird, but I Facestalked you last night," I heard her say.

"Facestalked?" I repeated.

"Yeah. You know, looked you up on Facebook?"

I was glad I was behind the curtain so she couldn't see me wrinkle my nose. That *was* weird. Well, it was weird until I remembered that I had done the exact same thing to Jonah.

"Your boyfriend's real cute."

I still hadn't taken down the pictures of me and Brad. I guessed I should do that. "*Ex*-boyfriend," I corrected as I walked out and joined her in front of the mirror.

"Oh. Wow. Sorry to hear that."

I shrugged. "It's okay. It's for the best."

She shrugged. "Well, you sure seem to have a lot of friends on Facebook."

I shook my head. "They're not my friends. They want to be able to tell others that they are, but they're not."

"What about that girl you were here with the other day?" she asked. "The blonde?"

"Andrea's not that bad, I guess. But she's not what a best friend's supposed to be."

Terri shrugged. "She really seems to like to shop."

"But that's not all friendship is about. For me, friendship is about . . . being able to stay on the phone all night talking about everything and nothing," I said. "And being totally coordinated during snacking sessions. And not having to talk in the car. And finishing each other's sentences."

Terri smiled. "That sounds like Harry and Sally," she sighed. I guess she saw the blank look on my face. "You know, from the Nora Ephron movie *When Harry Met Sally*?"

"What year did it come out?"

"Mm, late eighties, I think?"

"Yeah, I missed that one," I replied. "What was it about?"

She started pinning again. "It was about these two people who drove cross-country after college and had this debate about whether men and women can ever really be friends," she explained. "Sally thought it was possible, but Harry was convinced that one of the two was always going to have romantic feelings for the other."

"Well, obviously Sally's right. A girl and guy can totally just be friends. So then what happened in the movie?" I asked.

"So then they kept running into each other over the years, and finally they decided they would just be friends, and they were, for a long time, but that didn't work."

"It didn't?"

"No. Because what neither of them was willing to admit, almost until it was too late, was that, really, they were in love with each other," she said.

Why was I starting to sweat? Was it the Lycra? It had to be. Even though I didn't remember Lycra making me sweat before. "So then what happened?"

"So on New Year's Eve, Harry runs through the streets of New York to the party where Sally is and gives this long speech about how he loves all these different annoying things about her, and they end up together," she replied as she reached for a tissue and wiped her eyes. "Sorry. Just thinking about it gets me all teary. I just love movies where a person finds their person."

I was now sweating so much that there was a stain blooming near my left underarm. It was then that I knew it. Just as I knew how many sugars Jonah liked in his iced tea (three). And how sometimes he put Vicks VapoRub on his chest at night before he went to sleep just because he liked the smell. And how he tended to hum when he ate cereal (something that drove me absolutely bonkers when Ethan did it, but not so much when Jonah did). None of these things by themselves meant much at all, but all together they added up to everything.

Jonah wasn't just my best friend.

"Oh my God. Jonah's *my* person!" I cried.

"Excuse me?" Terri asked.

I turned to her and grabbed her arm. "Jonah isn't Montana's person—he's *my* person!"

"Who's Jonah?" she asked, confused.

I whipped out my iPhone and clicked on his Facebook page and handed it over.

"*That's* your person?" she said doubtfully.

I nodded.

"Oh, honey, but Brad is so much cuter," she said. "Don't you want a cute person?"

"No. I want *my* person," I replied. "And Jonah's kind of cute. In a Matthew Broderick kind of way."

"That's true," Terri said. "And if it works for Sarah Jessica Parker . . . So what are you going to do?"

I started to pace. "I don't know! What do you do when you realize someone is your person?"

She shrugged. "You tell them? I mean, I think that's what you do. I've got a real fear of intimacy thing going, so I never get that far, but from what I've seen in the movies, that's what it looks like you do."

I stopped pacing. "Right. You tell them," I said nervously. "You tell them, even though the potential for awkwardness if they don't consider you their person could be huge." I started pacing again. "But when do you tell them?"

"You tell them . . . now?" she suggested.

"I was afraid you'd say that," I sighed. "But you're right—I'll tell him now. Because, really, why *not* now? If you've realized someone is your person, you don't want to go any longer without them *not* being your person, right?"

"Billy Crystal said something almost exactly like that in the movie," Terri sighed.

I squared my shoulders and stood up straight. "Then now it is," I announced as I started toward the door. So what if he had essentially blown me off a few minutes earlier. No matter what happened—whether I got back to 1986, or ended up staying here—I had to tell him the truth. I couldn't live with myself if I didn't.

"Um, you might want to change back into your regular clothes before you go," she called after me.

"Right."

I changed and was just about to run outside when the door opened and Brad walked in. Oh no! This couldn't be happening. I mean, it *could* be happening, because it was *supposed* to be happening, but now that I knew for sure that Jonah was my person, I needed to put a hold on things.

"Andrea thought I might find you here," he said as he walked up to me.

"And she was right," I said nervously as I backed away from him. "But I've got something I have to go do, so—"

He grabbed my arm. "This is only going to take a minute. I promise."

I didn't have a minute! I didn't even have a second! I needed to find Jonah!

He screwed his eyes shut. "I don't know how to tell you this but today, when Andrea and I were hanging out at the Dell we had this Moment. . . ." He opened his eyes. "Huh. I guess I *do* know how to tell you."

"You did?"

"Yeah. We were in Abercrombie, and she was holding this purple-striped shirt up to me, and she looked up at me, and I don't know . . . we just . . . realized that we're meant to be together. Kind of like peanut butter and jelly. Or guac and chips. Or—"

I held my hand up. "I get it, Brad. You can stop." Now that I knew he wasn't going to kiss me, I was a little more relaxed.

"But before you start going all bath salts on me, I need you to know that nothing happened. Well, at least not yet. Because even though we're broken up, I felt like I needed to tell you first."

Wow. He really was a prince of a guy. "That's really sweet of you, Brad," I said, touched. "Seriously. Thank you. I appreciate it."

"You're welcome. And Andrea and I were talking about it, and she thinks it's fair that in the split, you get the table on the Ramp—well, until the Ramp comes down—and the bench in the quad, and the—"

I put my hand up. "It's okay. You can have all of it. In fact, I think I could probably benefit from a different point of view."

"You do?"

I nodded. "Yeah. I think this is good," I said. "I have a feeling you guys will make a great couple."

"Is that the psychotic part of you saying that?"

"You mean the psychic part? Yeah, I guess."

He smiled. "Thanks for being so cool about this. Andrea thought you'd freak out, but I told her you're not like that."

I smiled back. "You seem to know me pretty well."

He opened his arms. "Even though we're broken up, can I still have a hug?"

I nodded and walked into them. A hug was safe. A hug would not take me anywhere. At least I hoped it wouldn't.

"You're really awesome, Zoe," he said as he hugged me. "You'll find someone else."

As he eased up on the hug, I realized I was still here. Or there. Or wherever it was that I was. Phew.

"Maybe. Maybe not. Either way I'll be okay," I replied. And I would be. Even if Jonah didn't agree that we were each other's person.

As I tilted my head up to smile at him he leaned in, and before I knew what was happening, his mouth was coming straight toward me. "Wait! What are you—" I yelped. Before I could stop it, his mouth was on mine, sucking away like a jellyfish. The kiss seemed to go on forever, and the entire time all I could think about was where I might end up when it was over.

And then, finally, it was over.

"Wow. That was *awesome*," Brad said after he pulled back. "I figured that because I'm not Facebook-official with Andrea yet, a good-bye kiss wouldn't be considered cheating." He cocked his head again. "You okay?"

I opened my eyes and looked around. "What year is it?" I demanded.

"What kind of question is that?" He laughed. "It's . . ." He paused and took out his iPhone. "It's 2016. You know that."

"Oh thank God." I sighed.

His phone *ding*ed with a text. "I should get going. Andrea scheduled a photo shoot for a new photo to put with our changed relationship status. I guess I'll see you around."

"Yeah. See you on Monday. Back at school. Bright and early," I replied, excited.

After he left, Terri looked at me. "I've never heard anyone who was so looking forward to a Monday morning before."

"Yeah, well, I guess I'm weird that way." I was weird in a lot of ways, I guess.

She held up the dress. "So I'll have this for you in a week. Okay?"

In the light of 2016, it suddenly seemed kind of tacky. "Actually, I think I'm going to pass on the dress if that's okay."

"Not a problem. With the amount of traffic I got in here last week because of you, I owe *you*."

I started to go again before I realized I didn't have my bag. "My bag—"

"Check in the dressing room," Terri said.

As I ran back in there, I heard the front door open.

"Welcome to Terri's. I'm Terri. What can I do for you, hon?"

"I was looking for . . . I guess she's not here, though." He sounded disappointed.

I froze. It was Jonah.

"You talking about Zoe? Yeah, she's here. She's just in the dressing room," Terri said. "Oh, and the fact that I know you're Jonah and that she would be the one you're looking for has nothing to do with the fact that we were talking about you," she added. "I just happen to be very intuitive."

I pulled my shirt down and looked at myself in the mirror. After the day I had had, I looked like I had been dragged five miles down Coldwater Canyon by a car and then thrown in the washing machine and put through the heavy-duty spin cycle, but whatever. I walked out to find Jonah standing there in the middle of the store, hat off, hair sweaty, like he had just run a marathon.

"You're still here," he said, relieved.

"Yeah."

"I saw Brad as I was running over here, and I thought that—"

"He had kissed me?" I asked.

He nodded.

"He did. But nothing happened," I replied. "Well, other than the fact that it feels like a vacuum cleaner got hold of my tongue."

A smile began to bloom across his face. "So it didn't work."

My lips began to twitch as I began to smile as well. "I guess not."

He came closer to me. "Is it bad to say that I'm glad?"

I took a step closer to him. "No, it's not bad. Not at all."

"But that means you're stuck here. Probably for good."

We were so close I could smell his breath. It smelled . . . like Jonah. Not minty fresh, not gross. Just normal. "Seems that way."

"Listen, I was wrong about you," he said. "I had an idea about who you were, and I judged you based on that, and I really had no interest in being proved wrong. But you pushed and pushed, and the more we hung out, the more I got to know you, and the more I got to see that you're not this stuck-up elitist person that the world thinks you are—" He cringed. "Sorry. That makes you sound so—"

"Horrid? Yeah. It does," I said. "Because I was. Well, this version of me was. Is." I shook my head. "I don't know what I'm saying."

"You don't have to say anything. You can just let me talk. Because if I don't say this now, I'll lose my nerve and I'll never say it, and it'll go on to be my big regret in life, and if I were a song-writer, every single song I ever wrote would end up being about it in some way, even if I tried to hide it, and critics would catch on and write something like 'get over it already, man,' and then—"

Poor guy. Jonah could babble at times, but this was impressive. It meant he was super nervous. "Jonah. It's okay. Just say what you need to say."

"Okay. This is going to sound completely crazy, but in light of everything that's going on, I guess, really, not much could sound crazy."

Talk about the understatement of the year.

He took a deep breath. "So like I was saying, the more I got to know you, the more it makes me think that maybe . . . you're my person."

I was shaking at this point. And not even trying to hide it. "Really?" I said softly.

"Really."

"I'm so glad you said that because I don't think you're my person—"

His face fell.

"—I *know* you're my person."

At that we both smiled. Because I was near a mirror, as I did, I got a glance of myself and saw a piece of something smack in the middle of my front tooth, but I didn't care.

"Well. If we're each other's person, now what?" he asked.

Yeah. Now what? I had been so freaked-out about realizing that my best friend was my person that I hadn't got any further than that. "I don't know," I confessed.

He moved closer. "I have an idea how we can start."

"You do?"

He nodded as he leaned in. "Yeah."

As his head bent toward me, I relaxed. Finally I was about to be kissed by the right person. And then just as his lips hit mine, I freaked. But if I was kissed by the right person, I'd go back to 1986!

"Wait—you can't kiss me! You're the right person!" I cried.

But it was too late. Before I knew it his lips were on mine, and I could immediately tell that, yes, he was definitely the right person, and this was definitely the right kiss, and it went on and on and on, and I felt like I was soaking in a warm bath with lots of bubbles, and it felt so good that I didn't want to stop it, even if I ended up as Marie Antoinette's BFF.

But then it did stop, and I came to and opened my eyes, and Jonah was smiling at me and still holding me.

"We're still here," I said, dazed.

"We are."

"But . . . is it still 2016?"

He took out his smartphone and looked at it. "It appears so."

Frankly, I didn't care what year it was.

As long as I was with him.

Epilogue

WHATEVER FEARS I HAD ABOUT BEING stuck in 2016 with all the technology quickly went away. When you see a mother ask her two-year-old to find something for her on the iPad and the kid does, you realize that if he can do it, you can, too. As far as my family went, they may have looked different (i.e., perm-less) but they were still the same in all the ways I was used to (read: super into work, trying way too hard to be cool and act younger than they were). I had once heard this saying: "The more things change, the more they stay the same." Years 2016 and 1986 were the same in enough ways that I figured 2016 was as good a place as any to be. Not only did I have Jonah, but now I had Montana as well. And I was looking forward to taking away the negative connotation from the word *popular* and giving it a different spin.

Because high school is all about the drama of the hour, let alone the day, by the time the Ramp came down—about two weeks after the vote passed—so much had happened that barely anyone paid attention. Brad and Andrea hooking up was big news for a few days. That is, until they broke up when Andrea walked in on Brad examining Cassandra Levin's tonsils in a bathroom at a party a week later. I felt bad for Andrea—so bad that I asked her if she wanted to go hang out at the Dell after school one day and do a little retail therapy—but oddly enough, she and Cheryl from the Go Greeners began spending a bunch of time together.

I had thought that the campus TV station would do a report on the Ramp coming down, seeing that it was such a historical moment, but they felt that Penelope Strickland refusing to unchain herself from a tree because she was protesting the fact that the school refused to carry rice milk in the cafeteria was bigger news. So when it finally came time for the destruction (the administration was allowing me to swing the first hammer, which was nice of them), there were only a handful of students on hand to watch. Pretty much the ones who happened to be in the cafeteria right then, and, of course, my friends—Montana, Nerdy Wayne, and Jonah.

There was a smattering of applause after I brought the hammer down on one of the steps, and then everyone dispersed.

"Do you think you could do that again?" Jonah asked. "The picture I took is all blurry."

"Mm, I think the moment's passed," I replied.

"I guess you're right."

Montana gave me a hug. "Awesome job, my friend. If I were you, I'd write a piece about it tonight, while it's still fresh in your mind, and try to see if you can get it picked up by the *Huffington Post* or *Salon* or something like that. Colleges would go nuts for that stuff."

I shook my head. "Can't. I have plans tonight." I grabbed Jonah's hand. "He's taking me to see Depeche Mode."

"Who?" Nerdy Wayne asked.

"It's an eighties band," Jonah explained.

Wayne and Montana tried to look interested, but failed.

"They're not so bad," he said. "I'm kind of getting used to them."

"Okay—for you to go to a concert where there's eighties music? This *really* must be love," Montana teased.

Jonah and I looked at each other. It was. And it had been the whole time.

It had just taken me twenty-some-odd years to figure it out.

ACKNOWLEDGMENTS

This book was written during a period where I a) fell in love; b) moved from New York to Louisiana; c) got pregnant; d) got married; and e) gave birth. So the fact that it even got written is a miracle. While I may have been the one with my butt in the chair typing the words (or, during my pregnancy, lying down and balancing the computer on my bump), it could not have been born without the help and support of many. It's always scary working with someone new, but Dana Bergman at Puffin provided genius feedback and guidance on the manuscript, along with my editor Jen Bonnell, who has been my literary midwife on all eleven of my book babies. My agent, Tina Wexler at ICM, is a brilliant editor as well and the perfect first reader. The days I knew I was meeting Charlotte Aaron for coffee after a writing session made my fingers fly faster. Trying to write in a new space with something other than two cats around is asking a lot of person, but my husband, Lewie Blanche, went above and beyond to make sure that I was comfortable, physically and emotionally, and showed me that princes do indeed exist. And lastly, when I showed my daughter, Colette, this book, and she shoved it in her mouth and started gumming it with a huge toothless smile, I realized that this—and everything I've written in the past and will write in the future—is for her.

TURN THE PAGE
for a look at
Robin Palmer's

Inspiration for
the Disney Channel Original Movie
GEEK CHARMING

chapter one: *dylan*

One day as I was watching *Oprah*, waiting for her to get to her "Favorite Things for Spring" segment (she has *the* cutest taste in accessories), I heard this self-help guru guy say that the word for *crisis* in Chinese is actually two words: *danger* and *opportunity*.

The reason I looked up from *Vogue* when the guru said this is because I have one of those lives where there's always a crisis going on. Like 24/7. My best friend, Lola Leighton, says that I'm just a drama queen and that they're not *real* crises, like, say, the kind she would've had to deal with if her parents hadn't adopted her from the orphanage in China. Okay, yes, when you put it in that context, I guess Lola's right. But since I live in Beverly Hills and not a third-world country, my crises and the crises of nonadopted kids are bound to be different, you know?

Take, for instance, the time I was driving home from the Justin Timberlake concert at the Staples Center and I was all by myself because I had a huge fight with my boy-friend Asher after I caught him staring at Amy Loubalu's boobs like *seven* times that night even though he swears he wasn't, and my BMW conked out on the 405 freeway at midnight and I had to wait an *hour* for Triple A to arrive. Now, that, in my book, is a crisis—especially since I was wearing a miniskirt and tank top because it was a million degrees out. I mean, if a serial killer who liked girls with long blonde hair and blue eyes had driven by at that moment, I would've been dead meat. The only "opportunity" there was the opportunity to be chopped up into a million little pieces.

As far as I'm concerned, sometimes a crisis is just a crisis. Like what happened last week with my Serge Sanchez bag. Yet *another* crisis—and the only opportunity there was to see what $1,200 worth of red leather would look like after it dried out. (FYI, it turns out that it doesn't look so bad—sort of a cross between my two favorite nail polishes, OPI's I'm Not Really A Waitress and Essie's Scarlett O'Hara.)

It was Tuesday afternoon and I was at The Dell, which is a huge outdoor mall on the border of Beverly Hills and West Hollywood that my dad happens to own, with Lola and Hannah Mornell, our other best friend. The day before I had seen these absolutely *darling* J.Crew red gingham ballet flats that I just had to have because I knew they'd look so cute with my black capris and a white shirt I had bought the week before. Very 1960s movie-starlet-ish, which was going to be my new look for fall. So I had gotten the shoes (plus two dresses, some tank tops, a cashmere hoodie, and some lip gloss) and the three of us were hanging out in front of the fountain deciding whether we should go to Urth Caffé for sugar-free iced vanilla lattes or Pinkberry for frozen yogurt when the Crisis-with-a-capital-C occurred.

"Omigod, Dylan," said Hannah as she clipped a tortoiseshell barrette onto her short auburn bob. Hannah is incredibly preppy for L.A. standards. While I may buy something from J.Crew occasionally, like the ballet flats, almost her entire wardrobe is from there. B-o-r-i-n-g, if you ask me, but I do believe in freedom of speech in fashion choices, so whatever. "I can't believe I forgot to tell you who Jennifer Bonnell saw at Pinkberry on Sunday afternoon!"

"Who?" I asked, with my face tipped up to the sun as I tried to get some fall rays.

"Amy Loubalu."

"So?" I said.

"So," said Hannah, "she just *happened* to be talking to Asher."

My head snapped down so fast I'm surprised I didn't break my neck.

This is when the Crisis began.

"She is *so Single White Female*-ing me!" I cried. *Single White Female* was a movie I once saw on HBO about this woman whose roommate starts dressing like her, and gets the same haircut, and then steals her boyfriend and *kills him.*

Lola rolled her brown eyes as she put on some lip gloss. "Um, excuse me but she looks nothing like you. If anything, she looks like me."

"Um, don't take this the wrong way, but if you haven't noticed, you're Asian," I said.

"Yeah, but we both have long dark hair," she replied.

"She has a point," added Hannah.

Okay, so maybe Amy didn't *look* like me, since I'm blonde and she's brunette, but she was obviously trying to copy me by stealing Asher away from me. People like to say that when people copy you, it's supposed to be flattering, but I don't see it that way. Frankly, I find it very lazy. I've worked very hard to be the most popular girl in the senior class at Castle Heights High and it's not fair for some girl to think she can just ride on my coattails.

As I continued going off on Amy in front of the fountain, I was waving my arms a lot, which is what I tend to do when I go into what Lola calls DQM (Drama Queen Mode). Just then my Serge Sanchez bag—which had been hanging on my right arm like it always was because I was terrified of having it stolen—went flying into the fountain. Apparently my arms had gotten really strong from Pilates because it's not like the bag just sort of plopped over the edge so I could easily fish it out. It went soaring all the way

4

into the middle, and since it's such a huge fountain, there was no way I could get it out myself.

After that I did what anyone in my situation would do—I started freaking out and threatening to sue until Hannah pointed out that not only did I not have a reason to sue because the whole thing was my own fault, but since my dad owns The Dell, I'd be suing him and that probably wouldn't go over very well. When I realized Hannah had a point, I did the next best thing that someone in my position would do—I started looking around for a guy to jump into the fountain to fish it out for me. Not to sound full of myself or anything, but getting guys to help me out with stuff is never a problem, whether it be trig homework or opening my locker, which is always getting jammed due to the fact that I like to keep a few different outfits in there at all times in case I have a fashion mood change. The only problem is that most of the guys you find at a mall at 4 P.M. on a weekday are either old or gay, so the chances of one of them agreeing to jump into a fountain fully clothed to fish out a handbag aren't so good, even when you start screaming that there's a reward at stake.

I'm sure I was causing quite a scene, but it's not like you could blame me. I mean, if *you* had put yourself on the wait list at Barneys New York a year earlier for the Serge Sanchez Jaime bag and then used all your Sweet Sixteen booty to buy it, you'd be freaking out, too. Not only was it *the* bag of choice for every celeb who had been on the cover of US Weekly or People over the last few months, but I—Dylan Frances Schoenfield—was the only nonstarlet high school girl in all of L.A. who had scored one so far.

"Miss. Miss. MISS!" I heard someone say as I sat there on the edge of the fountain with my head between my legs trying to get my breathing back to normal.

My head popped up. "What?!" I snapped.

In front of me was a pimply-faced security guard, dressed in overalls and a straw hat to go along with the whole "Dell" theme. Everyone who worked at The Dell—from the parking-garage people to the bathroom attendants—were forced to dress up like farmers or milk-maids. Ridiculous, I know. You can thank my dad for that. I tried to talk him out of it because not only is it corny, but farming and shopping—unless it's for eggs—don't really go together, but Daddy says that if you want to succeed at something, you have to have a gimmick. He may be a genius when it comes to real estate, but the truth is he's kind of a geek. I mean, I love him to death but he's utterly hopeless when it comes to being creative—especially if it happens to be fashion-related. In fact, after my mom died a few years ago, I had to take over her job of picking out which shirt and tie he should wear with his suit in the morning. I'm not complaining, though. Sharing my incredible talent for color coordinating and accessorizing with the man whose name is on my Amex card is the least I can do.

"Uh, you're gonna have to quiet down or else I'm going to have to remove you from the property," Farmer Security Guard mumbled.

"Excuse me, but my father happens to *own* this property," I shot back.

"He does?"

"Yes. He does. I'm Dylan Schoenfield, daughter of Alan Schoenfield of Schoenfield Properties."

"Oh." He shrugged. "Then I guess it's okay," he said, shuffling away.

I turned toward the fountain to get an update on my bag and saw it bobbing along in time to Christina Aguilera's "What a Girl Wants" that was blasting over the sound system. Another one of Daddy's gimmicks was to have the spray of the fountain synchronized to the music, like you see at the hotels in Las Vegas. I just hoped that it didn't switch to something with a really fast beat or else I'd *never* get my bag back.

"My poor bag!" I cried as Hannah and Lola stood on each side of me and patted my shoulders. I couldn't remember being this devastated since the time Asher blew off my Sweet Sixteen dinner for a Lakers game. "What am I going to do, you guys?" I panicked as a brown-haired guy with thick-framed glasses walked toward us.

"Get your dad to buy you a new one?" asked Lola.

The guy was so busy trying to juggle his knapsack, doughnut, and Coke that he tripped on Lola's Marc Jacobs bag, which she had bought with *her* Sweet Sixteen money, and fell flat on his face right in front of me.

For a few seconds he didn't move.

"Are you all right?" I asked while watching with horror as my bag bobbed around in the fountain.

When I didn't hear a response, I tore my eyes away from the fountain and looked down at him. Because of the glare of the sun, it was hard to see if his body was rising and falling with his breath.

"Um, hello?" I said.

Nothing.

I started to get scared that maybe he had broken his neck and died instantly, which would not have been good because not only would his parents probably sue Lola's parents but they'd probably also try to sue my dad as well. Daddy likes to say that suing is what people do for fun in L.A.

As Hannah ran to the edge of the fountain and reached her arm toward the bag (as if *that* was going to do anything), I watched with horror as it got caught on a water jet and started whipping around like it was in a T-ball tournament. Extending my foot, I carefully poked the guy with my shoe. Obviously if he was dead it wouldn't matter if I did it carefully or uncarefully, but I was raised to be polite and courteous. "Excuse me, but ARE. YOU. ALL. RIGHT?" I yelled as if he were deaf and non-English-speaking.

Still nothing.

This was now officially terrifying—both the idea that I might be a witness to an accidental murder *and* the fact that my Sweet Sixteen booty was about to go down the drain. Literally. "Omigod! Omigod!" I shrieked. "Someone call an ambulance!" I announced to the mallgoers before turning to Lola. "And you—be a best friend and go help Hannah try and get my bag. *Now,* please."

Lola stopped examining her own bag for scuffs and rolled her eyes before getting off the fountain ledge and slowly walking over to the other side of the fountain. Unfortunately, unlike Hannah, who was being *productive*— she had somehow gotten hold of a pole from one of the mall cart people and was using it like a fishing pole to try to rescue my bag—Lola just stood there and scratched the side of her nose as she watched. I'm not one to talk bad about people, but sometimes I couldn't *believe* how selfish and self-centered Lola could be.

"*Oooofff,*" the maybe-dead guy finally said as he reached up and put his hands over his ears.

"Oh, thank *God.*" I sighed. Even though my bag had moved on to being shot up in the air like a cannonball (not a good sign), I was relieved he was alive (good sign).

A moment later the guy struggled to his feet and slowly started bending his arms and legs like one of those puppets with the strings that Marta, our housekeeper, once brought back for me from one of her trips to visit her family in El Salvador.

"Did you break anything?" I asked anxiously as my bag made a graceful arc in the air before plummeting back down.

"I don't think so," he said, wincing as he wiggled his fingers.

Up close I could see that he was around our age, and that he was wearing a T-shirt that said GEEK GANG. I don't mean to be mean or anything, but why someone like him would choose to wear a shirt that announced such a thing to the entire free world when it was obvious just looking at him that he was a geek was beyond me.

I looked back at the fountain. Just as it seemed that Hannah had hooked the strap of the bag with her pseudo fishing pole, the pole slipped out of her hand and started floating away and the bag began to slowly sink.

"If you're okay, then I need you to do me a huge, huge, HUGE favor," I demanded as the guy crouched down on the ground.

"My inhaler! Where's my inhaler?" I heard him mumbling over and over as he rifled through the spilled contents of his knapsack, which included about twenty different pens, some magazine called *Fade In*, and a copy of the *Hollywood Reporter*.

"Your what?" I demanded.

"My inhaler. I have really bad asthma," he replied nervously.

Great. Just what I needed—*another* crisis.

"Here it is," he said. After he took a hit, his shoulders moved down from around his ears to their proper location. "Okay. Much better. Sorry, were you saying something?" he asked as we both stood up.

Was *anyone* other than Hannah able to get out of themselves for just one minute? I pointed at the fountain. "I need you to climb in there and get my bag. Like this *very second*."

He put his now-crooked glasses back on to get a better look. It took everything in me not to reach over and push his shaggy brown hair off his face. Didn't he realize the whole emo look was *so 2006*?

"You're kidding, right?" he said.

"Hmm . . . let me think about that . . . um, *no*!" I yelled.

"Do you realize what kind of diseases a person could get in there?" he asked. "In addition to leptospirosis, there's shingellosis, and—"

"What are you *talking* about?"

"I read about it on WebMD," he said defensively. He took another hit off the inhaler. "Plus, I'm susceptible to inner-ear infections, so I have to be careful not to get water in my ear."

By this time Lola had decided to be a friend and was putting her flirting skills to good use by going up to all the cart guys to see if they'd help, but from all the head shaking it was obvious that there was no mall community spirit in this bunch. I made a mental note to tell Daddy to send a mallwide memo talking about the importance of coming together in times of crisis to help people out.

"It's only like two feet deep in there!" I exclaimed. "It's not like I'm asking you to go deep-sea diving in the *Bahamas*. Please," I begged. "I'll give you . . . a hundred dollars."

He shook his head. "Sorry. I really can't help you." He crouched back down to put his stuff back in his knapsack. "Just ask them to shut down the fountain until you can get it out," he said.

"I don't have time for that!" I cried. As Christina was replaced by Gwen Stefani singing "I'm Just a Girl," my bag rose from the dead and started a wild modern dance solo in the air. "Can't you see this is an emergency?! What about two hundred?"

He shook his head. "Really, I can't. They canceled our health insurance because my mom didn't pay the bill for the last three months; so I'm trying really hard to not get sick right now. Which is kind of hard, because I don't have a very strong immune system to begin with—my mom thinks it's because I was three weeks premature."

I thought about explaining to him that there were these things called *tanning salons* and maybe if he got some sun and lost the Pillsbury Doughboy look, he wouldn't get sick because the sun is very helpful for colds and diseases, but since I was in the middle of watching my status go from It-Bag Girl to No-Bag Girl, I didn't have time to be giving out advice to strangers.

I turned toward the fountain for an update. The solo was over and my bag was back to sinking. Lola couldn't even get the T-Mobile cart guy—who had a massive crush on her—to come over and help.

I grabbed Geek Boy by the shoulders. *"Please*—you've *got* to help me. I'll do anything. I'll even—"* I was about to say *let you take me out on a date*, but then I thought better of it. "Be your friend on Facebook. Please—just tell me what it will take to make you go get my bag!"

As he took another squirt of the inhaler, his eyes bugged out and a huge smile came over his face. "I'll do it if you let me film you and your friends," he said.

"Eww!" I squealed. "What are you—some kind of pervert? That's totally disgusting!"

"No—I mean make a documentary about you! I've been trying to think of something to send in with my essay for my USC film school application and this is perfect. You know, like an 'inner workings of the in crowd at Castle Heights High' type of thing."

My eyes narrowed. "Wait a second—how'd you know I go to Castle Heights?" Maybe this guy didn't just *happen* to walk by me—maybe he was *stalking* me. Not to sound stuck-up or anything, but I have been known to have that effect on guys.

"Because I go there, too."

"You do?"

"Yeah."

"What are you, a junior?" I asked.

"No," he scoffed. "I'm a senior. Like you."

"Did you just transfer there or something?"

"No. I've been there all four years. We had Spanish together freshman year."

I couldn't remember ever having seen him before in my life. Which wasn't so surprising, I guess, seeing that none of the geeks ever came within fifty feet of The Ramp in the cafeteria, where my friends and I sat.

Hannah walked up to me, her barrette hanging off the edge of her bob and her shirt soaked. "Okay, I know we're best best friends and all, but I'm done trying to help." She pointed at Lola, who was now twirling a lock of her hair around her finger as she threw back her head and laughed at something the T-Mobile guy was saying to her. "Especially since *she* hasn't helped at all."

I leaned over the fountain as far as I could without falling in, but I couldn't even see the bag anymore. I turned to the geek. "Okay! Okay! It's a deal! Now go," I demanded.

"Really?" he asked.

I yanked the inhaler out of his hand and started pushing him toward the fountain. "Yes. Go! Go!"

Celine Dion started singing "My Heart Will Go On" from *Titanic*, and the bag rose from the dead yet again. Every time Celine hit a high note and sent a jet of water up into the sky, Geek Boy ran for cover behind the marble centerpiece like a duck in one of those amusement-park games. If I hadn't been so worried about my bag, the whole thing would have been hysterical.

By this time a huge crowd had gathered behind me to watch. "What a dork. Too bad we don't have a video camera—this would make an awesome YouTube video," said Lola.

"Sure, if you're into making bad karma for yourself, it would be," sniffed Hannah.

"It's amazing how some people *totally* lose their sense of humor when they're PMSing," snapped Lola.

"Um, hi, ladies? This is so not the time for catfights, okay? This is about me and my bag." It was rare that I made it all about me, but if there was ever a time, this was obviously the case. I mean, now that I had experienced how incredible the feeling of the leather from the Serge Sanchez felt against the skin of my arm, it wasn't like I could go back to a regular old Marc Jacobs bag or something like that. That would be like being content with a soft-serve cone from the mall after having tasted Häagen-Dazs. Not that I ever touched the stuff myself.

A huge cheer went up as Geek Boy finally caught the bag like a football and held it over his head in triumph as he walked toward us like an ocean liner sailing on the sea. "Here," he panted as he thrust my waterlogged bag into my arms after stepping out of the fountain. Judging from the way his face resembled a tomato, this seemed to be the biggest workout he had gotten in years. "Where's. My. Inhaler?" he gasped.

"Here it is," I said, picking it up from the ledge of the fountain and exchanging it for the bag. Other than the bag weighing about five extra pounds because of the water, it looked salvageable—especially when the guys at Arturo's Shoe Fix got their hands on it. But once I unzipped it, I could feel my face pale. "Oh no," I whispered. I could care less about whether or not my lip gloss was ruined, or if my wallet was wet, or if my pack of gum was all soggy, but as I pushed the buttons on my Weight Watchers points calculator and the screen remained blank, I could feel my heart start to race to the point where I wished I had my own inhaler.

I looked at him. "My calculator. It's *ruined*."

He took another hit off the inhaler. "So go to Good Buys and buy another one," he replied. "You'll get a great deal—especially with the Just-Because-It's-Wednesday sale going on." Good Buys was this cheesy electronics store in the mall. I kept telling Daddy that it was so *not* in line with The Dell's reputation for excellence, but he just ignored me.

"It's not a regular calculator—it's my *Weight Watchers* points calculator!"

He looked at me like I was crazy. "But you're so skinny. You don't need Weight Watchers. You need to *gain* weight."

I couldn't believe he would say something so rude. "Of course I don't need Weight Watchers," I replied. "And the reason I don't need it is because of this," I said, pointing to the calculator.

"I'll never understand girls. Oh, and you're welcome," he said as he started ringing out his T-shirt, exposing his squishy fish-belly-white gut.

Lola cringed. "Ew, dude—can we watch the nudity, please?"

"Welcome for what?" I asked.

"Getting your bag for you?" he replied.

"Oh. Right. Thank you." I threw in a just-bleached smile. "I very much appreciate it."

Now that the crisis was officially over, everyone went back to shopping.

"So here's what I'm thinking in terms of the documentary," he said.

"The what?"

"The documentary. The one you said I could make in return for getting your bag."

"Oh, that one—right," I replied. "Hey, can we talk about it tomorrow? This whole thing has been super traumatic and I think I need to go home and lie down. Come on, girls," I said to Hannah and Lola, who were now sitting on the edge of the fountain with their faces toward the sun.

As the three of us started walking toward the parking garage, Lola kept trying to edge out Hannah with her hip so that she'd walk just the *teensiest* bit behind us instead of next to me. So rude, I know, but I didn't like to get involved in their drama. While the three of us were BFFs, I was definitely the glue that held us together. Being the person that everyone liked the best could be exhausting at times.

"Okay, but I don't have your e-mail address. Or your phone number!" Geek Boy shouted. "I think we should schedule a preproduction meeting for some time over the weekend to talk about the logistics and how filming is going to work. I mean, obviously we could do more of a guerrilla-style type look and style, but while I was in the fountain I was thinking the look for this should be more polished. I'm thinking how Alek Keshishian did the Madonna documentary *Truth or Dare* back in '91. Even though we don't have a lot of time to prep, I'd like to make the most of the time we do have."

I walked back over to him. "Yeah, let's talk a little more about this documentary thing. Are we talking MTV-reality-series-like?" Maybe I could end up getting a deal there for my show. Maybe even a *talk* show. People were always telling me I was like a younger version of Oprah.

"No. I'm thinking more hard-hitting than that. More in the vein of something Barbara Koppel would do. Or the Maysles brothers."

"Do they go to our school, too?" I asked.

I couldn't imagine anyone would be so rude, but it almost looked like he cringed when I asked that.

"No, they don't go to our school," he replied with a sigh. "They're only two of the most important documentarians in the history of documentaries."

"If it's a pair of brothers and then that Barbara person, that's three," corrected Hannah. It was stuff like that that explained why she was in AP classes and me and Lola weren't.

"I stand corrected," Geek Boy said. "So can I get your number?" he asked, holding out a notepad and one of the dozen pens from his knapsack.

I wrote down my phone number and handed it back to him. "This weekend's kind of jammed but call me and we'll set something up."

"Great," he said with a smile. His hair might have been a lost cause, but he had very straight teeth. He held out his hand, which looked like a waterlogged prune. "I look forward to working with you."

I tried not to cringe as I shook it. "Uh huh. See you around," I said as I started walking away.

Poor guy. Between the fact that he looked like a drowned gopher and the fact that I had had my fingers crossed behind my back when I had agreed, I almost felt bad for him.

chapter two: *josh*

It's funny how when something's meant to be, all these things happen to just make them . . . well, *be*. Like in *Knocked Up*, when Seth Rogen gets Katherine Heigl pregnant—first it seems like they'd never make it as a couple and then they end up realizing they do love each other even though he's a schlub and she's gorgeous.

And like with the documentary.

Flashback to the night before the purse-in-the-fountain incident. Me and my best friend, Steven Blecher, were hanging out at this coffeehouse called Java the Hut on Vine Street in Hollywood, where Quentin and Judd (that's Tarantino, as in *Pulp Fiction* and Apatow, as in *The 40-Year-Old Virgin* and the above-mentioned *Knocked Up*) have been known to stop in when they're editing movies at one of the various postproduction places in the area. Quentin and I are buds. Okay, well, I met him once when he spoke at our school's Film Society, so maybe we're not best friends, but we *have* exchanged dialogue.

As Steven bickered via IM with some kid at NYU film school that he met in a MySpace group devoted to Steven Spielberg about where *Jaws* had been shot, I worked on my essay for my USC application. "Do you think I should tell them that my dream is to become the Woody Allen of the twenty-first century, or do you think they'll get that when they watch *Andy Hull*?" I asked Steven. Because the competition to get into the film school was insane, the week before I had decided I'd submit a short film with my application. My plan was to make one called *Andy Hull*, which I saw as being similar to *Annie Hall*—Woody's 1977 masterpiece—but instead of being about a nerdy, neurotic middle-aged guy, it would be about a nerdy, neurotic teenage girl. I even had my leading lady picked out—Diane Lowenstein, a girl who my friend Ari had gone to theater camp with the summer before.

"Dude, I told you to bag that *Andy Hull* idea," Steven said as he broke off a huge chunk of my brownie. "It's lame." Steven's a bit on the tubby side. My mom's always on me to lighten up on the sugar, but honestly, as far as I'm concerned, it's preparation for later when I'm doing night shoots and need a quick pick-me-up. "If you're going to blatantly rip off a movie that's already been made, at least find some Japanese horror one no one's seen instead of something so mainstream."

I shook my head. "That's way too 2005." I sighed and tipped my chair back. "I just need to face it—I'm undergoing my first official creative block. I feel like Nicolas Cage in *Adaptation* when he couldn't write the script."

I would have done anything for Quentin to walk in at that moment so I could ask him what *he* did when he was blocked creatively, but I had no such luck. Instead I had to wait a full twenty-four hours, until I ran into Dylan. If you had told me even a week before that Dylan Schoenfield of all people would have ended up being my muse, I would have laughed in your face. Not only is she spoiled and stuck-up, but she's also über-popular. Like Best Dressed/Homecoming Queen/Miss February in "The Girls of Castle Heights Calendar" popular. Like Dylan-Has-2,028-Friends-on-MySpace popular.

Me? I have 612. And most are fellow movie buffs. I suffer from the opposite problem: not many people at Castle Heights know who I am. It's not like I'm some weird loner who wears a Black Flag T-shirt and trench coat and army boots—I mean, I have friends, like the guys in the Film Society and Russian Club—but I'm a film geek. And proud of it, I might say. I already know that I'll be quoted in the articles about me in *Film Threat* ten years from now as saying that I didn't come into my own until my twenties, and I'm fine with that. Everyone knows that every artist who's any good wasn't popular in high school. Take Tim (that's Burton, as in *Edward Scissorhands* and *Beetlejuice*)—I highly doubt *he* was prom king at his high school.

To me, the idea of doing a documentary about cool kids in high school was as original as it got. Sure, it had been done, but everyone knew that even though *Laguna*

Beach was quote-unquote reality television, it was about as real as the idea of me getting crowned homecoming king that fall. My documentary—which, during the drive home from The Dell that day I had decided would be called *The View from the Top of Castle Heights*—would be a no-holds-barred look at the beautiful people. The good, the bad, the ugly—no one and nothing would be spared in my quest for the truth of what really went on behind the velvet ropes that led to Castle Heights' cool crowd. And because we were talking about popularity in glitzy, sunny Los Angeles rather than, say, gray, rainy Portland, Oregon, it would be even *more* intriguing to audiences.

READ ALL OF **ROBIN PALMER**'S
HIGH SCHOOL ROM-COMS!